Praise for *Regrets Only*

"Razor sharp . . . clever, brisk. Fans of Liane Moriarty, *Mean Girls*, and the *Real Housewives* franchise won't want to miss this one."
—*Publishers Weekly*, starred review

"Rich-mom politics, social scheming, and a delicious murder mystery collide with a bang in Kieran Scott's *Regrets Only*, a fast-paced, juicy read full of flirtation, danger, and lies. . . . *Regrets Only* is a perfect dose of twisty, decadent fun."
—Kristin Harmel, *New York Times* bestselling author of *The Forest of Vanishing Stars*

Praise for *Wish You Were Gone*

"Kieran Scott sharply unravels a web of secrets between friends and families at the heart of this suspenseful story. With hidden motives and complex relationships, *Wish You Were Gone* is a captivating thriller full of twists and surprises. I couldn't put it down!"
—Megan Miranda, *New York Times* bestselling author of *The Girl from Widow Hills* and *All The Missing Girls*

"Equal parts murder mystery and complex relationship drama, Scott builds her house of cards with a steady hand using dirty secrets and tangled histories. I was holding my breath until not just the last page, but the last paragraph."
—Chandler Baker, *New York Times* bestselling author of *Whisper Network*

"There are shades of Liane Moriarty in this tale of comfortable sub-urban lives thrown into upheaval by a mysterious death and the inter-twining fates of those left behind. With twist after twist I didn't see coming, *Wish You Were Gone* engaged me the whole way through and left me breathless at the end, the way the best domestic suspense fiction does."

—Meg Mitchell Moore, author of
Two Truths and a Lie

ALSO BY KIERAN SCOTT

Wish You Were Gone

regrets only

KIERAN SCOTT

G

GALLERY BOOKS

New York   London   Toronto   Sydney   New Delhi

G

Gallery Books
An Imprint of Simon & Schuster, Inc.
1230 Avenue of the Americas
New York, NY 10020

First Gallery Books trade paperback edition August 2023

GALLERY BOOKS and colophon are registered trademarks of Simon & Schuster, Inc.

For information about special discounts for bulk purchases, please contact Simon & Schuster Special Sales at 1-866-506-1949 or business@simonandschuster.com.

The Simon & Schuster Speakers Bureau can bring authors to your live event. For more information or to book an event, contact the Simon & Schuster Speakers Bureau at 1-866-248-3049 or visit our website at www.simonspeakers.com.

Interior design by Jaime Putorti

Manufactured in the United States of America

10 9 8 7 6 5 4 3 2 1

Library of Congress Cataloging-in-Publication Data is available.

ISBN 978-1-9821-5401-1
ISBN 978-1-9821-5402-8 (pbk)
ISBN 978-1-9821-5403-5 (ebook)

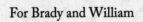

For Brady and William

prologue

I couldn't believe this was happening. I couldn't believe I was holding a gun trained at my eight-year-old daughter's head.

Everyone just calm down, okay? Calm down.

You don't want to do this. If you put the gun down, we can all just walk away.

Do you even know what you're doing with that thing?

I tried to breathe, but the air wouldn't come. Tiny dots prickled the edge of my vision. My finger twitched.

No, I thought. *No.*

What would my father do? What would he think if he could see me right now?

"Mommy?"

This was it. This was my chance. I said a silent prayer.

And fired.

*one
month
earlier*

paige

Why is the whole world against me?

Paige Lancaster twisted the thick, leather-covered steering wheel on the leased BMW SUV she wasn't 100 percent sure she could afford, sweat breaking out under her arms and above her upper lip. There were cars. Everywhere. People. Everywhere. Buses and kids and dogs and strollers. But there were no parking spots. And no one was moving from any parking spots. Everyone was just standing around, chatting. Gesturing effusively with their hands and laughing with their heads thrown back and their perfect teeth bared to the sun. Swear to God, the people in this town paid more for their orthodontia than they did back in L.A.

This couldn't be the way school pickup was run these days. School ended at 3:05. What time had these people arrived in order to park? Twelve thirty? What had they done to kill the time? Was there a mommy lunch date followed by yoga class on someone's front lawn, followed by a book club meeting and a freaking drum circle all so people could be here early?

Finally, *finally* someone up ahead pulled out. Paige accelerated, catching the scathing look of some mom with two long braids in her hair like Laura fucking Ingalls. *Screw you, Half Pint, I'm late to pick up my kid on her first day at a new school.* Paige stopped the car and hit her blinker. And now, she had to parallel park.

Fifteen minutes later, half the cars were gone, and Paige was finally out of her SUV. She hadn't parallel parked anything since her driver's test in eleventh grade. And that had been her mom's Honda Civic, not the tank she was currently driving. No one had ever uttered truer words than Cher Horowitz in *Clueless* when she'd said, "What's the point? Everywhere you go has valet." But she'd gotten through it. And her tires were only about a foot and a half away from the curb. Score. She shoved her keys into her messenger bag and jogged for the pathway that led to the school.

Fifteen minutes late. Where would Izzy be at this point? Had they left her at the side door by herself? Was she on the playground hanging upside down on the monkey bars? (Was that even something her daughter liked to do?) Or was she sitting in the front office, crying her eyes out, cursing the day her evil mother had taken her away from her nanny, Martha, the only responsible adult she'd ever known in her eight years on the planet?

Thirty years ago, when Paige had attended this very same school, Piermont Elementary (ugh . . . *thirty years?*), pickup had been a whole different ball game. Back then the teachers just *let the kids out the doors.* Parents didn't need to be there to receive them. They just *went.* To the playground. To the Country Five and Dime (which was now a Starbucks), to their friends' houses. Or to the chauffeured vehicles waiting out front. (Some chauffeurs were parents. Others were actual chauffeurs.) But now the parking lot out front was off-limits and every child had to be handed over to one of the three adults on their release forms, one by one, before 3:15. This was the procedure Paige had learned just this morning from the very stern assistant to the principal. The one she'd tried so hard to make smile with bad jokes and aw-shucks new-to-the-school pandering. It had not worked. And now she was clearly on the woman's shit list. One of the most powerful women in the school. Never underestimate the last line of defense to the person with the biggest office. It was something one of her first Hollywood showrunners had taught her.

Halfway up the path, the white brick walls of the school in sight through the autumn-hued trees, Paige's cell phone started to ring. She knew she should ignore it, but she'd just gotten off the phone with her agent before leaving the house to come here, and if Farrin Schwartz was calling back within half an hour it could only be good news. Paige suspected that Farrin routinely forgot she existed. If Paige didn't pick up, it was likely she wouldn't hear from the woman again for two weeks, if not two months.

But Paige couldn't wait two weeks. She needed a win. She needed something to write or revise or punch up or doctor. Anything to feel like her screenwriting career was not over. That maybe one day she'd be able to return to L.A. without her tail between her legs.

She paused to root around in her bag and had just about decided that her phone had disappeared to wherever it was that all of Mary Poppins's stuff appeared *from*, when someone said her name.

"Paige? No way. Paige Lancaster?"

A male someone.

Paige looked up into a pair of blue eyes so familiar she could have sketched them with her own eyes closed.

John Anderson. He was older. Blonder. Tanner. Softer. Crinklier. But it was definitely John.

"Holy shit, John?"

The twelvish boy next to John—practically his doppelganger—snorted, eyes trained down at his phone, as the world around them seemed to go quiet. But not because they were having some sort of rom-com meet-cute moment. No. It was because every mom within a ten-foot radius had heard Paige utter the word "shit" in the vicinity of the pristine ears of their children and had paused in place, as if some sort of sci-fi time-freeze device had been unleashed on the sleepy hamlet of Piermont, Connecticut. John blushed. Blushed! And Paige laughed. The world started up again, albeit with a few more scathing looks thrown her way. She was really racking them up today.

"How *are* you?" She leaned in to hug him and was relieved when he hugged her back, not stiffly, not awkwardly, but as if no time had passed. Her bag swung around him and knocked him from behind, the keys and sundry things inside jangling.

"I'm good. I just . . . I can't believe it's you. How long has it been? What are you doing here?"

She righted her bag on her shoulder and wished she weren't sweating. "Oh, it's been a minute," she said, and they both laughed. It had been twenty-four years. A quarter of a century, practically. How was that possible? "I just moved back. With my daughter, Izzy. We're going to stay with my mom for a while."

"That's great!" John said with a smile. A genuine smile. One that still weakened her knees, and she suddenly found herself on the verge of a giggle. And it had been *decades* since she'd giggled. "Welcome back."

"I guess that means you still live here, then."

"Yep. Well, moved back after college and grad school and a couple years living in the city. You know." He lifted one shoulder. "The usual. I'm so sorry about your dad. Everyone in this town loved him. I mean . . . you know I loved him."

"Oh, thanks. Yeah. He loved you too. Back in the day." She cleared her throat and cast around for a subject change. "This must be your son."

John did a double take at the kid and laughed. "Yeah, yes. Sorry. Bradley, this is my old friend Paige. Paige, this is Bradley, my youngest. He's in sixth grade this year."

"Nice to meet you," said Bradley, barely looking up from his phone.

Youngest? How many kids did he have? And when had he started, five minutes after they'd broken up?

"How old is your daughter?" John asked.

Izzy. Shit! "She's eight. And I'm super late to pick her up, so I should go. But it was good to see you!"

He looked amazing. Was he married? Of course he was married. But his hand was in his pocket, so she couldn't see a ring. People did get divorced. John looked past Paige and his smile fell away. With his free hand, he removed the sunglasses he had hanging from the collar of his T-shirt and slipped them on.

"Yeah. Us too. I'll see you around."

John steered Bradley around her, making an abrupt exit. Paige slowly turned, wondering what the threat had been. Three women stood alongside the path, dappled with sunlight, eyeing her. Sizing her up.

Paige felt instantly inferior. Pretty girls. Rich girls. Mean girls. The myth that they stopped existing after high school really needed to be debunked. She decided she would just walk past them. Pretend she hadn't noticed them noticing her, even though she was sure they had noticed that she had noticed that they had noticed. Panicked, late, and experiencing serious sexual nostalgia was not the right frame of mind in which to be meeting the A squad. Hopefully these three could read body language.

"You must be the new mom!"

One of the women waved Paige down as she drew near.

So much for that.

"I'm Lanie Chen-Katapodis." The woman extended a hand. She was tall, East Asian, and completely, utterly perfect. Not a hair out of place. Not a crease in her crisp, white shirt, which was tucked into a pleated, T-length skirt at her teeny, tiny waist. Her nails were gelled, her skin was flawless, and her hair was pulled back from her face in a skinny, tortoiseshell headband that would have looked ridiculous in Paige's curly, blondish-brown mess of a mane. There were big diamond studs in her ears and an even bigger diamond engagement ring on her left hand along with a band of sapphires. She wore a gold necklace featuring four diamond stars that hung prettily over her collarbone. "I'm the membership chair of the Parent Booster Association. You're Paige Lancaster, right? This is Dayna Goodman," she said, gesturing to a woman whose raven hair was cut into a sleek, asymmetric bob. In linen overalls and a white crop top, which offered a peek of her perfect abs, she had that laid-back ease of a woman who'd been comfortable in her skin since birth. "And this is Bee Dolan, our finance chair."

"Hello," said Bee, gently running her hand over her cloud of white-blond hair. She wore the sort of flowy, silky, colorful clothes that could have been pajamas or high fashion.

"Your Izzy is in class with my Dickinson and Dayna's daughter Devyn." Lanie gave a tinkling laugh. "Say that three times fast."

"Stepdaughter," Dayna corrected. Her eyes flicked over Paige, not unkindly. "How do you know John Anderson?"

"Oh. We're just old . . . friends." Paige blushed so hard her body temperature doubled. "What do you do in the Parent . . . Booster . . . thing?"

"Me?" She laughed. "I just heckle them from the cheap seats."

Paige laughed. Maybe a bit too loudly. But Dayna seemed pleased.

"It's so nice to meet you," Bee said. "It's Bee. B-e-e. Like Honeybee, which is my actual name. But nobody other than my mother calls me that." Bee shook Paige's hand vigorously. She had a very firm handshake and wore many, many rings. As she leaned in, Paige noticed she wore a necklace with four diamond stars arranged each about an inch apart. It was the same necklace Lanie had on, and a quick glance at Dayna confirmed that she had one as well. "Where are you from? You have a very artistic aura about you."

This totally unfounded compliment nevertheless pleased Paige. Like somehow this woman recognizing her aura could save her career. "L.A. But I grew up here."

"I'm so sorry," Dayna said.

"Sorry?"

"That you had to grow up here."

Paige blinked. Was she being serious? "Aren't your kids growing up here?"

"Stepkid. One." Dayna pulled out her phone and started to text. "And to say she's growing up is giving her far too much credit."

"Dayna! The girl is eight!" Lanie said with a laugh. "Ignore her. She's in a surly mood. Apparently, the heater stopped working at her hot yoga class. Literally, all Dayna does is work out."

Paige checked out Dayna's cut arms. She could believe it.

"Don't apologize for me," Dayna said. "She's from L.A. She gets it." She turned away, focused on the phone.

"Do you take Bikram?" Bee asked. "To be fair, the heating system is, of course, integral to the practice."

"I . . . no." To Paige, yoga looked like self-torture.

"Anyway, we just wanted to welcome you and let you know that membership to our PBA is available on our website. Piermont PBA dot org." Lanie enunciated each word deliberately so that Paige would be sure to understand. "Once you sign up, you'll have access to our full directory, including your child's class list and all the parents' contact information!" She had a tiny birthmark, Paige noticed, just above the left side of her top lip, which only served to make her more beautiful. "You can even make payments for all of our events through the website. All you need to do is create an account, enter your credit card information, and you're good to go!"

"I'm sorry, what's the PBA, exactly?" Time was ticking, and she had no idea where Izzy was.

"The Parent Booster Association," Lanie said slowly. "It only costs fifty dollars a year to join, and all you have to do is go to our website to purchase your membership."

"Our next meeting is this coming Monday," Bee offered. "We're going to be discussing the diversity in the arts program. And maybe you could sign up for the Thankful Dinner committee? We're low on volunteers this year."

Dayna snorted but covered it with a cough when Lanie shot her a wide-eyed look. The second Lanie's back was turned, though, Dayna shot Paige a look that quite clearly read, *There's a reason they're low on volunteers.*

"Right, I just don't really know if I'm the PTA type," Paige said.

She knew instantly that this was the wrong thing to say. The smile wilted on Lanie's face. What was wrong with her? *Read the room, Paige-y. You don't tell the people who clearly live and breathe the PTA that you're not the PTA type.* But could they not tell this from her acid-washed jeans and her motorcycle boots and her suede jacket? Her lack of makeup? Her being now twenty minutes late to pick up her only child who was a product of a one-night stand nine years ago? Not that they had any way of knowing that last bit.

"It's just . . . We just moved here and I . . . I wouldn't want to volunteer for something and then not have the time to fully commit."

"Oh. Are you a *working mom*?" Bee whispered the last two words.

"It's the P*BA*," Lanie said. "We're not affiliated with any national organization. We're completely self-funded and we have plenty of working moms who are super involved. We run all kinds of enrichment programs for our children—"

"And provide new books and interactive materials for the library," Bee put in.

"Because otherwise there would be nothing published after 1990," said Dayna.

"And offer enrichment classes in art and technology," Bee added. "Creative writing . . . chess . . . robotics . . ."

"And we spearhead our charitable giving and social events!"

"That all sounds amazing. But I really have to go," Paige said, inching down the path. She needed to get away from these people before she stuck her foot any further into her mouth. And besides, Izzy was probably in the back of a van halfway to the Canadian border by now. Part of her wanted to tell these women how very much they did not want her anywhere near their precious organization. She couldn't remember the last thing she hadn't utterly fucked up.

"It's really a lot of fun!" Lanie rose up on her tiptoes now and lifted her chin to better see Paige, who was making her getaway.

"I'll check out the website!"

Paige turned and ran to the school, hoping that last promise was good enough to keep them from completely writing her off. The side door, where the stern lady had told her she was to be between 3:05 and 3:15 to pick up Izzy, was locked, so she tore around to the front of the school, where only a handful of parents and kids milled about, getting in their social hour. There were also a few luxury automobiles lined up at the crosswalk to filter out of the parking lot, so clearly some things hadn't changed. Paige wondered what a person had to do to get parking lot access around here.

Paige walked up to the front door of Piermont Elementary and was buzzed in by security—something they did not have when she had been a student here. Inside the cozy, sunlit front office, Paige found her sweet-faced daughter in tears.

"Izzy! I'm so sorry," she said, dropping to her knees on the hardwood floor.

Izzy threw her pudgy arms around Paige's neck. "I thought you went back to California! I thought you forgot about me!"

Paige's heart broke into a dozen jagged pieces. "Never. I would never forget about you. Mommy's just *really* bad at parallel parking."

She looked up at the woman hovering over her and gave a self-deprecating twist of her lips. But the woman didn't so much as blink. She was young—much younger than Paige—and plain, with very pale skin, a round face, and straight, chin-length auburn hair. She wore small, square glasses and a shapeless black dress with a shapeless gray cardigan over it. Was she a nun? Did she teach here? Could nuns teach in public school?

Paige stood up, clasping Izzy's hand. Her eyes finally found someone she recognized. "Principal Spiegal," she said to the woman standing behind the front desk. At least she wore a kind, sympathetic smile. "I'm so sorry. I didn't realize you had to get here at the crack of dawn to get a parking spot."

"Not the crack of dawn," said the nun. "If you arrive on any of the side roads adjacent to the school at or before 2:55 p.m., you'll have no trouble getting a spot."

Paige's face burned at the clipped, judgmental tone. She already felt like a failure at parenting. She didn't need this chick piling on.

"It happens all the time with new parents," the principal put in placatingly. "We must have forgotten to mention it at your intake this morning." She smiled down at Izzy, who sniffled up at her. "But Izzy was fine. She was a brave little trouper, right, Izzy?"

Paige wanted to hit someone. A brave little trouper? It wasn't as if Paige had left her here overnight. She noticed for the first time that there were two little kids behind the nun, pushing their faces into the windows overlooking the small front parking lot. One boy and one girl. They both had hair the exact same shade as the nun's, but curly, so they must have been her kids.

So, not a nun.

"Well. That's good to know," Paige said to the principal. "Thanks for understanding."

She started past the woman who'd chastised her about the parking, tugging Izzy along.

"Being this late to pick up a child from school can leave them with permanent fears of abandonment," the Not-a-Nun said. "You should try harder to be on time. I have my office in town and leave work at two thirty to get here on the days I pick them up."

"Thanks again." Paige directed her comment to the principal. "Izzy what do you say to ice cream for an after-school snack?"

"Yay!" Izzy cried, jumping up and down.

"See? Already forgotten," she said to the room. "Thanks for keeping an eye on her."

She let the door slam behind her before Not-a-Nun could lecture her about too much sugar in her child's diet.

lanie

"She didn't even put the web address in her phone."

Lanie stared after Paige Lancaster, blinking against the sunlight. That had been one of the strangest encounters she'd ever had with another mom. Including the time her son, Austen, had been invited to a party at Chuck E. Cheese by one of the little boys from his fencing class. Those moms had been . . . interesting. They had all seen fit to show up to a social event in sweatpants and flip-flops, and not a single one of them had carried their own hand sanitizer. Lanie tugged her vanilla-scented bottle out of her bag and sanitized her hands right then and there, just thinking about all those germs. Then she adjusted her wedding band and engagement ring and checked her manicure. Still perfect.

"Yeah. That was *bizarre*," Dayna said with a snort, validating Lanie's off-put feelings. "She just took off while you were still talking." She lifted her phone to use it as a mirror, flicking her long, dark bangs away from her green eyes. Then she snapped a selfie, turning to make sure her abs made it into the frame. "Thanks for calling me surly, by the way."

"But you are surly," Bee pointed out, her fine, white-blond hair floating up on a breeze. "In the best possible way, of course."

Dayna sighed and put her phone away. "I'm just saying, I get insulted enough at home. I don't need it from you guys, too."

Bee reached out and touched Dayna's arm in her soothing, earth mother way, the wide neckline of her floral caftan sliding down her shoulder. "Have you called that counselor I recommended? She's such an incredible mediator. I really think that if you and Maurice could just find a way to reconnect, things would improve immeasurably."

Lanie tuned out for a moment, glancing around for her kids, whom she found balancing at the curb alongside the path with a handful of other munchkins. She couldn't imagine life in a marriage like Dayna's, which sometimes sounded more like a work contract than anything else. Dayna watched her husband's daughter from his first marriage, shuttled her around to activities, made sure she was bathed and fed and loved, and had sex with him twice a week. In return she got to live in one of the wealthiest suburbs in the Northeast, buy whatever her heart desired, and attend as many fitness classes as she could handle. Lanie's marriage wasn't perfect—at least not currently—but it had been and could be again. Plus, she knew Michael loved her. Well. She knew that he loved their kids, anyway. Maurice seemed to love two things: wine and his yacht.

"It's too bad Ainsley's not here," Dayna said. "You know she wouldn't have taken no for an answer."

Lanie felt this comment like a gut punch. She hated being compared to Ainsley, because she knew there was no way she could ever measure up. Ainsley was the president of the PBA and had been running it without a hitch for the last six years. She presided over their meetings like they were intense-but-fun Forbes 500 board meetings, and every party and fundraiser she threw was more fabulous than the last. Ainsley had the perfect marriage, the perfect house, the perfect, successful kids. Lanie didn't exactly want to *be* Ainsley, but Ainsley *was* power in this town. So being Ainsley-adjacent had always been important.

Ainsley, though, was on her way out. In just a few short weeks she would be retiring from the presidency and handing the reins over to Lanie. It was vital that the transition be seamless and drama-free. Which it wouldn't be if Lanie didn't have her 100 percent membership enrollment by the night of the election. She was running uncontested, but still. The last thing she needed was people whispering about whether or not she was able to fill Ainsley's shoes.

Because Dayna was correct. If Ainsley had been here—instead of getting her highlights done in Manhattan—Paige would already be a card-carrying member of the PBA. No one said no to President Ainsley.

"What if she doesn't join?" Lanie asked. "We have to have a one hundred percent enrollment rate. We've never *not* had a one hundred percent enrollment rate." Her heart was starting to do that fluttery thing it did when she was certain she was forgetting something. She fanned her face with her hand.

"Maybe she just needs some incentive," Dayna said, sounding oddly like a mob boss from a Scorsese film. She crossed her arms over her chest in a way that made her toned biceps bulge.

"Like what?"

"I don't know . . . tickets to something?" Dayna looked at Bee. "Do you have anything good in your stash?"

Bee's white-blond eyebrows knit together as she considered. Of course, Dayna was talking about tickets. Having spent ten years as a socialite and moderately respected painter on the New York art scene before marrying and moving out to Connecticut, Bee was the most well-connected of her friends, at least when it came to the arts. She was always able to produce tickets to the ballet or some major art installation or Fashion Week or Broadway.

"Not at the moment. I just gave the last tickets to the Monet opening to Felicity for her mother's birthday. But I'm happy to make a few calls. There's a new ballet opening at the Met!"

"I didn't really get a ballet vibe off her," said Dayna.

Lanie bit down on the inside of her cheek. This was a nightmare. For the past two years she had served as membership chair of the PBA, and for the past two years she had staked her entire reputation—the school's entire reputation—on their enrollment rate. It was on their letterhead for goodness sakes. *PIERMONT PBA*, it read. *100% enrollment thanks to* you! She was the one who'd insisted on getting new stationery printed, a new logo designed. She couldn't have it redesigned to read *99% enrollment rate thanks to everyone but the new mom!*

Lanie turned and started to walk. She couldn't stand still when she felt like this. Like her insides were trying to twist their way out.

"Where's Dickinson? Have you seen her?"

"They're all over there, busy destroying nature." Dayna lifted a palm. A few yards away, in the woods, a pack of children was jumping up and down on a fallen tree that bounced like a trampoline due to the fact that it was still semi-attached to its stump.

"Lanie, it's okay. Really," Bee said. "She was clearly in a rush. I'm sure that as soon as she gets home, she'll go on the website, read about all of the amazing programming we have, and she'll be so impressed she'll join right away."

Bee touched Lanie's wrist and Lanie instantly calmed. Bee's touch was always cool. Like the sun's heat didn't even affect her. Lanie breathed in and watched her eight-year-old daughter atop the tree trunk. All the parents told their kids to stay away from it, mostly because they weren't sure whether it was on school property or belonged to the house it had fallen behind, and no one wanted to get involved in a lawsuit. Litigation could get so unpleasant among neighbors. Of course, there were at least twenty of them crawling all over it right now, including her own trio—Dickinson and two of her siblings, ten-year-old Austen and five-year-old Haddix. Marcus, Lanie's eldest, was twelve and a member of the Young Investors Club, which met after school today. He was the reason she and Ainsley had become acquainted in the first place—his first playdate had been with Ainsley's son back in kindergarten. To this day, she could remember so vividly the day she'd met Ainsley. It was clear from the moment their eyes met that Ainsley was a person Lanie was going to have to get close to if she ever wanted to be somebody in this town. At the time she'd thought she was just making a strategic friendship. But really, it was a deal with the devil.

The old log was perfectly harmless, Lanie knew, but in her mind's eye she saw the thing finally giving under the weight and snapping free to trap her kids. She saw Austen's skull split open. Haddix's little limbs crushed. Dickinson's beautiful face splintered. She closed her eyes and breathed.

"Why don't you just throw a party and invite her?" Dayna suggested. "You haven't had one in, what, a week?"

"Dayna," Bee scolded. "It's been at least a month. But this makes perfect sense. If you throw a party, she can meet everyone and get a sense of the community."

Lanie's eyes snapped open and a smile spread across her face. "Yes! Of course!" A party! A party was always the answer. And she knew it was the answer in this particular case by the way the fluttering in her chest instantly eased. "I was thinking about doing an autumn leaves decoupage project! I'll invite Paige and her daughter and introduce them to everyone, and then she'll *have* to join."

"Decoupage? Oh, I *love* that," Bee said. "And I have a friend who can supply the glue at cost."

Lanie and Dayna exchanged a smile behind Bee's back. Having a friend who could supply glue at cost was *so* Bee.

"And there's that new cupcake place in town you've been wanting to use," Dayna pointed out. "Every time I come out of spin class, I have to physically restrain myself from going in there. It's like a cruel joke, them opening right next to CycleBar."

"Oh my gosh, yes! Those little pumpkin-face cupcakes in the window are darling!" Lanie was already typing notes and ideas into her phone. She had, of course, promised Michael she would stop spending so much time and effort on random, midweek parties. He claimed they stressed her out too much and it wasn't good for her mental health, but she suspected he wasn't thinking so much about her anxiety as he was about coming home from work to a house full of screaming children and wine-soaked parents. He'd also balked when he'd seen the bill for her back-to-school brunch.

"Did you have to invite sixty people?" he'd demanded.

"I invited eighty-five," she'd countered. "You're lucky those twenty-five moms had other plans."

Of course, what those other plans were, she'd yet to suss out. Twelve of them worked full- or part-time, and at least two of them had been getting procedures done to deal with whatever effects the summer sun had left behind. But the other eleven still had some explaining to do.

Michael, if she was being honest, hadn't been super excited about the renovations she'd made to the guest bathroom this month, either. And that had pissed her off. He never even used the guest bathroom, so who was he to criticize the Nicole Miller bamboo-pattern wallpaper she'd chosen?

Though, if she were being *super* honest, it did look tackier than she'd expected.

"We'll do it a week from today," Lanie said, shaking it all off with a swish of her keratin-treated hair. "I'll order the invites as soon as I get home." She tapped a reminder into her phone, just in case. Lanie almost never needed reminders, but she always felt more comfortable once they'd been set.

"Fantastic!" Dayna said. "Now that that is settled, can we please talk about the sexual tension between John Anderson and the new mom?"

"Dayna!" Bee put a hand to her chest as if scandalized.

"You caught that too?" Lanie said.

"Are you kidding? Devyn could have caught that, and she's the least athletic kid in second grade." Dayna loved insulting her stepchild. Though not to her face, of course. Lanie hoped, anyway.

"I wonder what the deal is. Old friends, she said?"

"Oh, it was more than that," Dayna said conspiratorially. "The question is, how *much* more?"

"Dayna! Stop." Bee was starting to get upset. She was never good at playing these games. The very idea of people being dishonest or untoward put her into existential crisis. Which was half the reason she'd had to get out of the New York City art scene to begin with. "John would never cheat."

Lanie was with Bee. The very idea of John being anything other than the perfect husband he'd always been held up to be, made her feel hot around the collar. She couldn't believe they were even talking about it.

Dayna clucked her tongue. "God. I was just kidding."

"Maybe they're colleagues?" Bee suggested, toying with the wide sleeves of her silk caftan.

"She doesn't look like the type to work in hedge funds," Lanie said, allowing a touch of sarcasm into her voice. Paige, in her opinion, looked more like the kind of person who would clean the hedge fund's toilets. Not that she would ever say something like that out loud.

Bee looked back in the direction of the school, her eyes going unfocused in that way of hers. "It's so weird, isn't it?"

"What?" Lanie said.

"To think of our husbands out there, meeting people we'll never meet, having inside jokes with people we'll never know. Having *lives* we know nothing about."

The fluttery thing was back. Over by the old log, someone screamed. Lanie flinched, but her kids were fine. It was an I'm-having-fun scream, not an I'm-being-crushed-by-hundreds-of-years-worth-of-petrified-wood scream.

Still. The sound of it ping-ponged around her chest, leaving gaping holes behind. Bee looked her in the eye and Lanie felt caught out. Like her friend was reading her innermost thoughts.

"I should go," she said, forcing a smile that was convincing to no one. "I have a party to plan."

nina

Nina Anand didn't get people. Even now, hours after the end of the school day, she still felt irritated by that episode in the front office. How could someone simply forget to pick up their child from school? And on her first day in a new town, a new class, with a new teacher and strangers all around. It made no sense. As far as she was concerned, it all stemmed from the fact that people couldn't be bothered to (a) figure out who they were and what they were capable of, and (b) make informed decisions about what they should do with their lives based on that assessment. Within minutes of meeting someone, Nina could tell whether they had it together enough to be a functional adult and therefore, have children. This new person, Paige Lancaster, clearly did not have it together. Anyone over the age of thirty who thought it was appropriate to wear artfully torn acid-washed jeans was not ready to be an adult. And Paige was obviously well over thirty. Probably over forty. Why she ever thought she could handle being a mother was beyond Nina.

She had also noticed that Paige was not wearing a wedding ring. Nina was not one to judge, but, well. It terrified her that a person like that didn't even have someone supporting her at home.

As she sat with her back up against the soft, velvety bench at Coffee Room, Piermont's favorite organic coffee shop, she breathed in through her nose and out through her mouth, trying to calm her nerves. Understanding people as she did and being able to predict their behavior was one of her great comforts in life. Take Ainsley, the PBA president, for example. Ainsley was so easily definable it was a wonder her name didn't appear in the dictionary. She was undeniably type A. Powerful, organized, and perfect. A lot like Nina, in fact, who cared that people recognized her worth. And tonight, if she played her cards right, Ainsley would not be able to ignore her any longer.

At the tables around Nina, people sipped their chai lattes and texted on their phones, manicured fingernails clacking against glass screens. A tiny dog in a Prada carrier snored on the floor two chairs over and a toddler in the corner was being tutored in Mandarin by a stern-looking college student, his mother pacing the sidewalk outside as she barked into her phone. Just another weekday evening in Piermont, Connecticut. If her parents could see her now . . . Well, her father would probably try to steal her wallet and her mother would give her the finger from her grave. Nina had been born with a plastic spoon in her mouth, and every day her surroundings reminded her of how far she'd come.

The door swept open and a couple of other moms from school sauntered in, their high-end athletic gear spotted with sweat, hair artfully pulled into topknots. Nina tried not to roll her eyes. She knew none of them would notice her, let alone smile at her or greet her, which was fine with Nina. She had never been good at small talk, which was the only talk people around here knew how to make. If any of these women had ever bothered to get to know her, they would have found out that she was the sort of person one could call if they needed Styrofoam balls for a school project or got a flat tire in the rain. She had no problem lending out her favorite mixing bowls or helping someone decide on paint colors. She might not have been a gossipy person, but she was practical. And everyone needed practical people in their lives, didn't they?

Maybe not in Piermont. They had nannies and maids and drivers for those sorts of things.

A uniformed police officer walked in and sauntered over to the counter. Nina's fingernails dug into the tops of her thighs under the table. Now at the counter, the women from school let out a raucous round of laughter. The officer seemed amused by them. Nina stared at the door, willing Ainsley to appear. She didn't relax until the cop had taken the coffee that had been waiting for him and slid back out the door.

Seconds later, with Nina still breathing heavily, the door opened again and there she was—President Ainsley in all her glossy, blond, crisply ironed glory. Nina sat up a bit straighter, but instead of joining her, Ainsley walked over to the other moms, her bootied feet clicking on the tile, and kissed each of them coolly on the cheek. Nina's face grew hot, waiting for Ainsley to notice her. Did the woman not even remember why she'd come here? Should Nina get up and go over there? Or would that seem too aggressive?

After another five minutes of extreme discomfort, Ainsley glanced over and spotted Nina in such a false way that it was obvious she'd known exactly where Nina was all along. She said something to her cohorts, who shot Nina looks that could only be defined as startled, then went to the counter and ordered a coffee. Then finally, *finally*, she sashayed over and pulled out the chair across from Nina's.

"Hello! So sorry I'm late," Ainsley said, placing her small straw bag on the table. "I had an appointment that went long."

"It's fine. I had some work to finish up," Nina lied, gesturing at her bag. She never left work without finishing what she'd intended to do for the day.

Ainsley sat and crossed her legs at the knee, regarding Nina as if she were about to interview her for an assistant's position. No squeals and air-kisses for her. Not that Nina cared. "So. What was so important that it couldn't wait for the next PBA meeting?"

"Well, as you may know, I run an accounting firm here in town."

Ainsley looked at her blankly. Nina cleared her throat.

"Anand and Associates? It's one of the largest privately owned firms in the state, and last year I was named one of the top five businesswomen under thirty-five in *Connecticut Monthly*."

Ainsley's eyebrows rose. She was impressed. This gave Nina a hit of adrenaline.

"Proceed."

"Well, we recently had a private security firm run a check of all our systems, and something that the gentleman said in the meeting caught my ear. He said that they've just recently discovered a major hole in the encryption algorithm for a very popular accounting software."

"And?" Ainsley said impatiently.

"The accounting software is QuiFi 2020. The exact accounting software Bee Dolan uses to keep the books for the PBA."

Nina laid down a paper copy of the article the security officer had pointed her to, feeling triumphant. A little voice in her head sang *ta-da!*

"So what you're saying is . . . ?"

It was all Nina could do to keep from rolling her eyes. Ainsley wasn't an idiot. Everyone knew she used to work at the very same hedge fund her husband now ran. And the PBA was a well-oiled moneymaking (and donating) machine, thanks to her.

"Our money is completely vulnerable. Tens of thousands of dollars, and it's very easily hackable."

At least, Nina assumed it was tens of thousands of dollars based on her estimations of the amount of cash the PBA had taken in at fundraisers last year and the amount it had expended on its various programs. She did not have access to the actual account. Although anyone could have the account number if the PBA had ever issued them a check, only Ainsley and Bee had the passwords.

Ainsley scanned the article and was silent for a long moment. Nina knew this was something Ainsley would take seriously. And now she would have to take Nina seriously. They would work the problem together. Come up with a solution. Present it at the PBA meeting. Then everyone would see what Nina had known all along—that the flighty, crunchy, oddly self-important Bee Dolan was not qualified to be the PBA treasurer. That simply being BFF and wearing matching necklaces with Ainsley and her squad didn't make one qualified. That occasionally, people had to look beyond their inner circle if they wanted things to be done correctly.

"Have you told Bee about this?" Ainsley asked finally.

Her coffee was delivered to the table by a handsome young barista with a spray of acne across one cheek. They smiled at each other, and Ainsley thanked him by name. Nina didn't even know they offered table service here.

"No. Not yet. I thought you would want to know first." In fact, she thought Bee Dolan was an incompetent idiot who was too oblivious to even understand what Nina was talking about.

"Good." Ainsley took a sip of her coffee. "You were right about that. But I'm not sure why you dragged me all the way down here on a Wednesday evening. You could have just texted me."

Nina felt stung. Reprimanded.

"I thought we could talk about solutions," she said gamely. "The PBA could switch over to the system we're now using at my office." She started digging through her bag for the folder she needed, but found her hands were shaking. "Or I did some research and there are a few other well-reviewed, but less-expensive programs that are just as—"

"Great. Email those to me, would you?"

Ainsley gathered her things, picked up her coffee and stood.

"You're leaving?"

"I have a lot to do, Dina," Ainsley said.

"But I made a spreadsheet." Had she just called her *Dina*? Surely not.

"Of course you did." Ainsley smirked. "Just send me the information and I'll talk to Bee about it."

"Ainsley, I'm not sure you understand the severity of the problem," Nina said. "Even the most inexperienced hacker could easily access those accounts."

"Like I said, I'll have Bee look into it. It is, after all, her job. It's almost as if you think our exec board is incompetent. Is that what you think?"

"I . . . no. Of course not." Had she really just said that? She did think the board was incompetent. At least, one member of it. She opened her mouth to correct herself, but Ainsley efficiently cut her off.

"Good. That's good to hear. Because I wouldn't want you to feel you had to leave the PBA based on our inadequacies."

Nina's face burned. She didn't understand how this had gone so sideways. She had been certain that Ainsley would be appalled by the lack of security on the account. That she would be impressed by the research Nina had done. That they would pore over the spreadsheet together and leave this meeting with a list of action items. And she certainly didn't think she was going to get tossed out of the PBA.

"I would never quit the PBA," she said. "That's not—"

"Good. Because you know how proud we all are of our one-hundred-percent enrollment rate." Ainsley glanced sideways in the direction of the Lulu Lemons, who were clearly straining to listen in, and then she turned a beaming smile at Nina. "Thank you *so* much for meeting with me, Dina. It's always good to hear from our members."

Then she adjusted the strap of her bag on her shoulder, waved to the peanut gallery, and strode out of the shop without so much as a cursory glance back.

Nina could hear the women behind her twittering and giggling, and knew it was all about her. About *Dina*. She placed her hands on her thighs and pinched the flesh through her tights as hard as she possibly could, gritting her teeth against the pain until tears stung her eyes. Only then did she release her grip and breathe.

It was fine. It would all be fine. Except that it wouldn't. Because, as it turned out, type-A Ainsley wasn't quite as predictable as Nina had thought.

paige

Paige leaned back from the table at Aldo's that night, reached up under her baggy sweater and undid the top button on her jeans. Her stomach expanded over her waistband, the jagged line it had cut in her skin throbbing. She'd only been away from L.A. for a couple of weeks, and it was possible she'd already gained five pounds. But she really hadn't realized how much she'd missed East Coast Italian food. And bagels. And having a Dunkin' on every other corner.

It was possible she was eating her pain.

"I told you this place had the best Italian in the area," her mother said, smiling over the top of her wineglass. Elizabeth Lancaster's blue eyes twinkled in the dim lighting that seemed to be calibrated to erase her lines and sunspots. She looked much younger than her sixty-seven years inside this cozy neighborhood haunt, which Paige might have thought was her real reason for loving the joint, if not for the fact that the food was, in fact, divine. She had ordered the veal saltimbocca, while her mother had gotten scallops with vermicelli in a delicate wine sauce, and they'd tasted from each other's plates, moaning and groaning over the flavors. They'd also devoured an entire order of cheesy garlic bread and a bottle of very crisp, very muscle-relaxing white wine. Izzy was still chin-deep in a plate of spaghetti and meatballs, and that girl was the pickiest eater on the planet. Paige had come here expecting the sort of fights they'd had over every meal that wasn't sugar-based and was pleasantly surprised when Izzy hadn't shut down the second the plate was placed in front of her. All things considered, Paige was feeling mighty fine.

"Thanks, Mom," she said. "And thanks for not rubbing it in that I didn't *make* dinner. Again."

Her mother placed the wineglass down. "You're still getting settled. Our deal can kick in next week."

Their deal had been struck when Paige's mother had agreed to let her and Izzy move in for an unspecified period of time, and involved Paige not only cooking dinner every other night but doing the bulk of the yard work (most of which she currently had no idea how to do), and running any errands that necessitated going out in the dark, because Elizabeth's eyesight was getting bad and she didn't love driving at night. Paige would have done all of this for her mom even if she hadn't been giving her and Izzy a roof over their heads.

Paige's mother had basically been her best friend her entire life. She was an only child, and her mom had treated her like an equal for as long as she could remember, allowing her to choose her own clothes even in kindergarten, and consulting her whenever they leased a new family car. It was because of this policy that she hadn't been stuck driving a Ford Taurus around town as a sixteen-year-old, but a much cooler Jeep Wrangler. (Her father would have preferred to put her in a tank.) Paige had never been the type of girl to have a big posse of girlfriends, and the girls she did hang out with sort of came and went throughout middle school and high school. She'd had a much easier time making friends with boys and had hung out mainly with John and his crew back in the day. So whenever she needed a little girl talk, her mom had been her go-to. Over the last few years, since her dad had died four years earlier, she and her mom had talked on a daily basis, sometimes twice daily. When Izzy was born, her mother had even come to stay with her for six months and helped her interview a long line of totally unqualified nannies until they finally found Martha, who had been a godsend up until the day Paige and Izzy had moved out of the bungalow in the hills and started the long drive back East. Paige was still unsure that she would have survived those first months of motherhood otherwise. Newborn baby Izzy had been her least favorite version of her daughter so far.

"Marie! Oh, Marie, I'm so glad you're here. You have to meet my daughter, Paige."

Paige looked up to find a pretty, curly-haired, very Italian-looking woman about her age approaching the table with a big, toothy smile. Right. There was one thing she didn't love about her mother. The woman was an extrovert and was always trying to convert Paige into the same.

"Hey! Right!" Marie said, reaching across the small table to shake Paige's hand. "You're the mom who was late to pick up her kid today."

She said this with such an affable smile that Paige had a hard time not liking her for it.

"Ummmmm, guilty?"

"God, I'm not surprised. Pickup is a fucking minefield," Marie said. "Oh shit, sorry." She blushed and looked at Izzy, who was oblivious to the fact that any of them were there, let alone that they were cursing. "Crap, I did it again."

"It's okay," Paige said with a laugh. "She's heard worse."

Her mother raised her eyebrows, which Paige chose to ignore. But please. The kid could pick up more colorful language than that on one ten-minute drive down La Cienega.

"Anyway, it's half the reason I've got my kids in aftercare. So I don't have to deal with that madhouse."

"Thank you!" Paige said, vindicated. Maybe her mother was right to call this woman over. "They acted as if I'd stolen the Ten Commandments or something."

"Sounds about right," Marie said. "You'll get the hang of it. But listen, since you had a rough day, tonight, dessert is on the house. Chocolate torte all around?" she said, looking to Paige's mom for confirmation.

"Oh, you *have* to try the chocolate torte," Elizabeth gushed. "And a cappuccino!"

Paige's brow wrinkled. "You work here?"

"Well, if you two would have let me introduce you," Elizabeth said. "Marie Mancuso, this is my daughter, Paige Lancaster. Paige, Marie owns this place and is the head chef. She also has two kids in grade school."

"Wow. Go you," Paige said. "Your food is incredible."

"Thank you." Marie gave a little bow of her head. "Come in any time. Any friend of Elizabeth and Frank is a friend of mine."

"You knew my dad?" Paige asked, feeling the pang she always felt when she so much as thought the word *dad*, let alone said it.

"He was one of my favorite people," Marie said, and reached over to clear a few of the empty plates. "And listen, don't pay any attention to the other moms. They're ninety-percent well-meaning, only ten-percent *asshole*." She whispered the last word, eyeing Izzy again.

"Thanks." It wasn't until Marie had walked away again that she thought to wonder how she'd heard about the late pickup. Was it Not-a-Nun who'd blabbed? Or had it been the PBA Three, which was how she'd started to refer to those women who'd accosted her on the pathway? Maybe John? Would he really have gossiped behind her back about what a crappy mother she was? She couldn't imagine it. How fast was the gossip mill around here, anyway? And why did anyone care? Izzy was fine. It was none of their business.

It definitely hadn't been John.

She still couldn't believe he was here. That she'd seen him. That she'd touched him. She could still so clearly remember the last time her skin had touched his. That Christmas break freshman year in college, when they'd had uninspired sex in his bedroom at his parents' house and then he'd told her he'd met someone else. She hadn't even gotten her bra back on yet, but he'd said the guilt was eating him alive and he couldn't take it one more second. Paige had slapped him across the face, fastened her bra, and bolted. She still felt a little warm every time she thought about it. The anger and the humiliation of that moment, both.

They'd gone away to separate schools swearing it would be different for them—that long distance couldn't touch their love. But they hadn't even lasted the full year. She'd been shattered when he told her. Even though she'd been hooking up with Lucas Fisher for the last two weeks while studying for finals. "Tension Breaks," she and Lucas had called them, showing up unannounced at each other's rooms when their eyes got too crossed from staring at calc problems or Shakespeare plays. She had never told John about Lucas, though, instead allowing him to think he'd been the sole perpetrator of their breakup. Which today, hindsight being twenty-twenty, she could see had been a shitty thing to do.

She knew it was weird that she remembered everything about her high school relationship so vividly, even now that she was in her forties, but it was likely a by-product of having never fallen in love as an adult. For the last twenty years, Paige had concentrated on her true love—her career. Until that had blown up so spectacularly in her face. Now it was time to concentrate on her other true love—her daughter.

"I'm done!" Izzy announced. "Can I go play pinball?"

"Pinball?"

"They have an old machine from when this place used to be a pool bar." Her mom waved vaguely toward the back of the restaurant.

"Marie's dad didn't have the heart to throw it out." Leave it to Izzy to have noticed. Elizabeth started digging in her purse. "She'll need quarters."

Paige's phone buzzed on the table. It was facedown against the tile tabletop, and when she turned it over, she saw a text from an unknown 203 number.

HI, PAIGE!

Seriously? Using a greeting comma in a text? WTF?

YOU AND IZZY ARE INVITED TO A FALL FOLIAGE DECOUPAGE
PARTY!!! MY HOUSE NEXT WEDNESDAY! RIGHT AFTER SCHOOL!
CHECK YOUR EMAIL FOR THE OFFICIAL INVITE! HOPE YOU CAN
MAKE IT!!! XOXO

Holy crap, that was a lot of exclamation points.

"Mom?" Izzy prodded.

"Here you go, sweetie." Elizabeth handed a few coins to her granddaughter.

Izzy cheered and ran off toward the bathroom alcove where, when Paige craned her neck, she could see there was an old Wild West pinball machine.

"Say thank you!" she called after Izzy. But Izzy ignored her.

"Ugh. Sorry. Seems like Martha didn't bother with the whole manners thing."

Her mother looked as if she was about to ask something, but then changed her mind. "It's fine," she said. "You can work on it with her." Paige felt stung. Wasn't her mother supposed to tell her she was crazy and Izzy was amazing and she'd never met a more perfect kid? Wasn't that the grandmother's role?

Elizabeth nodded at the phone in Paige's hand. "Everything okay?"

"Yeah. Just a weird text, and I have no idea who it's from."

Marie sidled over with three white plates, each centered by a scrumptious-looking chocolate confection. She glanced at the phone over Paige's shoulder and snorted.

"Oh yeah. I just got that invite."

"Wait. You know who this is from?" Paige asked.

"Yeah. Lanie Chen-Katapodis." Marie nodded. "Wait until you meet her. She's, like, the social chair of the entire town."

Paige's heart sunk. That tall, gorgeous Asian woman she'd met at pickup. "Perfect hair? Fifteen-inch waist?"

"Oh, so you *have* met her!" Marie said with a wink. "Did she tell you about her PBA one-hundred-percent participation rate?"

"Oh my God, yes. But I didn't give her my cell number. Or my email," Paige said, quickly checking her inbox to find that, yes, there was an invitation through Paperless Post. Along with a few more exclamation points. "How did she get all my contact info?"

"Welcome to Piermont," Marie sang, placing the last plate of torte at Izzy's empty place. She lifted her palms. "Nothing you do will ever be private again. Congratulations."

Paige did not like the sound of that. There were certain things about her that no one needed to know. Least of all the picture-perfect Lanie Chen-Katapodis and her gabby friends.

"So, what the hell is a Fall Foliage Decoupage Party?" she asked, squinting at the screen.

"Just another way for all the Martha Stewarts in this town to make those of us who are less craft-corner-inclined feel like shitballs."

"Marie!" Elizabeth scolded, but with a conspiratorial smile.

"What? The kid's not here." Marie sighed and shook her head. "You haven't met Ainsley yet, have you?"

"What's an Ainsley?" Paige asked.

"Good. That's good. I'd explain to you what an Ainsley is, but it's better you enjoy this time in your life. The time in which you didn't need to know."

lanie

There was nothing in the world Lanie found more satisfying than watching her inbox fill with RSVPs from Paperless Post. Each new notification that appeared gave her heart a little thrill, and opening them to see the green font that indicated the responder had accepted, tugged her smile a bit wider. She knew it was maybe a teeny bit ego-centric, but it wasn't as if there was anyone there to witness her guilty pleasure. The kids were in bed, the lights were all out, and Michael was, of course, not home yet. It was nearly nine p.m. on a Wednesday night. Every other working spouse in town had been home for hours. But why should hers be?

She took a sip from her bottle of sparkling water—she would have preferred some wine, but she never drank when she was the only parent home alone with the kids—not even a sip, not anymore—and shook off the negativity as another round of RSVPs popped up. She had already secured Bits & Bites for the finger foods, ordered the adorable fall cupcakes from Piermont Cakerie, and talked Lonnie at Jewel's Handmade Ice Cream into bringing the truck over even though he always put it away in the garage as soon as Labor Day was done. The order to the craft shop was put in. All she needed to figure out now was whether to provide rattan baskets or metal buckets for the leaf-gathering portion. The rattan felt a bit more like fall, but the metal buckets were so quaint. She could just imagine them tied with gingham ribbons and little balsam tags with the kids' names handwritten on them. They were a dollar more each, but they would look just *amazing* in the pictures.

She looked at the clock. 9:03 p.m. Screw it. Her heart gave a nervous flutter as she clicked the buy button and saw the tax and express-shipping fees populate. This was all for a good cause, though. She needed to maintain the PBA's 100 percent membership rate. She needed to prove to Ainsley that she was leaving the PBA in good hands. Ascending to the presidency was all Lanie had wanted since she and Michael had moved to this town from Brooklyn seven years ago and enrolled Marcus in kindergarten. She had known, the moment she had met Ainsley, that no one was going to be taking the presidency from her until she was good and ready to give it up. So instead, Lanie started to lay the groundwork. First, by going to every PBA meeting and volunteering for every committee she could. Then there had been that fortuitous moment toward the end of Marcus's first-grade year when Margie Mellon took ill and had to step down as head of the Field Day committee. Lanie had seen her opportunity and stepped in, running the most efficient, safe, and fun field day that the school had ever seen, and she parlayed that into special events chair the following year. From there, she had worked her way up to membership chair, the position she was in now, which was basically second-in-command. Ask anyone.

For two years she'd been keeping track of the families: who had moved into and out of town, who had graduated, who had dropped out for private school, who had been left back. (That had only happened once—the school system really was excellent.) She had badgered people into sending in their membership fees, kept the meticulous records necessary to update the annual directory, dealt with that awful woman, Rosalie, at the printer's when she lowered the paper quality but upped the unit price. And now, after all that, her chance was finally here. Ainsley had announced at the last PBA meeting in the spring that she'd be stepping down this fall, and everyone had immediately looked to Lanie. She was in. All she had to do was get through the upcoming sham of an election. Part of her wished she had someone to run against and crush. She wasn't immune to the thrall of competition. But the fact that no one had even considered taking her on simply meant that everyone knew she was the best candidate for the job.

Ainsley had told exactly no one what had precipitated her decision to step down when she had a year of eligibility left. Definitely not Bee, since no one told Bee anything, ever, unless they wanted the entire world to know within the hour. Bee wasn't a gossip for gossip's sake. She simply couldn't help helping if she could, and that often meant uttering the phrase, "Don't tell anyone I told you this, but I need your help with . . ." And not even Dayna, who was usually Ainsley's primary confidant. She had told Dayna things she had never told anyone. Because Dayna was a vault—she would never repeat anything she'd been told in confidence—but she *loved* to let you know that she knew something you didn't. Which was why Lanie was sure Dayna hadn't been told. She hadn't once tried to lord her insider knowledge over Lanie. Dayna held all the secrets of Piermont's elite. It was honestly a wonder she hadn't been murdered yet. Or written a tell-all for six figures.

Lanie shuddered at the thought as another round of RSVPs popped up. She quickly opened them. DeeDee Fisher, in. Marie Mancuso, in. Felicity Klein, in. But where the hell was the RSVP from Paige Lancaster? Had she not received the invitation?

An alert popped up on her computer, letting her know that Michael was home. She clicked on the security system and saw him, clear as day, as he entered the front foyer downstairs. Their house wasn't the biggest in town—the homes in Ainsley's neighborhood took that prize—but it sat on a huge piece of property in the hills, too far from any other homes for anyone to hear her scream. When they'd found it, Michael, who'd grown up on a dairy farm, had fallen immediately in love and Lanie had capitulated, even though she would have rather been in one of the large colonials near town—right in the hustle and bustle of the shopping and entertainment district. Her one demand—aside from immediately updating the kitchen—had been to put in a good security system.

She closed out all the e-commerce windows on her computer, leaving only her email open, just in case Paige decided to RSVP, and waited for Michael to come find her in her office. It was just down the hall from the primary suite, so he had to pass it to get there. He couldn't have avoided her if he wanted to—at least not without looking like an asshole. And Michael hated nothing more than looking like an asshole.

She heard his footfalls on the hardwood floor of the hallway and realized her hands were slick. When had this all started, her being nervous to see her husband? She could so vividly remember running home from her job as a buyer at Barneys (may it rest in peace) and into his arms outside their Brooklyn brownstone, excited to hit the bars or try a new restaurant or even sit in the tiny garden out back and let him rub her feet. Back then, every time he saw her, his face had lit up. Now, as he entered the room, he looked at her as if speaking to her were nothing more than an onerous obligation he needed to complete before he could skulk off to bed.

She wanted to throw her water bottle at him. But she'd just spent a few thousand on a party, so instead, she smiled.

"Hi, hon! How was your day?"

"Exhausting. How was yours? Anything interesting going on around here?"

He put his phone down on the crafting table and unbuttoned the top button of his shirt. The sleeves were already rolled up, exposing his thick wrists—one of the first things that had attracted her—and the hair on his muscular forearms. Michael was Greek on his father's side, but it was almost as if he'd gotten only his dad's genes and none of his mother's Irishness. He had dark skin, thick black hair that even into his mid-forties showed no sign of going anywhere, and the most stunning green eyes Lanie had ever seen to this day. He was ridiculously fit, running most mornings and swimming on weekends and throwing in a few gym visits, to boot. Every time she was around her friends' paunchier, pastier, balder husbands, she was reminded of how lucky she was.

"Well, we got the date of Haddix's Thanksgiving Party. She's very excited to sing the turkey song for you."

He managed a half smile. "Just put it on the shared calendar. I'll be there."

"And Dickinson lost a tooth . . . do you have any cash?"

He tugged out his wallet and blew out a sigh as he opened the billfold. "Twenty okay?"

"Perfect." She reached across the room, and he held it out to her.

"Oh, and there's a new family in town. The Lancasters. So I'm throwing a little Fall Foliage Decoupage Party next Wednesday to welcome them." She turned away as she said this, to avoid seeing his reaction, tossing the twenty onto her desk.

"Another party? Really? Lane, I thought we talked about this."

"We did, and I thought you understood." She spun back around in her chair. "I'm the membership chair of the PBA. People expect me to keep up the social aspect of the organization." She stood up and crossed the room, swinging her hips the tiniest bit, the way she knew he liked. It was a cheap ploy, but God help her, it was something. She laid her hands lightly on his shoulders. She could feel the warmth of his skin through his silky-soft shirt. He was always *so* warm, as if the Mediterranean sun had been born into him and was radiating outward. She felt a little stirring "down south" as she and her friends jokingly called it when kids were within earshot. "And if I want to be president," she said, leaning in to kiss his cheek. "I have to do what needs to be done."

He pulled away before she could land her lips anywhere near him, and grabbed his phone.

"I don't even understand why you want that job," he said gruffly. "All it is is listening to those spoiled, rich housewives complain all the time."

"Okay, first of all, *I'm* one of those spoiled, rich housewives," she said. "And secondly, how do you know what being president of the PBA entails? You've never even been to a meeting."

She'd meant it as a standard, throwaway accusation. None of the dads went to the meetings. But the depth of the guilt that crossed his face made her pause. What the fuck was *that* about?

He tucked his phone in his back pocket. "You want me to go to a PBA meeting, I'll go to a PBA meeting."

Lanie's pulse thrummed in her ears. He hadn't answered her question. Being PBA president *was* mostly about listening to people complain, but how would he ever know that? She thought back to the last dinner party they'd attended at Ainsley's house. Had Ainsley talked at all about the job? Had Michael even spoken to her? No. The husbands had all been occupied by the baseball talk, while Ainsley told stories about the trip to Paris she'd just taken the girls on with her sister. Lanie had spent the entire night biting down on her tongue with envy at all the shopping Ainsley had done.

"Whatever." He closed his eyes and pinched his brow between his thumb and forefinger. "Just go ahead and throw your damn party and send me the invoice."

He turned, and instead of making a left toward their bedroom, he started back toward the stairs.

"Where're you going?"

"I gotta work out," he said.

"It's practically ten o'clock."

He dropped his arms heavily and looked back at her. "I know that, but like I said, I had a rough day and I gotta get out some aggression, all right? Don't wait up."

He disappeared around the corner, and she heard his footsteps as he trotted down the wide center stairs and headed for the home gym next to the garage. Lanie could remember when he used to take her to bed after a rough day and they'd have wild, all-night-long sex. Now he did burpees.

She turned back toward her computer to check her RSVPs.

paige

If there was one thing Paige was a master at these days, it was procrastinating. She knew she should be writing. Generating new ideas. Networking with other writers, producers, and development people back in L.A. She knew that the longer she stayed out of the game, the harder it would be to break back in. But every time she thought about calling one of the writers she'd come up with in the writers' rooms of the early 2000s, or reaching out to that producer she'd cold-pitched at the Golden Globe after-party—the one who'd actually seemed interested—she froze. She could imagine how the conversations would go. The disgust in their voices. The pity.

The trades said you parted ways over creative differences. Davidson says he fired you. So which is it?

Paige! How are you? I heard about what happened with that guy . . . what was his name again? And the babysitter?

Paige Lancaster. Wow. I thought you'd be in prison.

There was no justice in the world. People should have been talking shit about Richard Davidson. About how, after three years as one of only three women on a writing staff of fifteen, working on a show about a hard-ass female cop, Paige had been passed over for a promotion. Passed over for Dan Buchanan. A fucking frat bro from Wisconsin. Or, they should be talking about how her ex, Trevor, should be in prison. Not that he'd done anything that merited actual time under the current rules of society, but under the rules the way they should be—under the rules of a utopic, fair, and equitable society, that asshole should be doing life.

Huh. Maybe that was an idea for a new TV show. A utopia rather than a dystopia. She typed a few words into her laptop, then groaned and slapped it closed. The show would still need conflict, and any conflict in a utopia would instantly make it no longer a utopia. It wasn't as if she could pull off either, anyway. Paige was not a high-concept writer. She was not a world-builder. She wrote contemporary women. Drama with a hint of snark. Mysteries and crimes motivated by true emotions. And she was fucking good at it. Better than most of the people she'd carried on her back on the last three shows she'd worked on. Better than fucking Dan Buchanan, whose idea of a joke was anything punctuated by a loud, smelly burp.

She could just imagine LaToya Woods, the poised, sophisticated, highly talented and award-winning actress who played Frankie Chance, burping during a scene. LaToya would quit first.

Maybe she should call LaToya. She'd been hinting around recently that she was bored by the routine of a weekly broadcast TV show and that her character, Frankie, was on the verge of becoming stale. Maybe Paige should pitch her something.

She thought about it. And instead she tackled Izzy's room. She spent the morning reorganizing her daughter's shelves and closet—she'd taken over Paige's own childhood bedroom—and then reorganized all of it again. After that was done, she rummaged in the hall closet for cleaning supplies and scrubbed the bathroom floor tiles, which didn't really need scrubbing. She spent an hour online researching local music classes, because maybe she'd take up the guitar again, what with all this free time. Finally, after a lunch of donuts and coffee, she went back to the guest room, where her own stuff had yet to be unpacked, opened the blinds to let in the sunshine, and took to the bed with her laptop for one more try.

As soon as it was open, her eyes began to drift closed. Ten minutes or ten hours later, the front door slammed, and she woke up. There was drool on her chin and donut crumbs on her shirt. This was no way to live.

"Paige!" she heard her mother call. "Paige, are you here?"

Elizabeth Lancaster was always busy. Always on the go. She'd never had a career, per se, but she'd always worked. She had been in retail when Paige was a kid, helping her best friend run her kitschy vintage boutique downtown. She'd volunteered at the library, at the women's shelter a few towns over, and at the hospital, which was where she'd been that morning. And she'd been a member of everything. The Garden Club, the Women's Auxiliary Club, a local police wives club. And, of course, had run several book clubs over the years. Elizabeth had never gone to college, but Paige was pretty sure her mother was more well-read than she was, and she had been an English and philosophy double major. Elizabeth was more social, better connected, and just healthier overall. It was difficult to live up to. Which was likely why Paige had rebelled against all of it her entire life.

Still. There was no way she could let her mother catch her lazing around like this. She jumped up, swiped at the crumbs, and clicked her laptop closed. By the time her mother reached the top of the stairs, she was walking out of her room with purpose, looking—she hoped—bright-eyed and ready for an afternoon of flow.

"Hi, hon! How's it going?" her mother asked.

"Good! How're the hospital broads?" Paige swept past her mother and headed down the stairs, struck with a sudden inspiration that a change of scenery would help.

"I wish you wouldn't call them that," her mother said, following.

"Dad always called them that."

"And I didn't like it when he did it, either."

Paige took an apple from the basket on the kitchen island on her way through and breezed into the den, her mother on her heels.

"What do you think you're doing?" her mom asked when she arrived at the door of her dad's office.

"I thought I'd work in here," Paige said, biting into the apple.

"That's your father's office."

"I know that, Mom. And there's a desk and a desk chair and all kinds of office-y things," Paige said. "I can't keep working in bed. It's not conducive to . . . well . . . anything."

She cracked open the door.

"No, don't!"

Paige flinched at her mom's warning, as if a pack of rabid clowns was about to attack when she opened the door, but all she was met with was cool air and a musty, dusty scent that prickled her nostrils. She pushed the door wider and . . . holy shit, she missed her dad. Her eyes were instantly hot with tears.

The room was exactly as it had always been. Built-in oak shelves filled with books about history and civil rights and true crime. Heavy plaid curtains over the two windows. The folded, framed American flag commemorating her grandfather's death. Framed photos from Paige's flying-up ceremony, when she graduated from Brownie to Girl Scout, and her Communion, and her graduations. Her father's desk sat in the center of everything, with the larger French window behind it. There was a thick layer of dust on everything. Paige moved over to the closest window and shoved the curtains wide. The shaft of sunlight was blinding, and illuminated the dancing dust particles in the air.

"When was the last time you cleaned in here?" Paige asked, coughing, more to cover her unshed tears than anything else. This room was not up to her mother's usual standards. The rest of the house was spotless.

Elizabeth hovered in the doorway, her arms wrapped around herself. "Before your dad died."

"Four years ago?"

"I haven't opened that door since the day of the funeral."

Paige's chest tightened. "Oh God, Mom. I'm sorry. I didn't . . . Why?"

Her mother lifted her shoulders. "Just haven't been able to." She stepped inside and over to the nearest shelf, running a fingertip down the side of an award that had something to do with leadership excellence. "The very idea of going through his things, throwing stuff out . . . I've never been able to wrap my head around it."

Paige got it. This room *was* her dad. He had spent so much of his time in here, and while the rest of the house was filled with her mother's stuff, decorated in her mother's airy, Nantucket aesthetic, these were his things. Dad things. Still, though she was on some level satisfied to find a flaw in her mom's togetherness, she didn't like that it was this. Four years? It didn't seem healthy. "It's just stuff," she said.

"Not to me it isn't." Her mom smiled wanly. "This is all I have left of him. It's not so easy to part with after you've spent over forty years with someone. You'll see one day."

Or not, Paige thought. Did she even have enough life left to *spend* forty years with someone? Right now she couldn't even imagine wanting to spend forty straight days with someone. She wondered what her dad would think of her current situation. In the time he'd been gone, she'd managed to find a great job, lose the great job, and be forced to slink back home in shame. She had to do something. She had to turn this thing around. She couldn't disappoint her father.

"I can help." Paige sat down in her dad's chair, facing the door and her mother, and the leather slowly deflated under her, letting out a long, wheezing sigh. She placed her laptop in the center of his old-school desk blotter. "Or, you know, not. We don't have to do anything." She wasn't about to force her mother to clean out her dad's stuff. It wasn't as if she and Izzy were going to be living here forever and she wanted to take the room over. Though the bookshelves were covetable. "But is it okay with you if I write in here?"

Maybe being surrounded by her dad this way would motivate her.

"Sure," her mom said. "I think your father would like that."

Paige wasn't sure whether she really believed in heaven or hell, but she liked the idea that she might be making her father happy somehow. Everything else was such a shitstorm, she would cling to just about any bright spot at the moment. She turned on the desk light, and then, out of habit and curiosity, opened the top right drawer. A large, silver handgun slid to the front and clattered against the wall of the drawer.

"What the fuck?"

"Are you okay?" Her mother, who had turned to go, was back now, as Paige slowly stood up from the chair.

"Dad's gun."

Elizabeth walked around the side of the desk, clutching the collar of her cardigan sweater against her throat, and looked down. Beside the gun was a pair of handcuffs. "Oh."

"Oh? That's all you have to say? Is it loaded?"

"How would I know?"

"Oh my God. You have a kid in the house! What if Izzy found this?"

"Paige, I'm sorry. I told you, I haven't been in here in four years."

Paige reached for the weapon, realized she was still trembling, and paused. It wasn't even in a case or a holster. It was just lying there, ready to be grabbed, ready to be discharged.

"Jesus," she said on an exhale. She took a long, deep breath, steadied herself, and picked up the gun.

"Paige."

"Shhh!" Paige released the magazine and checked it. Four bullets.

"Oh my God," Elizabeth said.

Paige went to the small closet, slightly behind and to the right of the desk, and yanked it open. "Where's the safe?"

"I don't . . . I think your dad got rid of it."

"He didn't ever lock this up anymore?"

"We didn't have kids in the house."

"But what if someone broke in here and found it? What was he thinking?"

"Paige, you know your father. He was probably thinking he was Frank Lancaster, chief of police, and no one was going to dare break into his house. The man had a hero complex, as you may recall."

Paige looked around helplessly. She couldn't just have a gun lying around, not with Izzy living here. She moved aside a box on the highest shelf in the closet and pushed the gun toward the rear, shoving the magazine into the back pocket of her jeans. Then she yanked her phone out of her other pocket to google gun safes, just as its alarm went off. She nearly dropped the phone.

"What is that?" her mother asked.

"Shit. I have to go pick up Izzy." How was it already two thirty? She'd woken up that morning full of righteous determination to get something, anything, down on paper and make at least three networking calls. Now her day was over and she had zip to show for it. What the hell was wrong with her?

"I can go," her mother said.

"No. I have to." Paige pulled the ponytail holder out of her hair and fluffed out her sweaty curls. "You said it yourself. Izzy needs routine. She needs to know I'm gonna be there."

Her mother had treated her to a long lecture on motherhood when she arrived in Connecticut, and Paige had been too tired to shut her down. Some of it had seeped in, though, and as much as she hated being told what to do, she sort of relished it, too. She was just too exhausted to think for herself. Besides, her mom was an awesome mom. Paige saw no reason to resent or reject her advice.

Paige went to pocket her phone again, but it slipped and hit the floor, bouncing toward her mom's feet. "Shit!" Paige blurted again.

"Are you sure you should be driving in this condition?" her mother asked.

"What condition, Mom?" Paige demanded, and gave her armpit a quick sniff. *Ew.* "This is me. This is my normal condition."

She grabbed her jacket on the way out, hoping the scent of leather would cover her stench.

On her way through town, Paige noticed an electric traffic sign placed on the curb in front of town hall. It flashed, one line after another.

RECENT CAR THEFTS IN BORO
PROTECT YOUR BELONGINGS
REMOVE KEY FOBS AND CASH
LOCK DOORS

Car thefts? In Piermont? What the hell was this world coming to? Paige was about to turn down one of Not-a-Nun's suggested side streets—the woman might have been a nosy bitch, but Paige assumed her info was good—when she heard the siren. There were red and blue flashing lights in her rearview mirror.

"Fuck. You have *got* to be kidding me. Fuck!"

Paige made the turn she'd intended to make and there were already a few Audis and a Porsche SUV parked along the curb. She passed them by and pulled over, easing the car up far enough for the cop to pull in behind her. She put it in park and, hands shaking, turned off the stereo, trying to think back to what she'd done wrong. Her mind was a blank. But she was very aware of the semiautomatic pistol magazine digging into her ass.

It wasn't a crime to be carrying around a magazine, though. Was it?

Paige waited for the cop to take his sweet time getting out of the car. Two moms walking tiny dogs strode by, ducking to get a look at who the unlucky criminal was. One of them was Dayna Goodman, who smirked when she caught Paige's eye. Paige did her best to stare straight ahead and ignore them, but she knew that by the time she got to Izzy's door, every damn parent in the school would know about her latest infraction. She was getting quite the reputation and she barely even knew anyone in this stupid town.

The cop paused by her window. She rolled it down.

"License and registration, please."

Of course. She should have had them ready. But she appreciated the "please." She fumbled in her giant purse and dug out her California license, wondering if this was the kind of cop who would write her a ticket just for being an out-of-towner. At least the registration was easy to find. She hadn't had the car long enough to jam her usual supply of tissues, sunscreen, and lip balm into the glove compartment with it.

"Do you know why I pulled you over, Mrs. . . . ."

"It's Miss."

"Miss—" He looked at the license. "Wait. You're Paige Lancaster?"

For the first time, the cop leaned down so she could see him.

"Yeah, I'm . . . why?"

He took off his sunglasses and Paige's heart gave a little punch to her sternum. His eyes were a crazy, stunning blue, set off by his tan skin and dark hair. He tucked his mirrored sunglasses into his pocket and smiled, and *whoosh*, the air went out of her lungs. There was no way someone this hot was a small-town Connecticut cop. He was better-looking than half the extras they cast as uniformed officers on the show.

She really hoped he couldn't smell her.

"I'm Dominic Ramos," he said. "I knew your dad."

Right. Of course. Back in the day, Paige had been trained to hand over her father's police certification if and when she got pulled over, along with her other paperwork, but she'd lived in California so long she hadn't even thought of it in years.

"Thank you," Paige said, then blushed, realizing he hadn't said anything that merited thanks. "I mean, it's always nice to meet someone who knew him."

"He was a great guy. An incredible boss. I don't really love the new guy. Don't tell anyone I said that."

"I would never," Paige replied, wondering if they were going to get back to the business of her transgression or if they were just going to shoot the shit for a while. Not that she minded chatting up a hot cop under other circumstances, but more parents were streaming past them, and she refused to be late to pick up Izzy again.

"What're you doing back in town? If you don't mind me asking," Dominic said.

"I came back to live with my mom for a few months." No reason to tell him she'd been fired from her job and had fled L.A. That her beloved bungalow in the hills was now an Airbnb, she'd had to fire the nanny, and now she needed her mom to help with her kid so she could lick her wounds and put her life back together.

"Oh, I hope she's okay. Your mom. Anything I can do?"

"She's hanging in there." *She's doing better than I am*, Paige thought. Except for that whole office/shrine/gun thing. "I was on my way to pick up my daughter from school when you pulled me over."

Dominic looked up in the direction of the school building as if he'd forgotten where he was and what he was doing.

"Right. Sorry. I'll let you go. Just try not to speed in a school zone again, okay? Especially not around pickup time."

"Sure."

He handed back her license and registration and tapped his fingers on the window frame. She couldn't help noticing he had nice, large hands and no wedding ring in sight.

"Hope I get to see you around again," he said with a grin, then pointed one finger at her. "Though not as a part of a traffic violation."

She laughed. "Yeah. Me too."

The second he was back behind the wheel of his car, she shoved her door open. Her purse strap had just settled on her shoulder when the school bell rang.

She was going to be late. Again.

nina

Nina checked her last action item of the day off her list and closed her planner. It was 4:59 when she walked out of her office and clicked the door shut behind her. It felt good to have another day with a completed to-do list under her belt. On her way to her car, she dialed home.

"Hey there, beautiful." Ravi always answered the phone the same way, and it always made Nina blush. "I ordered from China Palace."

"Perfect. I could really go for a spring roll right now," Nina said. "I'll pick it up on my way home. Have the kids done their homework?"

"Everything but Lita's math."

"Of course."

She popped open the door of her Volvo SUV and slid behind the wheel, taking a deep breath of the new car smell she'd managed to preserve even though the car was now two years old.

"It's not her fault her mom's a math genius who loves to watch her work."

Nina smiled and started the car, placing the phone down as it automatically switched over to the Bluetooth. "I'll be home with dinner in twenty minutes, but tell her she gets no screen time until we're done with her homework."

"On it. See you soon."

Nina hung up and checked all her mirrors and the rearview camera before backing out of her space in the small parking lot outside 221 Park Lane. She loved the building that housed the offices of Anand & Associates almost more than she loved the modern home she and Ravi had recently renovated down by the water. She'd chosen the offices herself, after an exhaustive search of the redbrick and white clapboard office buildings that populated the quaint, historic town of Piermont. She'd wanted a place that was small enough to feel cozy, but big enough to expand into the successful firm she'd always envisioned for herself. When she first went into business, it had been just her and her then assistant, Shawn, who had since moved into New York City with his partner, where he was studying for his law degree. Now Nina had ten employees, which meant she was only four hires away from her goal for the company, and the brick, columned building overlooking Veteran's Park was serving them well. They could walk into town for lunch and eat in the park when it was nice out. Perks people looked for in their jobs these days. Everyone above assistant level had their own office—Nina detested an open floor plan— and when she did hire on another two senior and two junior accountants, she would simply rent the space next door and get the super to bust down the wall. No one had taken it in the seven years she'd been here, and she didn't foresee anyone banging down the door anytime soon. Ever since the pandemic, a lot of places had gone full-on work from home, and real estate around town was a steal.

Ravi, who was a music teacher/day trader, had started giving remote guitar lessons while everyone was sheltering in place, and had discovered that he could make a real living this way and not have to deal with the school bureaucracy that he often said was trying to kill him. Plus, while Nina had been near nervous breakdown levels trying to get her work done and homeschool the kids at the same time, Ravi had found he lovēd being a stay-at-home dad. Neither of them was shocked to learn that he had far more patience than Nina did, and when the fall rolled around, Ravi had happily quit his job and taken his virtual lessons international. He now had students as far away as New Zealand and as close to home as New York City. Nina still sometimes left work early to pick up the kids or take them to parties—that was the benefit of owning her own business—but Ravi did most of the parental heavy lifting. Which was just fine with her. She was happy to give the kids the best of herself when she was home, and she knew she was at her best and most content when she was being productive at work.

Nina eased the car from Park onto Main and sighed as she braked at a stoplight, looking out at all the pretty fall foliage.

She still couldn't believe Ainsley had dismissed her and her concerns so easily. That smirk on her face. The way she'd called her "Dina." She was certain Ainsley had done it on purpose. That she was mocking her.

Nina shook her head. She was doing it again. Every single time her mind was unoccupied it went back to that meeting. She hated it. She needed something else to focus on. But she'd been so certain that was her in, and now she had no idea what to do next.

She glanced right and considered turning down Fresia Lane. Instead, her fingers tightened harder around the wheel. She had promised herself she would not drive by Bee Dolan's house again. At least, not today. Nina understood her behavior had become obsessive. She wasn't a moron. But it wasn't as if she was doing anything wrong, really. She could drive down Fresia Lane if she wanted to. So what if it happened to be the street on which Bee Dolan lived?

The light turned green, and Nina stepped on the gas, proud of herself for not giving in to temptation, only to be cut off by a black Mercedes SUV making a left in front of her. Nina gasped and leaned on her horn, but the woman just took off as if she didn't notice. It took half a second for Nina to recognize that it was Bee Dolan herself behind the wheel. As if Nina had somehow conjured her into being. Oblivious Bee, as Nina privately called her. Oblivious to stoplights. Oblivious to car horns.

Nina saw red. Instead of going straight toward restaurant row, she followed the Mercedes.

What are you doing? a little voice in the back of her mind asked.

Driving by Bee's house once or twice or three times a week was one thing. Following her was another. Maybe she'd wait until Bee parked, and then calmly confront her about her reckless driving. Maybe she'd just follow her in case she made another dangerous maneuver. The woman could be drunk. Or high. Nina could call the police if she needed to. Anonymously, of course. Maybe she could prevent an accident.

Following Bee was providing a service to the community.

Bee zoomed through downtown, ignoring pedestrian walkways and breaking the speed limit by at least eight miles an hour. When she got to the crossing at Fieldstone Road, she hooked a left toward the outskirts of the business district. Nina should have kept driving straight up the hill so she could loop around to China Palace, but she didn't.

Are you a stalker now? Is that what we're doing here?

No. She just wanted to see what Bee was up to. What condition she was in. Maybe she could prove that the woman Ainsley was trusting with the PBA finances wasn't, in fact, trustworthy. Maybe she could even take over as treasurer of the organization. Stage a coup.

The Mercedes pulled into the parking lot of Oceanside Bank, a small local establishment that had been around forever and that, to Nina's knowledge, was patronized only by the elderly residents in town. A handful of her clients had savings accounts there, or safety deposit boxes where they kept the deeds to their homes or their wills.

It's not like it's illegal for a person to have an account at a bank fre-quented by old people, her logical voice told her. Maybe Bee's parents had an account there and she was running an errand for them. Maybe she kept her good jewelry in a safety deposit box. Maybe she was planning to leave her useless husband, Seth, and was funneling money into her secret account.

Seth had lost his job during the pandemic and had yet to find gainful employment. He was basically a hermit. No one ever saw him, as far as Nina could tell. He didn't attend any of the PBA events—even the ones where spouses were expected—and his car, an ostenta-tious red Bentley that used to always be seen driving through downtown on a Sunday morning, hadn't been spotted in years. But Nina knew exactly where it was. She'd seen the red paint peeking out from under a tarp in the Dolans' garage on one of her drive-bys when someone—probably Oblivious Bee—had left the door wide open.

Nina edged into a spot at the far end of the parking lot, and watched as Bee got out of the car, said a few words to someone in the back seat, then slammed the door and locked it. She waited for Bee to disappear inside the building, then put the car in reverse and did a slow loop of the parking lot, driving close enough to the SUV to see inside. Sure enough, one of Bee's kids was playing some game on his phone in the front while the other two wrestled each other in the back seat.

Nina almost drove into a parking divider she was so distracted. A person couldn't just leave her kids in the car in this day and age. She was 99 percent sure that it was, in fact, against the law. She found a parking spot and waited for Bee to emerge, which she did about five minutes later, shoving a heavy brown bag into her purse.

What the hell? Was that . . . cash? If so, it was a brick's worth. Who carried around that much cash?

Nina waited for Bee to pull out, counted to one hundred and twenty, then followed. But Bee's black Mercedes was nowhere to be seen. Without even thinking about it, Nina turned her car toward

Bee's house. Her heart pounded with adrenaline and curiosity, and she felt sick to her stomach with disappointment in herself. But she had to know what Bee was doing.

Bee lived near the center of town in one of the historical homes Piermont was so proud of. It had fallen into disrepair in recent years, likely due to the fact that the only income the Dolans had was from the sporadic art classes Bee gave in her backyard studio—a greenhouse she'd converted into art space. Nina had signed up Lita for a watercolors class last year and had been so unimpressed she'd pulled her after two half-hour sessions. Or attempted to pull her. Bee had refused to give Nina a refund, saying it was against her "policy," and the conversation had gotten so heated that Dayna Goodman had stepped in to break it up. In the end, Ravi had brought Lita to the remainder of the classes so as not to waste the money, but as far as Nina was concerned, her daughter had never produced a single painting that convinced her they hadn't thrown away the fee. Oblivious Bee was also a fraud.

There were two large trucks parked near Bee's house and a dumpster in her driveway. Nina slowed to a crawl as she approached, ostensibly to be careful of workers. She narrowed her eyes as she passed.

The first truck was emblazoned with the words B&B PLUMBING. The second had a more tasteful logo that read, CLAIRE'S KITCHEN DESIGN. In smaller type it read, WE MAKE YOUR CUSTOM KITCHEN DREAMS COME TRUE! The dumpster was full of broken cabinets and other detritus, a big chunk of countertop jaggedly pointing toward the sky.

Clearly, Bee was gutting and remodeling her kitchen.

But how? How the hell was she paying for all of this? Was Seth finally employed? Even if so, an expenditure like this seemed irresponsible after being out of work for dozens of months. Not that anyone ever expected Oblivious Bee to act responsibly.

Nina's car edged past the driveway, situated directly between the two trucks that were parked on the road, and only then did she notice that Bee was just getting out of her own car with her kids. She looked up at the exact moment that Nina was inching by, and they locked eyes.

Shit.

Nina had half a second to decide: stop and be friendly and say hello, or put her head down, gun the engine, and get the hell out of there?

She chose option two.

paige

The backyard at Lanie Chen-Katapodis's house looked like a gathering of Martha Stewart's army. The women were all impeccably turned out in well-fitting chinos and cozy cashmere sweaters, or crisp button-down shirts paired with colorful scarves. Even with the breeze, there seemed to be not a hair out of place, and even with the adults-only punch being served in mason jars, not a lip color smudged. Paige's first instinct upon stepping through the sliding glass doors onto the paver patio was to run. Her second instinct was to drop a nuclear bomb on the whole thing. Gingham and silk splattered everywhere.

"Welcome to Lanie CK's," Marie said, stepping up next to her. She and the restaurant owner had met out front before walking in together, because Marie had insisted that Paige needed a wingwoman. "Where cool went to die."

Paige chuckled. "At least it looks like the kids are having fun."

The yard was tremendous—these people had to own ten acres—with a huge field stretching out to thick woods along the perimeter. Up a few steps that had been built into a retaining wall, a swarm of children raced around with little silver pails, playing tag, collecting leaves and other trinkets of nature, and screeching happy childhood screeches. In the distance was what looked like a climbing wall and some sort of obstacle course, but it was tucked behind trees and difficult to make out.

Izzy clung to Paige's side like a smaller child might have, as Marie's two kids, who were older, ran off to the table where a few extra pails were displayed.

"Why don't you go play?" Paige said to Izzy.

Izzy shook her head and shoved her nose into Paige's hip. Her daughter hadn't done this since she was four and her nose was at her knee. Clearly, Izzy was regressing, and clearly, it was all Paige's fault for ripping her away from her nanny, from her school and home—even from Trevor, who had been a fixture in her life, until he'd gone and ruined literally everything. Paige did not belong in this yard. Not only because she was wearing leggings and an oversized tunic sweater that had looked carefree and earth mom to her when she'd left the house and now felt like a garbage bag—but because she sucked at being a mother.

"You're here!"

Lanie Chen-Katapodis floated over on a pair of wedge sandals with the skirt of her perfectly autumnal dress billowing around her knees and full-on hugged Paige. Not a quick, cheek kiss/pat-on-the-arm hug, but a real hug. Which, to her chagrin, Paige sort of appreciated. Bee stepped in to give Paige a double-cheek kiss, in the French way, and Dayna was just behind, sipping a colorful drink from a stemmed glass.

"We're so glad you're here, right, ladies?"

She shot a pointed look over her shoulder at Bee. "Yes. Right. Happy you came," said Bee coolly.

"Lanie's head might have exploded if you didn't," Dayna added. "I like your sweater. See? Not everyone dresses up for these things," she said to Lanie.

Paige might have been offended if Dayna herself wasn't wearing leggings and an oversized top. Hers was of the post-yoga, off-the-shoulder sexy variety, but still.

"Thanks," Paige said. "I feel like I never know quite what to wear."

She blushed. Why the hell did she say these things out loud? Dayna snorted. "I'm gonna go get you a drink."

Bless you, Paige thought.

"Hi, Marie," Lanie said, looking uncertain.

"Hey. Thanks for having me. It's been a while." Marie's voice was flat.

"Yes, well. I think it's about time we moved past all that unpleasantness, don't you?" Lanie waved a hand as if to bat the unpleasantness, whatever that was, out of the air.

Marie's smile was tight. "Not sure Ainsley would agree with you, but . . . sure."

A little girl with the most adorable chin-length bob, wearing overalls atop a red T-shirt like a modern-day Ramona Quimby, went straight up to Izzy.

"Come on, Izzy! Let's get your bucket!"

"This is Dickinson," Lanie said brightly, running her hand over the girl's hair. "She and Izzy are in class together."

Izzy looked up at Paige, who nodded with an encouraging smile. "Go ahead, baby."

"Okay." Izzy detached herself and slowly followed the little girl, who ran full tilt to the table. Her daughter looked back at her once, but then she and the girl were gone, up the steps and into the melee.

"Your daughter is beautiful," Paige said.

"I know, right?" Lanie looked over at the yard.

"Lanie has four kids. Can you imagine?" Marie said.

"Wow," Paige said. "All in grade school?"

"Yep," Lanie answered. "That's Austen, over there on the zipline with his friends." She pointed at a group of boys shoving one another around on a platform eight feet off the ground, a teenager poised below them acting as lifeguard, she could only suppose.

"And the baby is Haddix. She's in the bouncy house with the other kindergarteners."

Dickinson, Austen, and Haddix. "Were you an English major, by chance?" Paige asked.

Lanie's eyes lit up. "Yes! You guessed it. It's Austen with an *E*. My favorite novelist, my favorite poet, and my favorite children's book author. My eldest, Marcus, is twelve. He's inside with his friends and the Xbox. He was named after my husband's father."

"I was going to ask if you had to tie your husband up in the basement while you were naming them, but I guess he got one," Paige joked.

Lanie's brow furrowed. "No. Michael loves their names."

"Right. Of course."

Paige would have bet money that Michael, though she'd never met him, did not love his kids' names. Marie was clearly trying to stifle a laugh.

"What about you, Bee?" Paige asked. "Are your kids here?"

Bee was standing with her chin tilted up and her eyes closed, breathing deeply as the breeze toyed with her hair.

"Bee?" Lanie touched her arm.

"Oh, I'm sorry. Days like this I tend to wander. What was the question?"

"Her youngest is at ballet. The other two are in high school," explained Lanie.

"Ah! Yes. I have a sophomore, a freshman, and a sixth grader, heaven help me. They're all totally different and I can't understand any of them."

Paige and Marie laughed politely.

"Anyway, I'm so glad you both could make it," said Lanie. "Why don't we go join Dayna over at the bar?"

"Is Ainsley here?" Marie asked.

Lanie averted her eyes. "No, not yet. But she's on her way."

Paige glanced at Marie, who seemed to be steeling herself. The other night when Marie had warned her about this Ainsley person, she'd done so with a lightness in her tone, but a sort of edge in her eyes. Paige was intrigued, to say the least.

They followed Lanie to the outdoor kitchen, which was bigger than any kitchen Paige had ever had indoors, and ordered punch from the very handsome young bartender. Paige could feel the other moms assessing her, whispering about her, probably sharing the stories of her day-one lateness and her day-two cop encounter. She glanced around for Not-a-Nun and didn't see her.

No sign of John, either. After seeing him, she had, of course, Facebook stalked him. There had been nothing on his page about his family—his social media presence entirely career-focused. He worked for a day trading firm in Greenwich. She had no idea whether that meant he was in a position to make his own hours, but he'd been there that day to pick up his kid, so it was possible he'd be available for an after-school party, too. There didn't seem to be a single male parent present, though.

Piermont, Connecticut. Stuck in 1959 since 1959.

"Wait, they got you now, too?" a woman with ash-blond hair asked Dayna.

"Yep. Stole my laptop out of my car right there in the driveway." Dayna turned and handed Paige a pretty, pink drink that matched her own.

"No!" Bee said. "So, it's true? There are thieves infiltrating Piermont?"

"Only you could make it sound like a Robin Hood novel," Dayna said and sipped her drink. "But yes, even with Maurice's Fort Knox security, they managed to get away with my computer and a phone charger I had in my car. Although I think our security system is more intended to keep tabs on me than anything else." Dayna laughed wryly. "To be honest, I really don't think I locked the Tesla, but please don't tell Maurice that."

"Unreal," Marie said. "I wonder why this is happening all of a sudden. Do they have any leads?"

"The cops said something about gang activity," Dayna said. "Like it's some sort of initiation right. They drop kids off out here and tell them to get back to wherever they came from on their own and with something good."

"Like *Naked and Afraid*, but without the nudity," said Paige.

"Yeah, no. They were fully dressed. We have video, but they were smart enough to wear face masks and sunglasses."

Bee shuddered. "What a violation. There really is evil everywhere."

"Ainsley."

Everyone turned. It was Lanie who had spoken, but Marie grabbed Paige's arm as if for strength. A woman with gleaming blond hair pulled back in a braided bun, a tan that looked like it had been lifted out of mid-August, and a toothy smile, joined them. She wore snug blue jeans; a white top with crisp, cuffed sleeves; and a jaunty red-and-purple scarf tied artfully around her neck. Peeking out from below it, four stars sparkled—a necklace to match the ones that Lanie, Dayna, and Bee each wore. She looked like a former supermodel who now owned a cosmetics company and was comped front-row seats at whatever Fashion Week shows she wanted to attend.

"That's Ainsley?" Paige whispered as the woman, who was already surrounded by admirers, glanced in their direction.

"That's Ainsley," Marie replied. "And it's coming this way."

Sure enough, Ainsley strode over on long, surely toned legs, honing right in on Paige. She offered her slim hand. "Hello! You must be Paige Lancaster! I've already heard so much about you."

Paige gave her the firm Hollywood handshake she'd learned her first week on the job in L.A. twenty years ago and was gratified to see the woman wince. She could also tell that Ainsley was pointedly not looking at Marie, while Marie seemed suddenly very interested in the bowl of nuts on the counter.

"Really? That's odd. Since hardly anyone around here knows me."

"Oh, but my husband does." Ainsley accepted a champagne flute from Dayna with a quick thank-you. Champagne, not the frothy pink drink everyone else was sipping. "Rather well, from what I understand." She sipped her bubbly and eyed Paige shrewdly. Dayna and Bee looked on hungrily, and Paige got the sense there was some joke here that she wasn't in on.

"Ainsley," Lanie said, in what might have been a warning tone.

"Your husband?" asked Paige.

Ainsley tilted her head slightly. She had the longest eyelashes Paige had ever seen. And having worked on set for so long, that was saying something. "Yes, my husband. John Anderson? I hear you two go *way* back."

paige

Paige almost choked, even though there was nothing in her mouth. *This* was John's *wife*? "I . . . yeah, we . . . went to high school together."

There was a long, awkward silence. Lanie turned her rings around and around and around on her finger. Paige bit down on her tongue to keep from saying more. She would not give this woman the satisfaction of babbling about how yes, she and John dated, but it was *so* long ago and obviously meant nothing now and blah, blah, blah.

Slowly, never taking her eyes off Paige's, Ainsley smiled. She turned her face to the side as if to address the group that had gathered behind her. "Well, he certainly doesn't have a type."

Uncomfortable laughter. Paige hated this woman with the heat of a thousand suns.

"What brings you back to Piermont?" Ainsley asked.

"I just needed a change," Paige said tightly. "My mom lives here, and she wanted to spend more time with Izzy."

"Izzy! What a cute name! Which one is she?"

"She's over there with Dicky." Lanie pointed.

The girls were now comparing the leaves they'd collected. They had joined a bunch of other kids at the three decoupaging tables set up in the corner of the yard. Two women with matching pink bandanas and matching pink aprons were teaching the kids how to decorate glass vases with their leaves, using brushes and vats of white glue. Izzy had a huge grin on her face.

This is for her. You're here for her, Paige reminded herself.

Her heart swelled when she saw her daughter laugh at something one of the other kids had said to her. A true, uncontrollable laugh.

"Oh, she's adorable," Ainsley said insincerely. "She must have gotten her coloring from your husband. What does he do?"

God, it was like a surgical strike, this conversation. Paige was sure Lanie knew that she was not married, being so plugged in to everything that was going on in this town. And from the look on Ainsley's face, Paige got the distinct impression that Ainsley knew this as well. Her expression was too flat. She knew there was no husband. Paige glanced at Marie, who widened her eyes and took a slug from her mason jar. No help there.

"I'm not married," Paige said. "But in case anyone's wondering what *I* do, I'm a writer."

"I knew she was an artist," Bee stated.

"Have you written anything I would have read?" Lanie asked eagerly, trying, bless her, to save the situation. "I'm a huge reader."

"No, I write for TV."

"No way," said Dayna, clearly impressed.

"From Connecticut?" Ainsley asked.

"I'm between shows right now," Paige said blithely. "But I worked on *Chance Encounters* for the last three years," she added, wanting to impress them, and hating herself for it. LaToya's brilliant characterization of Frankie, coupled with Paige's writing, was what made the character so damn relatable—not that Paige's talent or contribution had mattered in the end—but she wasn't going to think about that right now. Women aged thirty-five to fifty-nine were their demo, so the moms at this party were sure to have watched it.

"Oh, Dayna, you love that show!" Bee said.

"It's my favorite guilty pleasure," Dayna said, eyes bright. "I can't believe you worked on it. I have *so* many questions."

"I'm sure she doesn't want to talk about work right now," Ainsley put in, shutting Dayna down.

"That's so exciting, though," Lanie said. "Hollywood! I've always wanted to go to the Oscars. Have you ever been?"

"No, but I've been to the Golden Globes. And the Emmys."

"The Emmys are not the Oscars," Ainsley said, reaching past Paige to pluck an almond from the bowl on the bar.

"Ainsley throws an *amazing* Academy Awards party," Bee said. "We have a red carpet and we all wear gowns. Last year she even had Wolfgang Puck cater."

Marie snorted and Ainsley's eyes flashed.

"We always do an Oscar pool," Dayna said. "But you'll probably kick all our asses at that this year." Ainsley stared daggers at Dayna, clearly not happy with how effusive she was being toward Paige.

"Speaking of parties!" Lanie said. "Ainsley, why don't you tell Paige about the Parents and Pinot Party?"

Another party? Paige wasn't sure she'd ever recover from this one.

"Oh, right. That's the reason we're all here, isn't it?" Ainsley said, and Lanie blushed. "Every year I host this party up at my house in the Palisades for all the parents in the PBA. No children allowed. Just four straight hours of great wine, great conversation, and great food. It's a week from Saturday."

The Palisades. John lived in the freaking Palisades? That was where the Untouchables lived. It was a collection of about a dozen custom-built homes up on the cliffs overlooking the ocean, each house more fabulous than the last. When they were kids, everyone had called their peers who lived up there the Untouchables because they took helicopters or limos to private schools in the city and spent their summers in Italy and their winters in Switzerland. For three months in their junior year, one of Paige's guy friends had dated a girl who lived in the Palisades, and the family had taken him to their vacation home on St. Barths, where he'd hung out with Leonardo DiCaprio and Tobey Maguire. And now *John* lived up there?

"It's always covered by *Connecticut Monthly* magazine. And there's a silent auction with the proceeds going to the PBA," Lanie put in. "Maybe you could donate something from Hollywood!"

Like what? The scarf I cried into the day I got canned? Paige thought. *Or the tire iron that got me my restraining order?*

"Oh, but you have to be a member of the PBA to attend, don't you, Ainsley?" Bee asked.

Holy shit. Had they written a script for this conversation?

Dayna smirked behind her glass.

"You haven't joined?" Ainsley's hand fluttered to her chest. "Wow, how has Lanie not strong-armed you yet? One-hundred-percent enrollment is practically her life's mission."

Lanie's smile wobbled a touch. If she'd written this script, Ainsley had gone off it, making that last bit sound like a dig.

"But yes, you do need to be a member to attend," Ainsley added matter-of-factly.

Paige was being manipulated, and in the most obvious way imaginable. She hated to be manipulated. But if she did what she really wanted to do and told these women off and made some grandstanding exit, then she'd have to take Izzy with her. And Izzy was having such a good time. Her daughter hadn't even looked over at her once in the last ten minutes. She glanced around at the cabal—Ainsley with her huge teeth, Bee who was clearly tipsy, Lanie whose expression was practically desperate, and Dayna who seemed to be mentally filing away everything everyone said for later scrutiny—and sighed.

She wasn't going to be here forever. May as well let Izzy have a life while she was. And if that meant spending an evening with these people, so be it. Besides, she was sort of dying to see this mansion John Anderson lived in.

"Fine. I'll join the PBA." She fished in her purse for her wallet, pulled out two twenties and two fives, and slapped them down.

Everyone stared.

"We really prefer Venmo," Lanie said.

BACK AT THE car a couple of hours later, Paige made sure Izzy was secured with her seat belt, then slammed the car door. Her daughter was full of sugar, had her face painted like a fairy, and swung her feet happily beneath her. Paige needed to hit something.

She looked around her immediate area. Nothing but green grass, perfect sidewalks, and luxury cars. A round of tinkling laughter went up from Lanie's backyard, where the party continued. Marie had left early to run the dinner service at Aldo's, and Paige had waited exactly fifteen minutes before following. No one had noticed her exit aside from Lanie, who had made sure Paige took the gift bag that currently swung from her wrist.

The gift bag. Paige peeked inside. Nestled in some crepe paper was a glass mason jar filled with what looked like autumnal potpourri. Bingo.

She walked behind her car where Izzy couldn't see her, pulled out the jar, and hurled it as hard as she could, letting out a loud, guttural cry. She couldn't believe John was married to that überbitch. She couldn't believe she'd just stood there and let the woman insult her to her face. The jar exploded in the middle of the street in a million tiny shards of glass, spewing acorns and cinnamon sticks and fragrant dried berries everywhere.

Just like that, Paige felt better. She got in the car and glanced in the rearview mirror. Izzy was sucking on a lollipop, oblivious to the world.

"Did you have a good time, baby?"

"Yes, Mommy!"

Izzy was happy. That was all that mattered. Paige put the car in drive and calmly drove away.

lanie

Lanie watched the security footage over and over again, not quite believing what she was seeing. Why would anyone smash a jar of potpourri on the ground like that? Someone could have gotten hurt. Any one of Lanie's guests could have driven over the glass and popped their tires, or worse—one of the children could have run over to investigate and . . .

Lanie didn't even want to think about it. Not just the blood, but the lawsuit.

She rewound it and watched it again. She and Bee and Dayna had spent hours making up those jars. Well, she and Bee had. Dayna had just sat there bitching about her husband and occasionally placing a jar in a gift bag. It was Bee's signature fall scent—the one she sold on Etsy that was always selling out. It was the nutmeg, she had told Lanie and Dayna. That's what gave it that little kick.

Was Paige allergic to nutmeg?

But no. She hadn't even opened the jar. Hadn't so much as taken a whiff. She'd just hurled the thing like it was a grenade and she was in the middle of a war zone.

ten
days
later

lanie

Where the hell is Michael?

Lanie surreptitiously studied the laughing, gossiping, dressed-to-the-nines crowd gathered in Ainsley's great room. She hated the idea of becoming a cliché, but that was exactly what she was. The upper-class suburban mom who seemed to have everything but was starting to lose hold of her husband.

She refused to think the word "affair." Refused. There would be no coming back from that downward spiral.

The atmosphere at the Parents and Pinot Party was tense. Or at least off. Lanie knew it could just be her imagination. Normally she spent the entire evening with Ainsley, Dayna, and Bee chatting with a rotating cast of couples and accepting compliments and gossiping about who might win the silent auction items. Tonight, though, Ainsley was MIA; Dayna was holding court in the dining room by the auction tables; and Bee was standing with her husband, Seth, in a quiet corner. Seth looked like a husk of his former self, to the point that Lanie was starting to wonder if he'd been stricken with cancer and Bee had somehow kept it from all of them. Lanie hadn't seen him in months—no one had—and yet it was abundantly clear he didn't want to speak to anyone. Bee, at his side, looked miserable.

But at least he was at her side.

Normally, not having to follow Ainsley around like some sort of sidekick or handmaiden would have made the night more enjoyable, but thanks to her dear husband's disappearing act, Lanie was tense as ever.

Lanie laughed at a joke her friend Felicity's husband, Colin Klein, had just cracked—a beat too late because she hadn't heard a word he'd said—and took a sip of her wine, glancing around the party again in an attempt to spot her husband. There were at least fifty people mingling throughout Ainsley's vast great room, and more in the dining room beyond, sipping their wine or beer or drinks among the tasteful flower arrangements and midcentury modern décor pieces— colorful ceramic vases placed just so on open white shelving, artful lamps and metal bowls filled with glass baubles. The lights were dimmed suitably low, casting everyone in the most flattering possible light. But it wasn't as if it would be difficult to find Michael in the crowd. He was taller and broader than most of the men in Piermont, and therefore usually not difficult to spot. Neither was Ainsley, for that matter. She was taller than all the other women, particularly in heels, and her blond hair reflected any light, turning her into a walk- ing sunbeam.

Teresa Fletcher raised her phone and Lanie automatically turned her profile to the camera and smiled, going for casual, engaged, pres- ent. One never knew when someone's random pic would end up in the society pages. She forced the smile to stay as Teresa moved over to the next group.

Michael knew how important this night was to her. He knew that she needed his support. And he knew that appearances mattered. People could say as much as they wanted that she was a lock for the PBA presidency on Monday, but if there was one thing Lanie knew, it was that a single wrong move could throw everything off course. One misinterpreted text, one rumor, one mistaken "reply all" and the whole thing could come crumbling down around her.

At least she was back up to 100 percent enrollment. Lanie looked for Paige but didn't see her. Maybe she was in the dining room. She wondered if Paige had bid on anything. Wondered if she even had the money to bid on anything. Maybe she was sitting on a pile of Hollywood cash and just didn't care much about clothes or feel the need to buy her own place. Part of her had hoped for five minutes that she and Paige might be friends. Lanie wouldn't have minded having someone with whom she could let down her hair and discuss literature. Every time she tried to start a book club it turned into a wine-drinking club for people to bitch about their husbands. But now Lanie couldn't seem to get that video of Paige and the potpourri out of her head.

"There aren't any . . . football games or anything tonight, are there?" Lanie asked Lauren Childs, who was herself an avid Patriots fan, so much so that she'd held a funeral-themed party when Tom Brady had defected to some team down south. Perhaps Michael and some of the other dads had snuck off to the man cave to watch some all-important game.

"College, yes. NFL, no." Lauren plucked a canapé from a passing tray, something small and green with a blob of orange goo on top. Ainsley had gone with a new caterer this year, and the food Lanie had seen so far was not appetizing. Sophisticated, yes, but almost all of it looked as if it would feel slimy on the tongue. "Why do you ask? I didn't think you cared about football."

"I don't." Lanie smiled and sipped. "Just curious."

Lauren lifted one shoulder and popped the canapé in her mouth.

"Where is Ainsley?" Felicity said, rising up on her toes to look around.

"Relax, babe. You know she'll come around eventually and remind everyone to pony up some cash at the auction tables," Colin said, taking a sip of his beer. "Because our school really needs the money." He rolled his eyes dramatically.

"Colin," Felicity chided.

"What? You know it's ridiculous. What are we gonna pay for next? Every kid in school to get their own Ferrari?"

"That would be sweet!" Lauren's husband, Eric, commented, and the two men fist-bumped behind Lauren's back.

"Guys, you know the work the PBA does is very important," Lauren said, eyeing Lanie as if she didn't understand why *she* wasn't making this speech. "We do donate to charity."

"Yeah, but what charities? Do you even know?" Colin challenged.

Lauren and Felicity exchanged a look, and then everyone turned to Lanie.

"Well, there's Toys for Tots and UNICEF," she began. "And every year Bee comes up with a list of smaller organizations for us to support."

They could be more transparent about it, Lanie supposed. Maybe that was something she'd change when she took over.

"Ugh, this party is so boring!" Eric moaned. "When can we get out of here?"

"Seriously, dude. Lanie, next year can we do something *fun* in the fall? Something with beer?"

Felicity and Lauren laughed, and Lanie, increasingly aware that neither Ainsley nor Michael were in this room, nor had they been for the last hour, laughed as well. She hated to think it, but was this why Michael seemed to know what it was like to be the PBA president? Because Ainsley had told him? Because they were . . . intimate?

"Don't worry, boys," she said, feeling daring. Feeling angry. Feeling like she could strangle someone. "This particular tradition dies with Ainsley."

"So, I'm dead in this scenario?"

Everyone froze. Lanie smelled Ainsley's perfume half a second too late, but once she did, it was all over her. Ainsley had come up right behind her, so close Lanie felt the silky fabric of her sleeve brush Lanie's arm as she slipped by. Lanie's heart began to pound so hard and fast she was tempted to reach out for a chair to hold on to, but there was no furniture nearby.

"Et tu, Lanie?"

Ainsley tilted her head prettily, her blond hair spilling over her shoulder in gorgeous, loose waves. She almost never wore it down, and every time she did, Lanie wondered why not. It was so glossy and golden and made Ainsley look at least a year or two younger when it was down. Tonight she wore a green-and-blue paisley dress, its long, flowing sleeves slitted so her elbows peeked out, and a voluminous high-lo skirt. It was cinched at the waist with a gold belt that perfectly matched her heeled sandals. It was like a much preppier, buttoned-up version of JLo's iconic Oscars look from back in the early aughts. She reached up to touch her star necklace, and it was all Lanie could do to keep from ripping it off Ainsley's neck. Bee and Dayna had both been beside themselves with gratitude when Ainsley had gifted the necklaces to them, as if it made them some sort of cooler-than-cool girl gang. But Lanie knew what Ainsley was really doing by giving them matching necklaces—she was marking them as her property.

Say something, Lanie thought. *Say anything*.

"I didn't mean you would be dead, obviously. It was just a metaphor for, you know . . . the fact that you're going to be—" Lanie fumbled. "*Not* be president. Anymore. Was what I meant."

Lanie saw Michael emerge from the next room, and his eyes locked on her. He must have seen her drowning because he came right over and slipped his large, warm hand around her waist. Was it a coincidence that the two of them had both suddenly reappeared at roughly the same time?

"Everything okay over here?" he asked. He handed her his drink, and she gulped it just to give her mouth something to do. Ugh. Scotch.

"We're fine." Ainsley reached over and squeezed Michael's arm just above the elbow. It was an intimate gesture. A familiar gesture. And it lingered there half a second too long. Right there, in front of everyone. "Lanie, I feel like I haven't seen you all night. Let's go find Dayna and Bee and drink a toast."

She held the same hand out to Lanie. The others were silent. Michael watched her, his expression unreadable. Lanie wanted to slap the offered hand away. She wanted to break the skinny little wrist that held it.

But this was Ainsley. And everyone was watching. So she took Ainsley's hand and forced a smile as they sashayed through the crowd.

paige

"This view is unreal," Paige whispered.

She was standing at a wall of windows at the back of John and Ainsley's great room, feeling a touch breathless as she gazed out at the endless ocean and the stars just beginning to pop out in the distance. Their home was the stuff dreams were made of. Growing up, she and her friends had occasionally driven around the Palisades, but she'd never set foot inside one of these mansions. It was the most exclusive neighborhood in the county, set up here in the hills with elegant, custom-carved NO TRESPASSING signs everywhere. She almost couldn't believe that John and Ainsley's kids hadn't gone to boarding school or private day school like the Palisades kids had when she was young.

It had to be John's influence. He'd gone to the Piermont public schools and he'd turned out just fine. Better than fine, from the look of things. This house had wings. Actual wings.

"Amazing, isn't it?" said Claudia Marks as she took a sip of her white wine. "Hard to believe we live in the same town."

Claudia was one of Marie's friends. They had been introduced after school the day before when Marie had told Paige that she wasn't going to make it tonight because she had to work, though it was pretty clear to Paige that she simply didn't want to be here. Or that Ainsley didn't want her here. Or both. Sooner or later, Paige was going to have to get to the bottom of that rift. But for now, she was glad to have Claudia to chat with.

"Hard to believe we live in the same universe," Paige joked.

A door behind Paige slid open, bringing with it a cloud of cigar smoke. Startled—she hadn't realized this was a wall of doors, not windows—Paige stepped out of the way and was surprised to see that John was the person coming through. Her heart gave a tiny flutter at the sight of him.

"Paige! Hey!"

John leaned in to give her a one-armed hug, holding his glass out to keep from spilling, and Paige did the same. It gave her a second to smooth the delight from her face before she had to face him.

"Hi, John. Your house is incredible," Paige told him.

John gave a sheepish laugh. "Thanks. It's . . . well, I didn't have much to do with it aside from the signing of the checks. Ainsley's the one with the eye." Was it just Paige, or had something in his eyes hardened when he'd said Ainsley's name? He glanced sideways at Claudia. "Hey, Claudia. Good to see you. How's Liam doing at Yale?"

"So far, so good," said Claudia. "So nice of you to remember."

"Hey, if not for him, Bradley would not have made it through fifth-grade math, so I'm rooting for him."

"I'll tell him you said so."

John cleared his throat and looked at Paige again. "So. You want the tour?"

"Do we have time for that? The party's only four hours."

John laughed a hearty laugh that sent goose bumps up and down her arms.

Married. He's married. To the queen bee to end all queen bees.

"We'll stick to the ground floor. See how far we get."

John put his hand on the small of her back, and Paige gave Claudia a *You good?* look, to which Claudia replied with an *It's your funeral* eyebrow raise. Apparently, *everyone* was afraid of Ainsley. But Paige let it slide off her back. She wasn't doing anything wrong here. The host of the party had offered a tour. This type of thing happened every day.

She did, however, notice that he didn't take her back through the large great room—it could have been called a ballroom, really—but around to a hallway that skirted most of the crowd. Did he not want to be seen with her? Or was he trying to get her alone?

"We bought this place when Michelle, our oldest, was just starting school. It needed some work, but nothing crazy. New kitchen and some bathrooms. There used to be an actual bowling alley in the basement, but Ainsley had it torn out and turned it into a gym that we almost never use. This part of the house is where we really live."

John opened a set of double doors and the lights flickered on. They stepped down a couple of stairs into an open-floor-plan family room with a kitchen at the back overlooking the ocean that was like something out of a Nora Ephron movie. The countertops were white marble, the cabinets shaker-style, and there was open shelving displaying stylish, contemporary bowls and plates. Pendent lighting hung over a large island that could seat ten people, and there was another dining table set in the middle of a sunroom that must have been gorgeous in the mornings with the sun coming up over the water. The couches were deep and looked lived in, unlike the midcentury modern chaises and lounges in the seating areas set up around the great room, and there were knickknacks and photos everywhere—on the fireplace mantel, lining the built-in shelves around the flat-screen TV.

"This is great," Paige said, taking a few steps into the room and sipping her wine. "This part of the house . . . it's more the type of home I imagined you living in."

"You imagined where I'd live?" he joked. Flirtatiously? No. Not possible. But it *felt* flirtatious.

"No. Not, like, before I knew you were still here." She turned to look at him, trying to quell her smile. "You never wondered where I ended up?"

"I didn't have to. Your dad used to show me pictures."

Paige almost did a spit-take with her wine. "What?"

"Yeah, we used to bump into each other at the coffee shop once in a while, and let's just say he was a very proud grandpa. He bragged about Izzy all the time."

Tears sprang to Paige's eyes. "Oh my God. I can't believe—"

"And he bragged about you, too, you know. Your career. The house in the hills."

Paige put her fingertips over her mouth. She would not cry at this party. She refused to cry.

"God, sorry. I'm an idiot." John put his drink down on a side table and grabbed a tissue, handing it to her. "I just thought you'd want to know."

"No. I did. I do! I just— Shit!" Paige put her purse down on the couch and used the tissue to dab under her eyes, waving at her face with her free hand in an attempt to save her eyeliner. "It's been four years and still, whenever his name comes up, I start crying." A choking sound escaped, despite her best efforts, and John pulled her into his arms. She pressed her nose into his shirt and let herself cry, just a little. He smelled ridiculously good. Fabric softener and cologne and just a hint of cigar smoke.

"Oh, isn't this sweet?"

John practically threw Paige off him, so abruptly that she stumbled and knocked his wine over. The glass teetered one way, then the other, and decided to spill forward, drenching the skirt of her dress.

"Ainsley," John said.

"Honestly, Paige, I thought you were a writer," Ainsley said. "Isn't the damsel-in-distress act a tad . . . overplayed?"

The woman was standing in the double doorway with Lanie, Dayna, and Bee behind her, looking like a goddess in her flowy green-and-blue dress. Her skin glowed like there was a permanent beam of sunlight trained on her.

"God, Ainsley," said John. "Can't you just—"

"Let me get you a towel!" Lanie slipped into the room and ran to the kitchen, returning with a tea towel to sop up the rapidly growing stain on Paige's skirt. There was no saving it, of course. Nor would there be any saving the cream-and-blue rug that was now covered in broken glass and wine that looked like blood splatter.

"Can't I just, what? I'd love to hear what you were about to say."

John took a deep breath. "Ainsley, this is Paige. She's an old friend of mine from high school. I was just showing her around the part of the house where I actually live."

"Oh, I know who she is. We've met. Funny how Dayna was the one who had to tell me your ex moved back to town."

Paige glanced over at John. So he hadn't told Ainsley? How the hell had Dayna known about their past?

"We dated for like a year," John said and chuckled, making Paige's face burn with humiliation. "And it was a lifetime ago."

Okay. Good to know how he remembered it.

"Where's the bathroom?" Paige asked Lanie, looking *only* at Lanie. If she looked at anyone else right then she was going to scream.

"Right over—"

"That one's being renovated. You'll have to go upstairs," Ainsley snapped. "But be careful. I don't need anything else getting ruined."

"It's up the stairs on the right," John said. "I'll show you."

"No you won't. It's time for the speeches, and we need to encourage last bids for the silent auction," Ainsley told him. "Unless you've completely forgotten we're hosting this thing."

Another sigh from John. He shot Paige a pained, apologetic look.

"It's fine," Paige said, just wanting to get the hell away from them. "Really, I'm fine."

She took the tea towel from Lanie and speed-walked over to the stairs. More lights popped on as she jogged up them, illuminating school photos of John's kids, framed along the stairway walls. At the top was a long hallway, lined with closed doors.

How fucking big *was* this place?

She tried the first door on the right and found the bathroom, thank God. The last thing she wanted to do was search this whole hallway. Paige slipped inside, locked the door, and screamed silently into the tea towel. Then she brought her fist down on the first thing she saw, a silver towel rod. It snapped right off the wall. Pain radiated up her arm. She experienced half a second of satisfaction at letting out her rage, at destroying something.

And then she took a breath.

And saw what she had done.

The hole in the wall. The paint peeling off in jagged shards. The screws hanging haphazardly from the end of the towel bar.

The guilt seeped in.

And the fear.

Shit. *Shit!* She had to get this anger thing under control. What the hell was wrong with her? She'd just destroyed private property. Her ex-boyfriend and his wench of a wife's private property. And for what? She didn't really like this dress anymore anyway.

Paige turned to look at herself in the mirror. She was a wreck. The tears had smudged her makeup and there was sweat around her nose and on her brow line. The wine had started to dry, making it look as if she'd been recently stabbed in the leg. She ran the water and grabbed a tissue to dab at her face, but it was no use. She looked like she'd just rolled out of a club on New Year's morning.

She stared into her own eyes and breathed. Clearly, Ainsley was right. John did not have a type. She couldn't believe what a fucking bitch that woman was. How could John have married her? He'd never been one of those guys to be taken in by a vapid mean girl just because she was pretty. Where had she even come from? How had they met?

Why did it matter?

Paige shook her head and scoffed at herself. She would take a few moments to pull it together and then she would sneak out the back door and go home. And then she really needed to figure out how to get this anger problem of hers under control before she had another restraining order taken out against her.

lanie

Lanie stood at the top of the stairs, clutching Paige's tiny purse in both hands. She knew a rage spiral when she heard one. But usually Lanie screamed into a pillow or did some cardio. It sounded like Paige had hulked out all over Ainsley's guest bath. She should just leave the purse on the floor and go. Or maybe she should get John in case he needed to call the police. What if Paige was having some kind of psychotic break in there?

She remembered the broken glass on her street. The bits of potpourri everywhere. The crashing sound as the landscapers cleaned it all up with their vacuum contraption.

Lanie was still deciding what to do when the bathroom door opened. Her heart vaulted into her throat. She was about to be discovered lurking.

Lanie plastered a smile on her face, ready to pretend she was just now cresting the stairs. That she hadn't heard a thing. That she was just coming up to return Paige's handbag and see if she was okay—which was the actual truth. At least the handbag part. What she'd really been doing was coming to tell Paige where the back door was and gently suggest she use it.

No one got a tour of Ainsley's private residence. And no one touched Ainsley's husband. And on the night of the Parents and Pinot Party, no less? The woman may as well have shown up naked and then burned the place down.

She held her breath. But Paige didn't appear around the corner. Lanie waited a beat. Then two. Then three. Finally, she crept up the last few stairs and checked the hall. The bathroom door was closed. Had she been hearing things? She tiptoed over. No light under the door. A quick rap got no response. The hallway ahead was eerily empty, wall sconces lighting the way dimly back toward the main house. Lanie glanced quickly over her shoulder, then cracked open the bathroom door.

Her hand fluttered up to cover her gasp. When Ainsley saw this, Paige's life was effectively over.

nina

She had been waiting for her moment all night, watching Ainsley from the corner of her eye as Ravi chatted up the other dads, made jokes, told stories about his days playing dive bars in Boston. For a woman who was a social butterfly and the hostess of the party, Ainsley was oddly hard to get a bead on. Half the night it had seemed as if she wasn't even there.

Then, the speeches. It happened every year. One of the waitstaff would ring a tiny bell and everyone would move from the great room into the foyer, which looked like something out of a Disney film with its sweeping double staircase and ostentatious crystal chandelier. The catering company owned by Nina's client, Veronika Price, was handling the party tonight, and Veronika had asked Nina if this was something she really had to have her people do, or if Ainsley was hazing her. But no, the bell had been rung to summon Pavlov's dogs and now, here they were, gathered at their hostess's feet. Literally.

This year, like every other, Ainsley and John stood at the top of the stairs to address their minions. But this year, something was off. Ainsley's smile was as wide and freshly whitened as ever, but John looked—well—he looked ill. Normally he stood with one hand on the small of Ainsley's back and cracked jokes while Ainsley relayed her thanks and announced how much money had been pledged so far in the final auction, but tonight, he didn't touch her. He barely even looked at her. As she spoke, he threw back a scotch and then, realizing there was nowhere to put his empty glass, held it in front of him with both hands as if he was about to pee into it.

"In short, this has the potential to be the most profitable Parents and Pinot auction to date, so thank you to everyone who donated items and experiences, and an even bigger thank-you to those of you who are running up the tallies," Ainsley said, earning a chuckle from the crowd. "You still have an hour to bid, so make sure you don't miss out on that big-ticket item you were eyeing."

Nina's neck was beginning to hurt from holding her head back at this angle.

"And enjoy dessert!"

Ainsley threw her arms wide as an army of servers poured in from all directions, carrying trays of mini cakes and pies and fall donuts. People oohed and aahed and applauded.

"I heard there are mini apple fritters," Ravi told her, giving her waist a squeeze. "I'll go grab us some."

Nina watched John jog down the stairs and head straight for the bar. Ainsley went in the other direction, walking deeper into the house upstairs. Away from the party.

Her heart rate ticked. This was her chance.

Cutting through throngs of semi-drunk sweet-seekers, Nina jogged up the very stairs John had just descended. This place was the size of a palace, and there was no telling how quickly she might lose Ainsley. But she didn't need to look far. Ainsley was right around the corner, texting frantically on her phone, and the second she saw Nina, she dropped it. It bounced twice and landed at the toes of Nina's painfully tight heels. She bent to pick it up, glancing at the screen before handing it over.

WE NEED TO TALK. I'M CALLING IT OFF.

"Give that back." Ainsley snatched the phone.

"Sorry," Nina said. "I didn't see anything."

"What do you want, Nina?"

Oh, so Ainsley did know her name after all. But now that Nina had her alone, she couldn't for the life of her remember the speech she had planned. Ainsley's gaze darted past Nina as a raucous round of laughter went up in the foyer, and she knew she was about to lose the woman.

"I hacked in."

Ainsley paled. "You *what*?"

Maybe *not* the best way to start. But there was no going back now.

"I hacked into the PBA's financials." Nina reached into her purse and pulled out the folder of printouts—every transaction Bee Dolan had made in the last twenty-four months. The folder was a garish pink, ordered from Staples by her new assistant. Nina would never use it herself, but for some reason she thought Ainsley might appreciate the color—which now seemed like a stupid choice. "It was ridiculously easy to do. You don't even need to touch the firewall. I just ran a simple password algorithm, and I was in."

Ainsley took the folder from Nina and shakily flipped through the pages. "Oh my God," she said, and turned to the side. "Oh my *God*."

Nina almost smiled at Ainsley's distress. This was what vindication felt like. Now Ainsley would have to take her seriously. She'd have to ask for Nina's help.

"Do you have any other copies of this?"

"No, but I—"

"Good. Now I think you should leave before I go downstairs and tell the chief of police that you're hacking into private accounts. Though last I checked, he was the winning bidder on that Virginia golf outing, so I'd hate to ruin his night by having him make an arrest."

Nina blinked. The police? No. She couldn't. "You wouldn't," she said aloud.

"You just admitted to me that you hacked into the PBA's financials. You *handed me* evidence," Ainsley said, getting right in Nina's face. Up close Nina could see her pores. The tiny red lines in her wide eyes. "Don't you understand you've committed a felony?"

"I didn't—I wasn't trying to—"

"It doesn't matter what you were trying to do." Ainsley stood up straight, took a deep breath and transformed into her normal, composed self. "What matters is how it looks."

Nina reached for the folder, but Ainsley held it out of reach. "I'll be keeping this, thanks."

Then she turned and walked down the opposite set of stairs, holding her skirt up elegantly on one side, just like a true princess.

paige

Paige was lucky Ainsley had been looking down at her phone when she'd come around the corner. It had given her a precious half a second to duck into an alcove and hide. What she would have liked to do was punch the woman in the face, but that would not have been socially acceptable. Besides, she'd already destroyed Ainsley's bathroom.

Instead, she decided to wait until Ainsley rejoined the party and then find a back exit out of this place. A house this size had to have a couple dozen doors to the outside. She'd crawl down the cliffs out back to the beach if she had to.

After a minute, Paige heard someone join Ainsley. Heard their voices as they conversed, but couldn't quite make out what they were saying. She could tell it was growing heated, though, and she had this awful vision of Ainsley being shoved over the top of that pretty, sweeping, centerpiece staircase—the one that had to be around the corner at the other end of the hall.

Then Paige heard one word clear as day—*felony*.

She peeked out of her hiding spot.

It was Not-a-Nun. The woman even dressed the part for a party—she was sporting a fairly shapeless black dress with a beaded white collar. It might have looked chic on someone taller, but it did nothing for the woman's short legs. Her large bag—totally wrong for a party like this one—hung from the crook of her arm.

Ainsley held some sort of folder out of the nun's reach, then turned and disappeared from the end of the hallway. The nun's face was blotchy, as if she might be about to cry. What a fucking bully Ainsley was. Paige half wanted to go over to this woman and tell her to forget it—that Ainsley was just a bitch talking trash—but then the nun suddenly slapped herself across the face. Once. Twice. Paige bit down on her tongue and ducked behind the wall. She counted to twenty Mississippis before checking the hallway. Empty.

"Merciful Jesus," she said under her breath. It was something her grandmother used to say whenever she and her cousins got out of control. And that was exactly how this night had gotten—totally out of control.

She needed to call an Uber and get the hell out of there. That was when she realized she didn't have her phone.

PAIGE BACKTRACKED, BUT her purse was not in the bathroom. It wasn't on the stairs to the living room. It wasn't on the couch where she was sure she had left it. It was just gone. Had someone stolen her purse? But who? Paige was pretty sure the damn servers at this party had more money than she did.

She stood in the center of the darkened living room and told herself to breathe. She'd definitely had her bag when John brought her in here earlier. The only people who had been with her were John, Ainsley, Lanie, Dayna, and Bee. The star necklace quartet. Paige glanced at the now closed double doors. Faintly, she could hear the sounds of the party beyond. She resigned herself to her fate.

"I'm going back in," she muttered.

Back in the party proper, things had gotten louder—rowdier—
drunker. Men and women crowded the bidding tables set up along the
vast dining room, and the jazz band in the ballroom had kicked it up a
notch, playing a version of the "Macarena" that Paige was hoping she
would be able to erase from her memory by first light. Paige looked for
Claudia, needing a friendly face and an ally more than anything, but
she didn't see her. She did see various clutches of women eyeing the
stain on her dress as she slipped by. Heard a few conversations stop
when she got too close. She did her best to ignore it.

*You don't care about these people. Just find your bag and get the hell out
of here.*

Maybe John could help her. Though that would be risking Ainsley's
wrath all over again. The very idea felt exhausting, but Paige didn't
know what else to do. She wove toward the back of the room and
stepped out onto the deck. Bulb lights had been strung and, though the
outdoor area had been packed earlier, there was no one out there now. It
was a cool night, and Paige walked straight ahead to the railing, looking
over the sheer cliffs and the rocky beach down below. Way far out on
the ocean, Paige could see twinkling lights. A cruise ship or a large fish-
ing trawler—it was hard to say. If she screamed at the top of her lungs,
would it carry across the water to the people on that boat?

"I'm only telling you this as a courtesy. You don't have to get all
emotional about it."

Paige flinched. Shit. Was that Ainsley again? What the hell? Was
the woman everywhere? She looked around, but no. She was definitely alone.

"But Ainsley, you promised—"

"God, Lanie, you sound like a child. I'm only doing what's best
for the PBA. Clearly I'm the only person in this town qualified to
run it."

Where the hell were those voices coming from? Paige was torn
between curiosity and terror that she'd be caught eavesdropping.

"How dare you say that?" Lanie snapped in a voice Paige couldn't believe was coming from Miss Perky. "How *dare* you? You know how hard I've worked. Don't walk away from me, Ainsley!"

Paige held her breath.

"Don't touch me, *Lanie*. I will destroy you."

"What the hell does that mean?"

"I know a few things, darling. About what you did during quarantine? Things I'm sure you don't want me repeating."

There was a long, loaded silence. Paige strained forward. The voices seemed to be coming from somewhere below her. Was there another deck beneath this one?

"I don't understand what happened." Lanie's voice was much calmer now. Quieter. Resigned? "What changed? You said you were going to step down."

"I know what I said. I changed my mind. And you don't need to understand. You just need to accept it."

There was a creak and a stomp, and before Paige could move, Ainsley appeared right in front of her. There were stairs, hidden from Paige's view by two large planters. They must have led down to the beach. Ainsley froze at the sight of Paige, her eyes wide, but then she smirked.

"You're really still here?" she said, looking her up and down. "Get a life." Then she swept inside imperiously. Seconds later, Lanie appeared, dabbing below her eyes with the fingertips of one hand. When she saw Paige, her reaction was slightly different.

She looked . . . scared.

"Were you listening in on us?"

"I was just looking for my purse." Paige stared pointedly at the beaded bag in Lanie's other hand. She held her arm out for it. Lanie placed it in Paige's palm and cleared her throat.

"I'd appreciate it if you wouldn't tell anyone what you just heard. I'd like to share the news myself."

"I don't even know what I just heard," Paige said truthfully.

Lanie gave her a skeptical look, then followed Ainsley back inside.

lanie

She didn't need more wine, but she poured herself some anyway, breaking her cardinal rule. It was after midnight. The party had ended an hour ago. She'd called an Uber and left even earlier than that, risking Ainsley's further irritation, but the slap in the face was the least Lanie could do after Ainsley had gone back on her word. As for Michael, she couldn't believe he hadn't come with her. He had a flight in the morning and was supposed to come home, sleep a few hours, then take a car service to the airport from here. But he hadn't even blinked when she'd said she was calling a car. Had he stayed behind to spend more time with Ainsley?

The sitter had been Venmo-ed, the kids were in bed, and Michael was still not home, still not answering her texts. They had fought. Again. He didn't understand why she was so upset over Ainsley's news. That she wasn't going to give up the presidency after all. He'd said she didn't need the stress. That she had enough to do with the kids and the membership chair responsibilities and dealing with the house. He just didn't get it. She was so close. *So* close. To have to give it up now, simply because Ainsley always got her way . . .

But then it had occurred to her. Maybe he was on Ainsley's side. Maybe it was more important to him that Ainsley got what she wanted. Maybe it didn't matter as much to him that his wife of fifteen years got what *she* wanted. Lanie slugged her wine. Everything was falling apart.

Michael had never understood why she cared so much about the presidency. That, in and of itself, was a huge problem. Lanie was an organizer. A people person. The most type-A woman she knew. She was tired of not being in charge. It was her turn. Her time. And Ainsley had just plucked it from her grasp like it meant nothing. Of course she was upset. No, she was pissed.

Did he not know her at all?

And then, of course, there was that other, much larger problem. Ainsley knew. She knew about what Lanie had done.

It had to have been Dayna. Obviously, it was Dayna. But when? And *why*? Dayna was the vault. She couldn't have told. She wouldn't.

But it was literally the only way.

Lanie's phone pinged, but it wasn't Michael. It was Felicity.

I NEED THAT PIC OF YOU ME AND LAUREN BY THE FIRE-PLACE! SO MUCH FUN!

Lanie caught her dim reflection in the kitchen windows. She looked haunted. Haggard. Like some kind of drug addict. She picked up her wineglass and threw it at the sink, shattering it to bits.

"Oh my God." Her hands covered her mouth. What was wrong with her? She grabbed a rag and started to clean it up and instantly nicked her finger. The tears were an immediate and disproportionate response. She braced her hands on the marble countertop and pressed into it, quietly heaving. The kids were upstairs in their rooms, behind closed doors, but Lanie had never been a loud crier. She had always been one to keep her emotions packed down deep, even when she was alone. She clasped one arm around her middle as she shook, trying in vain to hold herself together.

Her phone pinged again. She sucked the blood from her fingertip, but it was just a text from Lauren, asking when she was going to post her pictures. It wasn't as if she could blame her. Whatever the event, Lanie normally posted everything the second she got home, if not sooner.

Lanie gulped and, still heaving, perched on one of the stools at the kitchen island. She opened Instagram and shakily brought up the photos from this evening. There were so many—multiple snaps of almost every pose. Her eyes were so blurry it was near impossible to tell which ones were the best. Were Lauren's eyes closed in that one? Did Colin have his hand on the wrong woman's ass?

Lanie went back to the sink, ran cold water into her hands and splashed her face, then found a Band-Aid and dealt with her finger. She cleared her throat a few times, shook her hair back and took a deep breath. She could see her eye makeup running down her cheeks in the window, so she grabbed a paper towel and swiped. Then she went back to her phone and started posting.

SO MUCH FUN AT THE ANNUAL #PARENTSANDPINOTPARTY
TONIGHT!
@AINSLEYAAMES = #MVP #HOSTESS #PBAPREZ
FRIENDS WHO SIP TOGETHER STAY TOGETHER!!!
AMAZING VIEWS! AMAZING FRIENDS! #BLESSED

She hit share on the last post and put her phone down, the tears starting up again in earnest as the likes began to pour in, lighting up her screen like the Fourth of July.

What if Ainsley and Michael were together right now? What if Ainsley told him what she'd done?

Her phone pinged with another incoming text. This one was from Dayna.

AINSLEY TOLD ME. I'M SO SORRY.

Lanie started shaking. She texted back.

SORRY FOR WHAT?

It took longer than normal for Dayna to reply.

ABOUT THE PRESIDENCY.

Lanie started to text back.

HOW COULD YOU TELL HER?

No.

HOW MUCH DID YOU TELL HER?

She deleted that, too.

But what if Dayna had told Ainsley everything? Not just about what she'd done on that awful afternoon during the pandemic, but why. And what had come after.

A sinking realization came over her, leaving her so cold she started to shake. She was never going to be on solid footing again. For the rest of her life, she would always be wondering when the other shoe would drop. Ainsley could hold this over her head forever.

If Michael ever found out, her life was over. Michael would kill her. Or leave her. She wasn't sure which was worse.

Lanie stood up and grabbed her keys and called her mother, who answered on the first ring. Thank God the woman never slept.

"Lane? What's wrong?"

"Can you come over? The kids are asleep and I have to go out."

"At this hour? What's going on?"

"Nothing. I just . . . Please, Mom?"

"Of course. I'll be there in ten minutes."

Lanie went to the closet and slipped on her black trench coat, making sure her face looked okay in the mirror. She couldn't stick around for her mother's questions. She had to go back to Ainsley's and talk to her face-to-face.

Lanie just hoped Michael was out with the guys for a nightcap somewhere, or driving around, blowing off steam. She hoped against hope that he wasn't still at Ainsley's. Lanie wasn't sure what she'd do if he was.

nina

Nina slid into her house, praying Ravi wouldn't hear as she clicked the door closed. Still as stone, she waited. One Mississippi. Two Mississippi. Three Mississippi.

The house remained dark. Not a creak on the stairs.

She kicked off her sneakers and tiptoed across the high-gloss wood floors. She could have skated, really, but she had to get into her office fast. She had to hide this goddamned hot-pink folder.

She couldn't believe what she'd just done. Couldn't believe all she'd risked, sneaking back into the Andersons' house to retrieve it. Like an idiot, she'd printed out the fruits of her hacking labor on company letterhead. The words Anand & Associates were emblazoned across the top of each list of figures. If these pages were shown to the police, her chances for plausible deniability were nil.

From the moment Ainsley left her at the top of the stairs, Nina had kept an eye on the woman. Keeping a safe distance, she'd watched through French doors as Ainsley fought with John about Paige. Watched her put the folder down on the desk and seemingly forget it was there. This sheaf of papers that could ruin Nina's life, left aside like it was nothing.

Infuriating. That was the word for Ainsley Aames. She was infuriating.

Nina's plan had been to steal the folder back before she left the party, but she hadn't had the chance. Ravi had eaten too many fritters on top of too much wine and had thrown up in the hydrangea bushes outside like some common teenager. Which, now that she thought about it, was probably why he hadn't heard her come in. It was almost two a.m. He was in the deepest of deep drunk sleeps.

But it was okay. It was okay. It was all going to be fine. She had the folder now. There was no evidence. And Ainsley wasn't going to talk. Nina was sure of that.

paige

It wasn't as if she'd intended to run by John and Ainsley's house. She just wanted to tackle some hills, and that was where the hills were. Besides, their neighborhood had the most gorgeous views in town. Paige used to run this route all the time in high school when she had been the least accomplished runner on the cross-country team. Her father had mandated that she do a sport—any sport—so she'd of course chosen the one that allowed her to be alone as much as humanly possible. But while Paige had never been great at it, she'd grown to love it, and had become a lifelong runner. She craved the feeling of accomplishment, of thinking she could never get to the top of a hill and getting there anyway. Plus, she loved to listen to audiobooks, and now that she was no longer trapped in L.A. traffic for hours a day, this was the only time she had to do it.

She kept thinking about Ainsley's expression when she'd found John comforting her. Like she wanted to rip Paige's face off. Maybe Paige should explain. In the calm light of day when John wasn't around. She was still emotional about her father's death, and John was one of the few people who had known him. Ainsley was human. Wasn't she? She'd have to understand.

No, screw that. Why should Paige have to apologize? She didn't owe Ainsley anything. Ainsley wasn't better than her. Paige had been nominated for an Emmy. She'd won two Writers Guild Awards. She'd met Tom Hanks, for God's sake. Well. She'd been in the same room as Tom Hanks. Never got up the guts to go talk to him. But she could have.

She turned on the speed.

The sun was slowly rising up from the ocean and warming her face against the early morning chill. Her heart beat a bit faster as she turned onto John and Ainsley's street. There were very few houses up here, and the bends in the road made it so that she wouldn't spot their driveway until it was too late to turn back. Her breath shortened as she approached that last turn, more from nerves and anticipation than from the grade of the hill.

She should jog across the street and head back home, she knew. But she didn't. And the second she came around the bend she regretted it.

Cop cars. Four of them. Klatches of people. Hands covering mouths. Heads bent together. Tears. Someone was stringing up yellow caution tape across the driveway. John and Ainsley's driveway.

Paige's knees jellified and she bent forward, bracing her hands just above them.

John, she thought. *No.*

The strangest memory flitted across her consciousness. John, as a twelve-year-old kid, before she'd developed any sort of crush on him, popping wheelies on his BMX bike in the parking lot at the middle school. The cackle of his laughter just before his eyes went wide and he realized he'd rotated too far and was about to crack his skull. They'd all thought he was going to die that day. There had been so much blood. But all he'd ended up with was a bald spot with a jagged line of ugly stitches down its center. That scar was what had solidified John's popularity among the boys in her grade. She used to run her fingers over the line of rough skin under his hair when they were kissing. Her fingertips tingled now at the memory. It suddenly felt like five days ago, not twenty-some-odd years.

If something had happened to him . . .

But then there he was, standing on the brick front porch of the house, all the way up at the top of the drive, talking to a pair of plainclothes officers. He still wore the same clothes as when she'd last seen him. He was rubbing his forehead with one hand, nodding as people asked him questions. The relief Paige felt was overwhelming. She pressed one hand into the nearest tree and tried to catch her breath.

"Miss Lancaster? That you? Hey! You okay?"

It was that cop from the other day. Dominic. He walked across the street toward her in full uniform, the radio at his hip giving off bursts of static.

"Are you all right?" he asked again.

"I'm . . . I'm fine." She waved a hand at her face. "What's going on? What happened?"

Dominic's kind eyes softened further. "It's Ainsley Aames. Did you know her?"

"Did I? *Did*?"

Why was he using the past tense?

He nodded solemnly. "She's dead. Husband found her this morning."

Paige sat down on the curb. Her legs simply couldn't hold her anymore. She couldn't believe this was happening. She'd just seen the woman. They all had. Poor John. His poor kids. She put her head between her knees.

"Whoa, okay." Dominic crouched in front of her. "So, I guess you did know her."

"Barely," Paige said to the gravel beneath her face. "But she had a party last night and—"

"The Parents and Pinot Party. It's legendary." He looked over his shoulder at the house.

"What happened?"

"They don't know yet. He found her on the beach at the bottom of the stairs. Apparently, she took a bad fall."

Paige pressed her hand into the curb and shoved herself up unsteadily. Her breath was back, but her heart was still jackhammering away like a warning drum. The last time she'd seen Ainsley, she'd been at the top of those stairs. With Lanie. But she'd been fine then. She'd gone back inside to join the party, all haughty and full of herself.

Dominic popped to his feet, nimble as a gymnast, and held out an arm to her.

"Is John . . . how is he?"

"Shaken up, of course. I haven't talked to him myself. The detectives from county are with him now."

"Detectives?"

"Yeah, you know how it goes. They've gotta rule out foul play. Right now they're thinking she got too drunk at the party and it was an accident. But you never know. And the spouse is always the first person they talk to."

Murder. He was talking about murder. About *John* murdering his wife.

A lump rose in her throat. Just then, John lifted his head and, even from this distance, she could tell he'd spotted her. He straightened up slightly and his jaw set. She wished she could go over there and talk to him. See for herself if he was okay. Tell the detectives John would never hurt anyone or anything. Tell them about that time senior year when he'd accidentally run over a squirrel and cried for half an hour.

"I really should get some of these people out of here," Dominic said of the little groups of mostly women who were standing on the other side of the street from where Paige had stopped. Gawkers who had positioned themselves around the end of the cordoned-off driveway. "Are you gonna be okay? Do you need a ride home?"

"No, I'm . . . I'm fine."

For the first time, Paige really looked at the other bystanders. Dayna stood among them, her face blotchy and red. Some were dressed in athletic gear like she was, others looked like they'd thrown on jackets over pajamas and run over here. Someone noticed Paige watching and nudged the woman next to her. They whispered and stared.

Suspiciously. Accusatorially.

"I think I'm gonna go," Paige said to Dominic.

It wouldn't be long before someone told the story about Ainsley finding Paige and John alone at the party. Until they all learned of their past as high school sweethearts. Paige had written for a cop show for years. She knew how this went. Maybe they looked at the spouse first, but they looked at former lovers second.

paige

"Izzy, you're eight years old. You don't need your grapes cut up for you anymore."

Paige stared down her daughter, whose tiny chin jutted out, her arms crossed over her skinny chest at the kitchen island. They had been arguing for fifteen minutes and were now at a stalemate. Over grapes.

"Martha cut them up for me!"

"Yes, when you were two and three. You're a big girl now. You can chew and swallow a whole grape." Paige pushed the bowl of grapes toward her and glanced down as her phone lit up. A news alert about a shooting in L.A. She really must change her settings. What she needed to know now was what was going on over at John's house, but it wasn't as if her phone was going to tell her that. There were no news alerts for Piermont, Connecticut, and she didn't have any friends to text her with updates. As far as she knew, Lanie and Marie were the only people in town with her number, and Lanie was certainly not thinking about her. As for Marie . . . well, Marie might have been throwing a "Ding-Dong! The Witch Is Dead" themed party.

"No! I want them cut up like Martha did!"

"Why don't you just cut them up for her, Paige?" said Elizabeth, who was pretending not to listen as she dried dishes with a towel. "She's barely eaten all day."

"Not helping, Mom." Her mother shrugged. Paige sighed and looked at Izzy. She picked up her phone. "Why don't I call Martha right now and ask her whether I should cut up your grapes?"

The flash of fear in Izzy's eyes was telling, but she reset her jaw. "Fine. Go ahead," Izzy said.

"Okay. Calling her now." She pretended to hit a contact and held the phone to her ear. "I'll just ask her if she was still cutting up your grapes like you were a baby."

"Paige," scolded Elizabeth.

"I'm not a baby!"

"Then stop acting like one!" Paige said, lowering the phone.

Izzy screamed and threw the bowl of grapes at the floor. The hard plastic ricocheted across the tile and Elizabeth gasped.

"Izzy! We don't throw things!" Paige said. "Go to your room right now!"

"I hate you!" Izzy shouted.

Paige shook as she bent to clean up the mess. All she could think about was the shattered potpourri jar. The broken towel bar. The shards of glass on her driveway back in L.A. A laptop, twisted and folded the wrong way.

She had thought Izzy hadn't seen. But of course, that was naïve. Paige wiped tears from her eyes as she stood.

"Izzy, we don't throw things that aren't for throwing," she said quietly. "Go to your room."

Izzy didn't move. The doorbell rang. They all looked over, a clear line of sight from where they stood to the front door. Through the cut glass, Paige saw the blue police uniform and her heart seized. She was the worst mother ever, and now she was going to be dragged downtown for questioning. It had only taken eight hours. She had given it twenty-four. But at least she'd already contacted a lawyer— her roommate from college, Lydia, who had gone on to Fordham Law. She wasn't in criminal defense, but she had a colleague on call in case Paige needed him.

"Who's that?" Elizabeth said.

"It's the police!" Izzy ran for the door and yanked it open. "Are you here to arrest my mom?" she asked brightly.

"Why would I do that?"

Paige's vision went hazy. It was Dominic Ramos's voice.

"Because she did something bad and then we had to move here."

"Izzy!" Paige said with a gasp, as Elizabeth shot her a questioning look.

Paige grabbed her purse, assuming she'd need it, and rushed to the door. She couldn't believe Izzy had just said that. Her daughter had no clue what had gone on back in L.A. She was sure of it.

Dominic's eyes were merry as they met hers. "What bad thing did you do?"

"No. Nothing. Kids." She forced a laugh. "She's just mad because I wouldn't cut up her grapes."

"Oh. Well last I checked, that *is* a capital offense."

"So are you going to arrest her now?"

Paige rolled her eyes. "Mom? Could you?"

"Yes, yes. Of course. Come on, Izzy. Let's get some new grapes and go out back on the patio." Elizabeth took Izzy's hand and led her back through the kitchen, grabbing the bag of grapes—and a knife— along the way.

Once her mother and daughter were gone, Paige's heart rate began to normalize, and her vision cleared. That was when she noticed Dominic was carrying a bakery box from Gino's.

"Oh yeah!" he said, noticing the track of her gaze. "I brought sfogliatelle. I remembered your dad was a fan." He noticed her bag on her shoulder and his smile faltered. "Oh. Were you on your way out?"

"No, I . . . uh . . . no. I just—" She took a deep breath. "Sorry, why the sfogliatelle?"

Dominic shifted his feet. "My mom taught me it always helps to ply a person with sweets when you're gonna ask them a favor."

Paige had no idea where this was going, but apparently it wasn't down to the station. "Smart woman, your mother," she said. She plucked the box from his hand by the string and stood aside so he could come in.

She led him into the kitchen and snipped the strings off the pastry box. The scent of the sugar and flaky pastry as she lifted the lid made her mouth water. It was the smell of her childhood. Her father was forever bringing these things home on Sunday mornings or after the various community meetings he was always attending. She took out two plates and popped open the coffee maker, surreptitiously swiping the fallen grapes and the bowl from the floor and into the garbage.

"Pick a pod, any pod," Paige said, opening a drawer beneath it. Her mother had rows of every kind of coffee imaginable, plus hot chocolate for Izzy. Dominic whistled, impressed, then selected a dark Jamaican roast.

"Excellent choice," Paige said.

"I figured Donut Shop would've been a little too on the nose."

Paige snorted a laugh and started his coffee, then put out the pastries and leaned back against the counter. "So, is everything okay? I mean, obviously it's not okay, but—"

"Yeah, it's not every day we have a high-profile death in this town."

"I can imagine," Paige said. "So. What's the favor?"

"Well, they're thinking the Anderson death was likely accidental."

Relief whooshed through Paige. "That's great!"

He tilted his head at her enthusiasm.

"I just mean because the alternative would be—"

There was a shriek of childish laughter from out back. Paige didn't know whether to feel gratified or annoyed that her mother had managed to change Izzy's mood so quickly.

"Having a murderer among us," Paige whispered, and rolled her eyes slightly because now the idea seemed so ridiculous. This was Piermont, for God's sake. Nothing remotely interesting ever happened here.

"Yeah, well, I'm not convinced there's not," Dominic said grimly.

Paige quickly pulled out a stool for herself and sat down. She reached for her pastry and took a huge bite, spraying crusty flakes and powdered sugar everywhere.

"Oooookay," she said, chewing. "Explain."

His coffee finished brewing and he plucked himself a cup from the dish drying rack, and another for her. She told him there was milk in the fridge and waited while he prepped his own coffee, feeling bad that she could no longer find the strength to play the good hostess. She did fish out a pod for herself and slapped it into the machine.

"I don't know, it's mostly a sixth sense. But the women I talked to this morning, they all said Ainsley never got drunk enough to be sloppy or even a little messy, not even at her own parties."

Paige thought of Ainsley last night and her snide remarks at Paige's expense. She thought of the odd encounter Ainsley had with Not-a-Nun, and then that tense conversation with Lanie. She hadn't *seemed* drunk. But then again, she'd told Lanie she would "destroy" her.

Who said shit like that?

It occurred to Paige, for the first time since this morning, that she wasn't the only one with a surface-level motive around here. Ainsley might have been the queen bee, but she had a lot of enemies. She hadn't seen Lanie among the crowd this morning, come to think of it.

"And the husband, they said, was wearing the same clothes he had on at the party last night," Dominic continued. "Pictures confirmed it."

"So maybe he passed out in his clothes."

"Maybe, but he hadn't gone to bed. Their room was completely perfect—bed made, no water on the bedside tables or anything."

"So?"

"So where did he sleep? Did he sleep at all? Or was he too racked with guilt over having murdered his wife?"

Paige swallowed. "Did you ask him these questions?"

"We tried, but he lawyered up."

"Oh."

"And then the M.E. said likely accidental, so . . . I don't know. Maybe I should just let it go."

"Maybe." *Please just let it go.* It wasn't that she thought John could have been guilty, but the last thing he needed was a criminal investigation. The next few weeks and months were going to be hard enough for him and his family.

Dominic took a long sip of his coffee and a bite of his pastry while Paige cast about desperately for a way to change the subject.

"Did you see or hear anything off at the party last night?" he asked her before she could think of a new conversational gambit.

The Not-a-Nun slapping herself repeatedly across the face? Ainsley threatening Lanie? John and Ainsley arguing because he had given her a hug? Something stopped her from mentioning these things, though. Probably the fact that Ainsley had been the bully in all situations, and she didn't feel like throwing these women—or John—under the bus for being victimized.

"I'm not really the best source," she told him. "I left pretty early."

"Oh. Not a party person?"

Paige considered her options here. She could keep her past with John a secret, but if she did that, he'd definitely find out some other way. Especially if he interviewed Dayna or Lanie or Bee, which he'd obviously have to do since Ainsley was the leader of their pack and they were so involved in the PBA. Hell, John himself might tell the police. If she didn't tell him, it would look like she'd hidden it for a reason.

"I left because Ainsley basically told me to. She caught me and John alone and she got pissed off."

Dominic tensed slightly. "Why were you alone with her husband?"

"Because he was giving me a tour of the house." She took another big bite of her pastry, averting her eyes. "I used to date John. In high school. So Ainsley wasn't super happy to find us together. But we weren't doing anything."

"Oh." Dominic stood up a little straighter. "That's . . . interesting." His brow knit and he took another sip of coffee, then coughed. And coughed. He doubled over coughing.

"Oh my God, are you okay?" Paige jumped up.

Dominic nodded as he fought for breath, pointing at his throat. "Wrong pipe," he rasped. "M'fine." He pulled out a stool and sat.

Paige got him some water anyway, then waited while he got hold of himself.

"I'm okay," he said finally, and cleared his throat. "So . . . you and John Anderson—"

"She was just imagining scandal where there isn't any," Paige said with a wave of her hand. "I haven't even seen the guy in over twenty years. He was just showing me their private living room and I got emotional and then she and her friends walked in."

"Why'd you get emotional?"

"We were talking about my dad."

"Oh." Dominic shifted in his seat.

"So, anyway, yeah. I didn't stay until the end." She narrowed her eyes. "Guess I'll never know whether I won that signed copy of *The Secret* . . ."

He tilted his head in question.

"Silent auction."

"Right."

"I didn't really bid on anything."

There was an awkward silence. Paige got up to rinse out her cup at the sink, wondering what Dominic was thinking. She shut off the water and turned to him. "I feel like we never got around to your favor."

He shook himself, as if refocusing.

"Right! I was going to ask you to be my eyes and ears inside the PBA."

"Um . . . what?"

"Hear me out," he said. "No one down at the precinct wants to look into this. My boss—the new chief, he's all about appearances and making sure this place is held up as some utopia. It took six weeks of sporadic driveway burglaries and car thefts for him to admit there was a problem and officially alert the town. So, the medical examiner says she fell; she fell. They don't want a scandal. But there's something else going on here. I can feel it. And if I can prove it, then maybe they'll let me take the detectives' exam. They keep passing me over, but if I'm right, they won't be able to ignore me anymore."

A warm tingle raced down Paige's spine. An inside informant. That was what he was asking her to be. A mole. The idea intrigued her. The idea that he thought she was capable of it intrigued her even more. But what did she know about investigation?

Plenty, actually. She'd written for a detective show for years. She had half a dozen L.A. cops of all ranks on speed dial and had sat with their on-set consultants for hours upon hours making sure everything was—if not realistic, then at least plausible. She'd given voice and motive and brainpower to one of the best cops on TV. She could do this. And her father would be so proud.

Plus, the sincerity and plain want in Dominic's words struck a chord in Paige. She knew from ambition, and she knew from being passed over. She wanted to ask him why he felt that way—surely this able-bodied young cop couldn't raise any of the traditional bigoted red flags within the department. But it felt like too personal a question, so she kept it to herself.

An informant. Interesting. Her career was in the shitter. She could barely write. She certainly couldn't parent. But this . . . this was something she could do. Maybe even do well.

"Can I ask you something?"

"Shoot." He took a bite of pastry, and then licked his lips, which Paige found momentarily distracting in the best possible way.

"If you're looking for a murderer, wouldn't I be a suspect?"

Dominic laughed. Paige did not.

"Sorry," he said. "You're serious."

"I am. I just told you I used to date the deceased's husband and she caught us alone together the night she was maybe murdered. I'm a writer, dude. I know what that means."

"Okay." He took a napkin from the metal napkin holder on the island and wiped his fingertips. He looked her in the eye. "Where were you at about one thirty this morning?"

Her heart thunked. They were really doing this. "Should I call a lawyer?"

"Up to you."

Well. This was very not by the book.

"I was in bed with my kid."

"Any witnesses? I mean, other than your kid?"

"My mom was here. Oh! And Teddy McFancyPants."

Dominic barely swallowed a laugh. "I'm sorry, who now?"

"Nanny cam. It's in a bear. His name is McFancyPants."

"Good enough for me," he said.

"Don't you want to see the footage?"

Maybe she was better at this than *he* was.

He shoved the rest of the pastry in his mouth. "Not necessary. But don't erase it, just in case we need it. I don't want to have to interview this McFancyPants directly. He sounds shifty." He took another, careful, slug of coffee. "Look, you're the daughter of the most legendary, decorated police chief this town has ever seen. Plus, it's not even an official investigation because no one believes me. All I need you to do

is go to meetings and parties and let me know if you overhear anything, you know, useful."

Paige considered it. There was just one thing holding her back.
Did she really want to spend more time around Lanie and Dayna and
Bee? They had all been there when Ainsley caught her and John.
They probably all hated her. And what had Lanie been doing with
her purse all that time? Had she gone through her stuff? Tried to
hack into her phone? Paige hated catty women, but catty women who
already had it out for her?

"I don't know."

His face fell.

"I just have a lot going on right now. And besides, those women
can't stand me, Dominic. Truly. I'd be surprised if they even invited
me to the next party."

"Just think about it, okay? It would really mean a lot to me."

God. Why was he so freaking sincere? And why were his eyes so
goddamned blue?

"Okay, fine. I'll think about it." She cleared the rest of their dishes
into the sink. "But seriously, I'm betting every last one of them lost
my number after last night."

Her phone pinged in her back pocket, and she fished it out after
flipping the water on over their plates in the sink. When she saw the
text she froze so completely, Dominic stepped up to glance over her
shoulder.

PBA MEETING WILL TAKE PLACE AS SCHEDULED. TOMOR-
ROW NIGHT AT PIERMONT ELEMENTARY LIBRARY. 7PM

Dominic raised one eyebrow. It was so sexy, Paige couldn't help
smiling.

"I *said* I'll think about it."

* * *

SHE WANTED TO do it. And she knew she was probably going to do it. But the idea was so ludicrous, she spent a good hour trying to talk herself out of it. When she couldn't, she told her mom about it, expecting her to balk. But no.

"I think you should do it."

"What? Mom, no. Why?"

Paige and her mother were sitting out in the backyard on chaise lounges, looking up at the stars. It was on an oddly warm autumn evening, and Izzy was fast asleep inside.

"Because it would be good for you. And good for Izzy."

Her mother took a sip of her white wine and leaned back, pulling a shawl around her shoulders as she gazed skyward.

"Good for me and Izzy to help some half-cracked cop with a murder investigation that no one wants him launching?"

Her mother snorted a laugh. "No. Good for the both of you for you to get involved."

Paige groaned.

"Honey, look. I know you don't want to talk about why you lost your job or felt like you had to move back here for a reset, and I'm trying to respect that." Her mother put her glass down on the table and jostled herself into a sideways position on her chair, resting on her hip now so she could look at Paige fully. "But if you really do want to get closer to Izzy and if you want her to feel more secure and have a social life, then you need to show her that you're invested in your new community and your new life. Joining the PBA, getting to know these women, attending these meetings and being part of something— that's going to be good for your emotional state *and* it's going to show her that she matters."

Paige decided not to point out that she would be getting to know these women in order to figure out if any of them pushed their sworn leader down a set of stairs. "But won't me attending all these meetings and events take me away from her more? I don't want you to have to babysit all the time."

"First of all, she's my granddaughter. It's not babysitting, it's hanging out with family." Elizabeth smiled. "Secondly, the meetings will be when she's winding down for the night, and half the events will involve her and all her little friends."

"And the whole murder thing?"

"Do you really think that poor woman was murdered?"

Maybe. "No."

"Then just call Officer Ramos after each meeting and tell him you didn't find anything out. Eventually he'll get bored and move on."

Her mother reached for her wine again, brought it to her lips, and paused.

"Or better yet, go out for coffee or a meal with him after each meeting," she said, eyes sparkling.

"Mom!"

"What!?" Her mother shrugged and sipped her wine. "He's very attractive."

Paige laughed. "I hadn't noticed."

"Maybe you'll even get inspired to write something new," her mother said. "Since that doesn't seem to be going so well."

"You noticed that, huh?" Paige asked.

Elizabeth shrugged. "All I'm saying is, there are all kinds of potential upsides."

"What about the downsides?" Paige said.

"Like what?"

"Like I'll have to leave the house. Be social. *Talk* to people."

Her mother smirked. "Welcome to personhood, kiddo. It may have taken you forty-some-odd years to get here, but we're glad you've finally arrived."

lanie

"I don't even remember the last thing I said to her. Was it that she had spinach in her teeth? God, what if the last thing I said to Ainsley Aames before she died was that she had spinach in her teeth?"

"I can't believe it. I can't believe she's dead. That one of us is . . . dead."

"The *best* of us."

"There's no way she fell down those stairs. She had amazing balance. Remember when we all took that barre class?"

Lanie couldn't seem to focus on who was talking. Her anxiety was through the roof. This was the meeting at which she was supposed to be named president. The night she'd been looking forward to for months, if not years. But now she had no idea what was going to happen. Was anyone going to bring up the presidency? She certainly wouldn't. That would not be appropriate. And she couldn't believe this was what she was thinking about, anyway. Ainsley would have been appalled.

Dayna stood right at her side as if they were still friends. As if she hadn't told Ainsley all the secrets they had shared in confidence. Bee, meanwhile, kept pulling fresh tissues out of her massive bag and blowing her nose into them noisily before crumpling them and shoving them back inside. For the first time in her life, Lanie wanted nothing more than to get away from these people. She wanted to run screaming for the door.

"Are you okay?" Dayna asked, leaning toward her ear.

"I'm fine," Lanie said through her teeth.

She stared past her immediate group of moms, past their tasteful stud earrings and artfully arranged messy buns, at a poster on the wall. It was an illustration of a diverse group of kids all leaning in over one book with the slogan: IMAGINE YOUR STORY. She wondered if Ainsley ever imagined this. Her life cut short. Lanie had a feeling that Ainsley would have enjoyed the idea of having a dramatic death—something that would cause scandal or that everyone would talk about. But she was certain she wouldn't have imagined *this*. A drunken tumble down the stairs. It was so *frat party*. Such an ignominious way to go.

She had been shaking so badly on the drive back over there Saturday night after her mother arrived to stay with the kids that she'd been sure she was going to crash. Then, when she saw that Michael's car was, in fact, still there, she'd almost crashed on purpose. She remembered wondering what it would feel like to slam her car into his, to feel the airbag explode. Wondered what he would do when he found her there, unconscious, behind the steering wheel.

She still didn't know what Michael had been doing there so late.

"The police put her time of death around two a.m.," said Caroline Roday, who lived just down the hill from Ainsley, in the house with the columns that had its American flag replaced every season to keep it from fading. It was technically outside the Palisades, but she acted as if she lived up there. "The party was well over by then."

"Two a.m.?" Lanie repeated. She'd been in her car at two a.m. Driving aimlessly, trying to tamp down her fury after seeing Michael's car still parked on the road. What time had *he* left Ainsley's house? She knew what time he'd gotten home, thanks to their security system—slightly after three. He'd slept in one of the guest rooms, something he did sometimes when he had business trips at all hours, and left so early she'd never laid eyes on him.

"I don't care what the police say. Someone did this to her," said Felicity. "And I think we all know who."

Lanie's stomach clenched. Everyone was looking at her.

"That new woman?" said Caroline.

Lanie let out a breath and gripped the top of the nearest chair. She had to calm down. Of course no one thought it was Michael. No one knew about her suspicions that he and Ainsley had been spending time together. No one knew he'd still been at her house so late.

But Paige. That was interesting. Lanie thought of the shattered glass on the street. The state in which she'd found Ainsley's hallway bathroom after Paige had left it. The way she'd pressed herself against John when she'd thought no one was there.

"Did you know she used to date John Anderson?" said Bee.

"I heard she was obsessed with him," added Dayna.

"I bet she moved back here to be with him," Felicity put in. "All she had to do was get Ainsley out of the way."

"Are you guys kidding me?" This from Marie Mancuso, who had been standing against the window, scrolling on her phone. "Paige no more pushed Ainsley Aames down the stairs than I did."

Silence.

Marie's arms flopped down at her sides. "Oh my God, I did *not* push her down the stairs!"

Everyone knew Marie hated Ainsley. Ever since last spring when they'd had their PBA Thank You dinner at Aldo's and Ainsley had been stricken with food poisoning and summarily launched a campaign to get the place closed down. It hadn't worked, because the restaurant had passed all health code inspections, but the damage from Ainsley's negative word of mouth was clear. The place was never as packed as it used to be, and Marie was forever running two-for-one and early-bird specials trying to lure people back.

Lanie sort of missed Aldo's. She'd been obsessed with their eggplant rollatini. It occurred to her that she could take the family there again, now that Ainsley was dead, and then she wanted to pull out her own spleen.

"I just keep waiting for her to walk through that door," Bee said.

Lanie turned to look. They all turned to look. But there was no one. Nothing but an empty doorway. When Lanie squared her back to the door again, she realized she was clutching her own arms tightly enough to give herself grip marks. She let go and shook out her hands.

"We should start the meeting soon," Bee said.

Bee's voice was creaky. She looked like death. Her doughy face was paler than normal and shiny, like a dumpling that had been left in the oil too long. There were flakes of mascara under her eyes. Around the library, people were crying, blowing their noses, shaking their heads, clinging to one another. Some husbands were even hugging their wives, kissing their foreheads, rubbing their backs. Not Lanie's husband, of course. Heaven forbid.

Sunday morning, Michael had texted her from the car service on his way to the airport that he was sorry about their argument and that they should talk when he got home. She'd texted back that Ainsley was dead. He'd called her instantly.

"What do you mean she's dead? How? When?"

Lanie had held her breath, trying to read into his tone. He was distraught, of course, but was it real? Had he truly been surprised? Or had he, somehow, known something?

"Lanie?" he'd said. "What the fuck?"

Or maybe he'd just been beside himself with grief over the fact that his lover had broken her neck.

"I don't know what happened," she'd told him. "All I know is John found her. Lauren called me because Caroline called her when she saw the police cars. But they don't have any more details yet."

"My God," he said. "That poor bastard. They don't think it was . . . I mean . . . did anyone mention anything . . . suspicious?"

Had he asked this because he already knew the death was suspicious? Because he knew she'd been murdered?

"Like what?" Lanie had asked. *Who would want to murder Ainsley?* she'd thought. *Okay, she was a bitch. But murder?*

Of course, Lanie had been crazy angry at Ainsley on Saturday night. For telling her she wasn't giving up the presidency after all. Offering no good explanation. *Threatening* her. Lanie could have killed Ainsley herself in that moment out on the deck.

That moment Paige had overheard.

"I don't know," Michael said. "Forget it. Forget I said anything. Shit. This is unreal."

"Did anything happen when you were there?" Lanie asked Michael now, gripping the phone so tightly it hurt. "I mean after I . . . left?"

There was a pause and it sounded like he'd entered a wind tunnel, but then he was back clear as day. "No, nothing out of the ordinary. I just hung out with the guys. It was totally stupid. Colin and Evan started playing some drinking game, and Colin got so blitzed he peed on the carpet. Luckily, Ainsley wasn't around to see that."

"So you weren't there long?"

She had just wanted to see if he would lie to her.

"Why do I feel like I'm getting the third degree here, Lane?"

"Sorry. Forget it. I'm just . . . Can you come home? I mean, can you fly out tonight or something?"

"I can't. We're stuck in bumper-to-bumper at the tolls. Even if I wanted to turn around, I couldn't. I'll be home tomorrow night."

Translation: I don't want to turn around. I don't want to come back and comfort you. She knew he'd told one of his college buddies he'd meet up with a group of guys that night at some bar near Harvard to watch Sunday Night Football and catch up, and he hated to back out on plans with his friends. It was like a moral compass thing. Or a bro code thing.

"Can't or won't?" she'd asked.

And it had all gone south from there.

"Lanie?" Dayna prompted. She seemed impatient. Clearly Lanie had missed something.

"I'm sorry. What?"

"Do you want to call the meeting to order?" Bee asked, gesturing at the podium. Someone had put out Ainsley's gavel. Bile rose in Lanie's throat at the sight of it sitting there, waiting for Ainsley to pick it up and rap it in her signature rhythm.

Tap. Tap. Taptaptaptaptap.

Lanie held her breath, not trusting herself to speak without vomiting on Bee's shoes. Her head was spinning and her pulse was skipping around in a way that couldn't be normal. It was all too much to process. And yet. Here she was. Finally. After all this time. The gavel was hers.

"Sorry," she managed, then covered her mouth with her fingertips, pressing firmly. "Yes, of course."

Lanie's knees quivered as she walked to the front of the room and stepped up to the podium. She had dreamed of this moment for so long. But every time she'd imagined it, Ainsley was there, smiling as she stepped aside, making way for her anointed replacement. The queen bee, ceding her crown.

But Ainsley had told her to her face she didn't think Lanie could handle the job. Why? What had changed?

The rest of the board took their seats at the long table to Lanie's left, leaving her own usual seat empty. She hesitated, then picked up the gavel.

Tap. Tap. Taptaptap—

The room fell silent and Lanie dropped the thing like it was a hot poker.

"Good evening, everyone. If we could settle?"

It was at that moment that the door opened. The entire room turned as one, breath suspended, as if they believed that by some miracle, Ainsley Aames would sweep into the room and forcibly shove Lanie out of her rightful spot at the podium.

But it wasn't Ainsley Aames.

It was Paige Lancaster.

paige

Dominic had chosen the wrong deputy, that was for sure. Showing up late had been a big mistake. But she'd promised Izzy they could finish one game of Chutes and Ladders before she left, and the game had taken *forever*. Whatever toy designer had placed that long-ass chute on square number 96 should be drawn and quartered. Though he or she was probably long since dead, now that she thought about it.

But it was clear that before Paige's arrival at the PBA meeting, everyone had been standing around chatting and gossiping, and that would have been the moment to overhear something juicy or at least interesting. Now that the meeting was starting, there would be nothing to report back.

"I think we should start with a moment of silence," Lanie said from her place behind the podium. "For Ainsley."

Instantly all heads bowed. Paige, who was sitting in a kiddie-sized chair in the kindergarten area of the library, because it was the last available seat and close to Marie, bowed her own head and almost tumbled sideways off the seat. She had to press her fingertips into the crusty rug at her side to keep from falling over. She wasn't sure what she was supposed to be thinking about during this moment of silence, but her imagination conjured up the image she'd been seeing all day: Ainsley crumpled at the bottom of a set of cliffside stairs, her eyes wide open and glaring at the sun, a trickle of blood out the corner of her mouth.

She hadn't seen any of this, of course, but this was what her brain supplied. And she knew why. In season two, episode 13 of *Chance Encounters*, the mystery revolved around a woman who had been found dead at the bottom of the stairs, and this was the pose the family had found her in. The woman, who was played as a corpse and in flashbacks by a lovely, underappreciated actress named Poppy Medina, even looked a bit like Ainsley. Paige wondered if this would come out in Dominic's investigation. Whether someone would find her name in the credits and think it looked fishy. Though she had contributed nothing to that particular script.

She really did need to find some other suspects for this crime, considering all evidence kept leading her brain back to herself. She looked around the room for Not-a-Nun and saw her sitting, ramrod straight, near the back wall. At some point Paige was really going to have to learn this woman's name.

Lanie cleared her throat. "Thank you." And everyone looked up.

Paige wondered if the moment of silence was sincere, or whether Lanie was covering up her guilt. Maybe both?

"I know everyone is still in shock and we—the board—really appreciate all of you coming out." She gripped the sides of the podium. "We all love . . . loved Ainsley, obviously."

Bullshit, Paige thought.

"But we're going to have to find a way to come together during this tragic time and keep things going. We believe Ainsley would have wanted it that way."

Paige looked over at Bee, but Bee was staring absently into the distance, her face wet with tears. Real tears, or crocodile tears?

Though she had a hard time imagining that a woman so focused on auras could be a murderer.

"So, I think we should talk about the most pressing decisions coming up over the next few weeks. Things that Ainsley—" Lanie paused as her voice cracked. "Sorry. Things that Ainsley would've normally handled herself. First, we need to deal with Halloween. . . ."

Paige wondered idly how Lanie was managing to sound so choked up. As Lanie launched into a laundry list of tasks that needed to be completed for an upcoming Trunk or Treat event, Paige's phone beeped with a text. She tugged it out and checked the screen. The text was from an unknown number.

CAN YOU TALK?

Paige typed back.

WHO IS THIS?

Instantly the three scrolling dots appeared.

SORRY. IT'S JOHN.

Paige's heart stopped beating in her chest.

"Hey. You okay?" Marie whispered.

Paige startled and dropped the phone. It bounced once, twice, and landed faceup near a bookshelf. The few people closest to her and Marie—those sitting in regular-sized chairs like mature adults—turned to look down their noses at her. Paige launched herself up, grabbed the phone, and shoved it back into her bag. She resettled and breathed in and out slowly, trying to calm her heart.

Why was John texting her? How had he gotten her number?

"I'm fine, why?" Paige asked.

"I heard what happened at the party. Ainsley walking in on you and John hooking up?"

Paige barked a laugh. Now every single person in the room turned to glare at her. Lanie pursed her lips together.

"Was something I said funny?" she asked.

"No! No, continue." Paige waved both hands. "Sorry."

"All right, as I was saying, we have two of our biggest events of the year coming up—the Halloween Trunk or Treat this Saturday, and then the Thankful Dinner in November. Ainsley played a huge role in organizing both these events, so we're really going to need some people to step up and help out."

"We were *not* hooking up," Paige whispered to Marie. "He was just giving me a tour."

Marie lifted one shoulder like *Whatever you say*.

Paige wanted to punch someone. "Who told you this? Was it Lanie?"

"I don't know." Marie narrowed her eyes. "I think it was Dayna? I can't remember, honestly, a bunch of people were talking about it at soccer last night."

Paige glanced around the room. While most people at the front were focused on Lanie, she saw a few people checking her out, giving her snide looks, flinching when she caught their eyes.

"They're just looking for drama. These people *love* their drama."

There was a commotion at the front of the room and when Paige glanced up, she was surprised to find Not-a-Nun standing next to the podium. People in the peanut gallery grumbled and whispered.

"What's going on?" Paige said. "Who *is* that woman?"

"Her name's Nina something or other. She has a very hot husband."

"I move for a special election to install a new president," Nina announced.

"What?"

Dayna stood up from her chair. "*I* move to install Lanie Chen-Katapodis as our new president, effective immediately."

Lanie demurred. "I don't think—"

"Does anyone second my motion?" Nina demanded.

"Does anyone second *mine*?" Dayna asked.

"I do! I second Dayna's!" Bee said.

"Wait, *you* don't want to be president, do you?" Lanie asked Nina.

"All in favor?" Dayna called.

"You can't just do an audible vote, Dayna. Not for an election."

"She's right. The bylaws state that—"

"But Ainsley *wanted* Lanie to be the next president," said Bee.

Paige noticed Lanie and Dayna lock eyes, something unspoken passing between them. She wished she had a notebook.

"This all feels a little morbid, don't you think?" some guy in the front row grumbled.

"I'm putting my name on the ballot officially," Nina called out. "I think this organization could benefit from new leadership."

And with that, the entire room erupted in shouting and debate, and Paige started to think she might get something for Dominic after all.

nina

Nina could not believe these people. She really couldn't. First of all, there were three times the regular number of parents present tonight for this meeting. Had they come because they cared about the PBA? Because they wanted to volunteer more of their time? Because they wanted to *help*? No. They were here out of morbid curiosity. Because they wanted to be part of the drama, the scandal, the story. Secondly, it was abundantly clear that no one on the board had a clue what they were doing.

Ainsley really had been running this thing entirely on her own.

So many of the experiences Nina had in life were like this. Like the annual mayor's Easter egg hunt (basically a bloodbath, with fourth graders stomping all over toddlers to get the plastic eggs), the movie nights in Veteran's Park (would it be that difficult for the town to invest in speakers made after the 1970s?), and the self-checkout lines at the ShopRite one town over (she hadn't used them since the green mango/no mask incident of 2020).

She and Ravi had a running joke. Whenever things went horribly awry and the solution was clear as day, they would look at each other and he'd smile and say, "If only you ran the world."

Well, she'd just taken her first step. Lanie and her entourage were not the solution. They were the problem. And on some level, Nina had to believe that Ainsley would have been grateful to her for stepping up and volunteering to helm the ship.

"Order!" Lanie shouted, banging the gavel with gusto. "Everyone, please! Let's come to order."

She slid her gaze sideways at Nina.

"Nina, would you please sit so we can discuss this like civilized people?"

Unbelievable. Lanie calling *her* uncivilized. With a roll of her eyes, Nina walked to the closest empty chair and sat. Once she did, Bee and Dayna sat as well, and gradually, the grumbling in the room went silent.

"Thank you," Lanie said. "Now, there is a motion on the floor to have an open election for the presidency. Does anyone—"

"Sorry," said Caroline Roday, leaning forward in her front-row seat to look over at Nina. "Are you even a parent in this district?"

Nina's face burned. She placed her hands on her thighs and pinched her skin, a quick, sharp hit. "Why would I be here if I weren't a parent in this district?"

"You could be a reporter. I saw a news van downtown earlier," some fleshy husband said. Then he looked her up and down with a dubious expression.

"I'm not a reporter." Nina took a deep breath, stood up again, and clasped her hands together tightly. "My name is Nina Anand. I have two children at the elementary school, Lita and Liam. I ran back-to-school night this year and I've been a member of this organization for three years, since Lita was in kindergarten. I think I could do an excellent job as president. I know for certain that I would be able to tighten up certain procedures I find lacking."

She said this while looking Bee dead in the eye. Bee stared back, blank-faced and clueless. Was it possible Ainsley had never shared Nina's concerns about account security with her?

Someone gave a long, low whistle, like they were impressed. At least, that's what Nina hoped it meant. Nina generally avoided speaking in public as much as humanly possible. Which was probably why she was sensing a serious tightness in her bladder. But she soldiered on. This was too important for her to give up now.

"And I can't be the only one who feels this way," Nina said looking around. Most of the people who met her eye quickly averted their gaze. "So, I think we need to take this opportunity to correct the problem."

"I'm sorry, did you just refer to Ainsley Aames's death as an *opportunity*?" Dayna demanded.

Nina's throat closed over. "I didn't mean—"

"Sheesh, maybe she really was murdered," the doughy dad added under his breath.

Once again, the room erupted, and this time it took Lanie a good five minutes to get it under control. "I think Nina had the floor?" she said wanly, looking exhausted.

"I apologize," Nina said. "I didn't mean that the way it sounded." She took a deep breath. "But again, I move for an open and fair election. It's time for new leadership, and I believe that if we simply let our current membership chair take over, all we'll get is more of the same."

Dead. Silence.

"I'm sorry, but don't you, like, have a full-time job?" asked Cori Levin, who looked about twelve, and talked like she was still in middle school, but somehow had twin seventh graders. "Yeah, you're that accountant!" She turned to the assembled crowd. "She helped my parents get their financial shit together so they could retire," she told everyone and no one. "It was a freaking miracle, you guys. My father *loves* to bet the ponies, and my mom collects these awful teacup set things? Oh my God, you wouldn't believe how much cash she's sunk into these hideous little—"

"No parent with a full-time job has ever been president of the PBA," Felicity interjected, cutting off what would have likely been a long ramble.

"Felicity is right," Lanie said. "PBA president is a full-time job in and of itself. We all saw the amount of time and energy Ainsley devoted to—" Here, Lanie paused to take a shaky breath. "We wouldn't want you to be overwhelmed, Nina. It's just too much for a working mother to take on."

"I second Nina's motion!"

Nina flinched, as did half the people in the room. It was that new mom. Izzy's mom. Lita liked Izzy and couldn't stop talking about the flower the girl had drawn in art class. Nina felt a stab of gratitude that someone was speaking up for her. Even if it was the woman who couldn't figure out school pickup and walked around at a party with a stained dress like it was perfectly normal.

"Excuse me?" Bee said.

"I said, I second Nina's motion on the basis of the fact that everything you all just said is bullshit."

The room erupted. Nina wrapped her arms around herself as other working moms crowded around her to offer their support.

"Good for you," they said.

"The stay-at-home moms have no idea what we can handle."

But Nina was looking across the room at Izzy's mother, who seemed to be getting into it with Bee and Lanie, probably about the rules laid out in the PBA handbook. Nina already knew the rules. A member had made a motion and another member had seconded it, and before this meeting was over, someone would have to get a handle on the people so they could vote.

paige

She would never have admitted it out loud, but holy crap, that had been kind of exciting! As the hordes of people moved out of the library and into the hall, Paige was feeling a surge of adrenaline unlike anything she'd felt since the day she'd lost her job back in L.A. Since she'd thrown her laptop across the room and unsuccessfully attempted to push over a potted palm tree.

Embarrassing, that one. Heat crawled up her neck even now at the thought of it.

But this was a different kind of adrenaline. It was a positive feeling. Like she was doing something good for someone. Maybe even something good for the town. Perhaps she should have gotten into politics.

Except, of course, the person she'd helped to change the system was potentially a murderer. Paige could have sworn she saw Nina pinching her own flesh under her arms as people bombarded her with questions, wrapping herself up in a hug as if for protection.

"Nina, hey."

Nina had been making a beeline for the front door of the school, more like she'd just performed a smash-and-grab than like a person who was interested in leading this group of people or garnering any votes, when Paige grabbed her arm. Nina yanked herself away and looked at Paige as if she'd assaulted her. Paige gulped. She remembered Nina smacking herself in the face repeatedly the other night after arguing with Ainsley. She took a step back.

"Sorry, I just wanted to introduce myself since we never officially met. I'm Paige Lancaster."

"Nina Anand. Nice to meet you." The woman's words were clipped. She didn't offer her hand.

"Listen, if you need any help with your campaign, I'm here," Paige told her. It seemed as good a way as any to spend some time with a prime suspect.

"Campaign?"

"Yes, for PBA president. Our motion passed, so . . ."

Nina blinked. "Right. Yes. Okay. Thanks."

Paige narrowed her eyes. Maybe this woman was more of a robot than a nun. A robot nun?

The back of Paige's skull tingled. Robot Nun. That could make an interesting animated series for adults, and she'd heard Hulu was looking for new content. Paige hated adult animation, though. Maybe she'd keep it in her back pocket in case things got really dire.

"I'll think about it," Nina said.

She produced a smile so tight it could barely be called a smile, and then she was gone.

"So. That was interesting," said Marie, sauntering over with Claudia and another mom Paige had yet to meet. "Paige, you remember Claudia. And this is our friend Indira."

They exchanged greetings and comments about how awful all this was and how crazy the meeting had been. The proceedings might have ended, but no one seemed in a hurry to go anywhere. Except for Nina. Most people had broken up into groups either in the library or out here in the hall to talk over what had just happened.

Paige scanned the faces around her, making mental notes for Dominic. When she'd arrived earlier it had seemed like most people were stunned about Ainsley's death, some crying, many reminiscing. Now most members of the group were more composed. Everyone except for Bee, who still looked like she could burst into fresh tears at any moment, and Dayna, who looked ill. They stood in a klatch with Lanie, who seemed to be holding court. It must be weird for them, not to have their fourth by their side anymore. Any of the three would be a good source of information for another time when they weren't so distraught. Lanie and Nina were at the top of the list of people who stood to benefit from Ainsley's death, considering both clearly wanted Ainsley's spot as president. In fact, now that Paige thought about it, she was pretty sure that was what Lanie and Ainsley had been talking about the night of the party.

I'm only doing what's best for the PBA. . . .

You said you were going to step down. . . .

Was the presidency of some small-town school organization enough to kill for?

"It still seems premature to have this meeting at all," Indira said as they found their own corner to gather in. "Do we really need to figure out who our next president will be before we've even had a funeral?"

"We should just let Lanie have it," Claudia put in. "She's been waiting long enough." She shot Paige a guilty look. "No offense."

"None taken. It's not like I think Nina has to win. I just didn't like the way they were talking to her in there. So she works. That doesn't make her a bad mother."

"It's not about being a bad mother. We all work," Indira said, gesturing at Marie and Claudia. "It's about the time suck."

"Ainsley treated PBA president like a full-time job," Claudia put in. "She was always rushing off to meetings, getting quotes, drumming up support from local businesses, scouring for new event ideas, attending the board of education meetings, organizing volunteers. She was so dedicated."

"She used to work, too, you know," Indira said. "She and John ran that hedge fund together."

"Why did she stop?" Paige asked.

Shrugs all around. "No one ever asked Ainsley why she did anything."

"I heard they were having money problems, though," Claudia said, leaning in. "Jessie saw one of those red collection notices on the mail table over the summer when Danielle had that pool party."

"Really?" Marie asked. "Is that why they sold the Range Rover?"

"I thought that was because their daughter Michelle wanted something more environmentally friendly," Indira said. "I saw her driving a Prius just before everyone went back to school."

"She was president of the high school's sustainability club," Claudia said. "She's the one who got all the restaurants in town to switch from plastic straws, remember?"

"Oh, God. Right. That was super fun." Marie rolled her eyes.

"Ugh, those poor kids," Indira said. "To lose their mom so young. I don't know how my kids would survive if something were to happen to me. Peter would be a disaster as a single dad."

Paige wondered how old Michelle and Danielle were now. Older than Bradley, clearly, if they were driving and their friends knew what a red envelope meant. But how could the Andersons have money problems? Their house was on par with some of the homes of A-list producers she'd been in back in L.A.

"Well, I heard Ainsley was having an affair. Or at least that they were no longer sleeping in the same room," Indira said under her breath.

A little bell went off in Paige's head. So that was why the sheets in John's room hadn't been touched. This was a normal occurrence.

"*I* heard it was one of the other *dads*." Claudia lowered her voice to the point she could barely be heard.

"Who?" Marie asked, wide-eyed.

"I have no idea."

"So . . . what?" Marie said. "You think John found out and—"

"No," Claudia said. "No! Of course not. Everyone *loves* John."

Indira and Claudia both looked Paige up and down as they said this. Assessing, quantifying, theorizing. Paige wanted to tell them off but held her tongue. She was supposed to be making friends here. But there was also a little, uncomfortable flutter of nerves in her belly.

If Ainsley was having an affair, that gave John an actual motive.

PAIGE MET DOMINIC at a Starbucks a few towns over. It had started to drizzle during the drive, and Paige was feeling both tense and excited as she attempted, once again, to parallel park. She ordered herself a caramel latte, and when she found Dominic sitting at a back corner booth nursing a black coffee, she truly felt like she'd become a character in one of her own projects. She had no idea you could even order a black coffee at Starbucks.

"Hey!" His face lit up as she approached, and he sat up a bit straighter. "How was it?"

"It was . . . interesting." She dropped her bag on the bench and shucked off her wet jacket. "People are definitely tense. And suspicious."

"So they think it could be murder, too?" he asked, looking almost too excited.

"Well, some of them do, I think. But it could just be people with nothing better to do." She lifted a shoulder and averted her eyes. "You know how it is in small towns."

"I've worked here for ten years. I know." He took a swig of coffee. "But were they suspicious of anyone in particular? Did you get any details?"

Paige hesitated, thinking about the rumored affair. She knew she should say something, was even on the verge of doing so, but all it would do was make John look like a suspect. And Dominic had already said John wasn't talking and was hiding behind a lawyer. *Well, good for him*, she thought.

"Someone mentioned that John and Ainsley were having money problems. There was apparently a collections notice at their house and something about downgrading cars."

Dominic took out his little pad and made a few notes. "That's something I could look into."

"And I did remember a couple of things from the party. I overheard this weird argument between Ainsley and one of the other moms. It was pretty intense."

"Who was it?" he asked.

"Nina Anand," Paige said. Dominic's face was a blank. "Apparently she's an accountant?"

"What were they arguing about?" he asked.

"I don't know. It was kind of hard to tell. But Ainsley said something about a felony."

Dominic stared at her. "And you didn't think to mention this yesterday?"

"I mean . . . people say stuff like that all the time and it doesn't mean anything. And Ainsley seemed like the type of person who would exaggerate for effect. But Nina did seem pretty upset afterward." She slurped her coffee, and her teeth ached from the sweetness. "Also, I kind of thought you were there to arrest me, so forgive me if I spaced."

With a thoughtful frown, Dominic made a note.

"And there was also this thing between Ainsley and Lanie."

"Lanie Chen-Katapodis."

"Yes. Ainsley kind of . . . threatened her?"

Dominic's eyebrows rose. "How so?"

"She basically said she would tell some big secret Lanie has if Lanie didn't back off."

"Back off what?" Dominic asked.

"I don't know for sure, but I think Lanie was supposed to take over as president of the PBA this week and Ainsley had decided not to step down. Lanie was really not happy about it."

"What did she say, exactly?"

"I don't remember the exact conversation." Paige winced. "It was late, I wasn't supposed to be hearing what I was hearing, and all I wanted to do was get out of there."

"That's okay. This is good."

"It gets better," Paige said. "As of tonight, both Lanie and Nina are running for PBA president. They both want to take Ainsley's place."

"So you think one of these women might have killed Ainsley to get the presidency?"

"Stranger things have happened," Paige said. "But honestly? Part of me thinks it's all a little far-fetched. What if everything I over-heard was just run-of-the-mill mom drama?"

"But what if it wasn't?"

Paige sighed and took another swig of her coffee. The rain was really coming down now, spattering the plate glass windows like gun-shot.

"Can I ask you a question?" she said, wanting to lighten the mood. "Shoot."

"What's a Thankful Dinner?"

"Oh, man." Dominic grinned. "I love the Thankful Dinner. They show this video montage of all these little kids saying what they're thankful for and they always have this ridiculous corn souffle . . ."

She raised her eyebrows at him. "I guess the way to a man's heart really is through his stomach."

They locked eyes and she blushed, realizing what she'd just said.

"Well, this guy, anyway." He took a slug of coffee and set the mug down with a clatter. "So, did you talk to anyone else at the meeting?"

"Marie Mancuso. She and my mom are friendly," Lanie said. "She introduced me to two other women, Indira and Claudia. They're the ones who told me about the money troubles, but I didn't get their last names. Apparently, one of their daughters is friends with one of John's daughters."

She stared down at her coffee. The milk swirling in the light brown liquid. Should she tell him about the affair? It was on the tip of her tongue. What kind of undercover informant was she if she didn't give him the most important nugget of information?

But it was just a rumor. She had no proof. She decided to dig into it a little on her own. See if there was any meat to it. If there was, she would tell him. It wasn't as if she had any actual loyalty to John, and if he *had* somehow murdered his wife . . .

Her brain refused to complete the thought.

"Talk to anyone else?" Dominic asked.

"Just Nina."

"Nina. The one who had the intense argument with Ainsley?"

"I seconded her motion for president, and then volunteered to help her with her campaign."

"Good! That's good." Dominic nodded as he wrote something down. "You gotta get in there. Make friends with these people. That's when you'll get the real dirt."

"Well, I'm trying," Paige said.

"Just be careful." He suddenly turned serious.

"Why?" she asked. "What do you mean?"

"Well, I wouldn't want anything happening to my best informant," he told her with a grin.

Paige's heart fluttered at his flirtatious tone.

"Or your only informant?" she countered.

"I like 'best,'" he said. "Let's stick with 'best.'"

Paige smiled. "Best" had a nice ring.

lanie

Lanie's hands shook as she shucked off her dress and reached for her favorite silk nightgown. She had never considered herself an anxious person until the pandemic. Somewhere around month three of the mandatory lockdown, when the governors of New York, New Jersey, and Connecticut all collectively decided that no one in the tri-state area should yet be allowed to leave their house to do anything other than food shop, she started to feel that uncomfortable flutter in her stomach. She'd cut back on caffeine, tried to meditate (which had turned out to be impossible with four small children throwing blocks at one another's heads in the next room), and basically eliminated her sugar intake. When none of that had worked, she'd stopped watching the news or looking at the papers Michael had delivered to the house every morning. He'd flip through them at the breakfast table while sipping his coffee before retreating to his home office to work, and Lanie would sit there trying not to let the headlines take root inside her chest.

None of it worked. Not meditation. Not Xanax. Not wine. Until finally, she'd hit rock bottom. She still couldn't believe Dayna had told Ainsley about what had happened. Ainsley, of all people. But she wasn't going to think about that now.

She pulled her nightgown on and huffed a sigh. She couldn't believe Nina. How dare she? The presidency was Lanie's. She had worked her ass off for it. But she hadn't been about to power grab it less than two days after Ainsley's death. She had intended to run things quietly and unofficially for a few weeks and then, once the situation normalized, everyone would just unanimously agree that it was time for her to take over.

Her hands were still shaking. She needed some wine.

This election is going to be a joke, she thought as she poured herself a glass of rosé and brought it back up to her bedroom. *Everything is going to be fine.*

Later, the glass drained, she lay in her bed, staring at the dark ceiling, her arms flat at her sides, wondering about Ainsley. She wondered if Ainsley had known she was dying. Whether she had been scared. Whether she had felt loved. Whether she had known where she was going and who would be there to receive her.

Ainsley had been a churchgoer. Saint Mary's Catholic Church in the center of town. So, it would seem she had faith that she was going to be welcomed into heaven. But Lanie had a hard time imagining Ainsley going gently into that good night.

She was definitely more of the rage, rage type.

The thought made her laugh, and then her eyes filled with tears. She placed her hand over her abdomen. At least she knew that Ainsley had never known her biggest secret. The secret she'd never told a soul.

The bedroom door opened, letting in a shaft of light from the hallway. Michael paused, one hand on the door. The other held his briefcase with his suit jacket folded over his arm. Lanie's stomach clenched, and she sat up.

"Were you . . . laughing?"

"No! Yes. Sorry." She sat up and turned on her bedside lamp. Her heart pounded in her eyeballs. "What time is it?"

He sighed, bowing his head. "It's after midnight."

Normally she would point out that he'd said he'd be home at ten. Normally she'd be all over him about it. Not tonight. She sat up a little straighter. Waiting for him to look at her.

She hadn't laid eyes on him since she'd left the party on Saturday night. Except on the security feed. So much had happened since then it felt as if a year had passed.

He put his briefcase and jacket down on the chair next to him and looked up. "Are you okay?"

Lanie jumped out of bed, her soft nightgown sliding down her legs, and threw her arms around his neck. He hugged her back, holding her tight.

"I can't believe she's dead, Michael. I can't believe it. I know she was a pain in the ass, but it's going to be so weird around here without her."

"I know. Have you heard anything else? About what happened?"

She shook her head as she pulled back, keeping her hands on his shoulders. "People at the meeting tonight were saying she was murdered." She rolled her eyes. "But that's just the gossips. Always looking for the next scandal."

"It's not completely ridiculous, you know. Ainsley did piss off a lot of people."

"Michael." She scolded him, but felt gratified. Would he say something like that if he and Ainsley had been spending time together? Or had he said it *because* they'd been spending time together? To throw her off his scent?

"Sorry, I know you're not supposed to speak ill of the dead and everything, but you know it's true. *You* were pissed at her that night. You've been pissed at her for years, Lanie."

He moved past her, going to the closet to shuck his clothes. Lanie stood there, stunned. What was Michael saying?

"So you think I killed her?" She snorted a laugh. But then again, she'd wondered the same thing about him, so who was she to be offended?

Michael looked back at her from the darkness of the closet, his face half in shadow. "No. I'm just saying she knew how to push people's buttons. Even yours. And you're the most levelheaded person I know."

You don't know anything.

"I'm pretty sure even John wanted to strangle her once or twice."

"Michael!"

He raised his palms. "Sorry. Sorry. I just . . . forget it. Can we change the subject?" He stepped out of the closet in his boxers and T-shirt. "I'm wiped and I have to go to D.C. tomorrow."

Maybe if he didn't travel all the time he wouldn't be wiped all the time and they *could* have an actual conversation instead of the overtired sniping she'd grown almost accustomed to. He walked around her and yanked the sheets free from their tuck on his side of the bed. They both climbed in from opposite sides.

"I'm sorry. I'm really just tired." He rolled toward her and kissed her forehead perfunctorily.

"It's okay. I'm sure it's been a long day."

He reached up to rub both his eyes with his hands, then let his arms fall at his sides. He looked haggard. As if he hadn't slept in days.

"Maybe we'll go out to dinner when I get back. Do something together, just the two of us."

Lanie smiled. "I'd like that."

She was about to turn out her bedside light when she noticed a scratch on the back of Michael's left hand. A long, fresh, jagged red scratch that looked as if it had been made by a pin or a nail or . . . a fingernail?

Lanie swallowed.

"Ouch," she said. "Where'd you get that?"

Michael had been rolling over, away from her, but he paused to look at it. "Oh, they're doing construction at the office. I caught myself on some crap they left in the stairway." Michael always took the stairs, fitness junkie that he was. "Good night."

"'Night," she said. "Love you."

But there was no response.

nina

"Can't sleep?"

Nina sighed as Ravi came up behind her at her desk and put his hands on her shoulders.

"What's wrong?"

He turned and sat down on the edge of her desk, which was immaculately clean, his leg pressing against the arm of her chair. Giving a yawn, he scratched at his beard and trained his tired eyes on her. Nina hesitated. She hated seeming weak. Even in front of Ravi. Especially in front of Ravi. As far as she was concerned, she was batting way out of her league from the moment they'd met just after college, and she still sometimes wondered at the fact that she'd been allowed to stay in the game this long. Ravi was cool. He was popular. He was a musician, for God's sake. And he was gorgeous. People like Nina the Nerd didn't land guys like Ravi the Hot Guitarist. Nina had seen the covetous way the other moms looked at him. And she kind of loved it.

"I don't know why I volunteered to be president," she confessed, squeezing her eyes shut so that she wouldn't see his reaction. "I think it was a huge mistake."

"What? No! That is definitely not true," he said. "Nina, you should be running the PBA. You totally deserve a leadership role. You kick ass at every project you take on and you'll kick ass at this, too."

She opened her eyes. "But I didn't really think about what it meant. On a practical level, I mean."

"Explain." He tucked his hands under his arms and focused on her.

"Campaigning. Public speaking. Community relations . . . you know me. None of those things are my strong suit."

Ravi laughed. "Okay, but that stuff is mostly about winning the election. Once you're president, can't you delegate the things you don't want to do?"

Nina leaned back in her chair, deflated. It wasn't lost on her that he didn't disagree. He thought these were weaknesses of hers as well. But she couldn't blame him. Because it was true. She just . . . sort of wished he'd argued the point.

Stop being such a girl, she told herself. *He's helping you work the problem.*

"I suppose that's true," she said. "But then how do I win? What if I need to make speeches? Press the flesh? Talk myself up?"

Ravi scratched at his beard again, looking off across the room. "What about a campaign manager? Maybe that woman who stood up for you at the meeting? Patty?"

"Paige." Nina sat up again with the smallest jolt of adrenaline. "That's not a bad idea, I guess. Although she seems a bit of a mess. Just looking at her makes me imagine junk drawers full of unpaid bills."

Ravi laughed. "Your worst nightmare. But that's okay. Because you have zero junk drawers full of unpaid bills."

She blinked at him, stumped.

"Meaning you'll balance each other out. You can do the organizing and she can do the strategizing and the socializing."

"You know, she did offer to help me at the end of the night. You could be on to something, Mr. Anand."

He stood up and clapped his hands together. "Yeah, that's why they pay me the big bucks." They both laughed and he leaned down to kiss her temple. "Will you come back to bed now?"

"In a minute," Nina told him, waking up her computer. "I'm just going to google her and see what her background is."

Ravi rolled his eyes good-naturedly. "I'll see you in the morning, then."

Nina smirked. They both knew there was nothing she loved more than a Google deep dive.

"Five minutes," she lied. "I swear."

AT 3:07 THAT morning, Nina sat straight up in bed. She'd heard a crash. Was it a window? Was one of the kids up? No. A car alarm was going off.

"Ravi!" She shook her husband's shoulder. "Wake up!"

"What?" He looked at her bleary-eyed for half a second, then heard the alarm. "Wait here."

She wasn't about to do any such thing. They both headed downstairs through the house to the front windows, which had a view of the driveway.

"Shit," Ravi said.

Nina's car was blaring like a carnival, the lights flashing on and off. There was broken glass all over the driveway.

"Call the police," he said, and opened the door.

The cops came pretty quickly. The driver's-side window of Nina's car had been shattered, but nothing had been stolen, because she kept nothing of value in her car. The police said this was an escalation of the recent criminal activity in town. The burglars had only hit unlocked cars up to this point. Had avoided anything messy.

"Lucky us," Ravi said, and put his arm around Nina.

It wasn't until she was using the wet/dry vac the next morning that Nina noticed a scrap of paper in her center console. It hadn't been there the day before. She reached for it, unfolded it, and stopped breathing.

In carefully printed capital letters, it read:

**IF YOU TELL ANYONE, YOU'RE GOING DOWN
WITH US**

lanie

Lanie woke up on Tuesday morning full of energy and the desire to get shit done. Odd, considering it was also the day of Ainsley's wake. Maybe it was the fact that she'd slept like the dead. Or maybe it was the fact that she had decided to believe Michael about the origin of the scratch on his hand. Or maybe it was just the weather. The day dawned bright and crisp and full of the scents of turning leaves. Fall always invigorated Lanie. The first day of school had been her favorite day of the year as a child. All those clean, fresh notebooks; the sharpened pencils; the promise of new things. While most of the world made New Year's resolutions on the first day of January, Lanie always made hers on the first day of school.

This year, the resolution had been to win the presidency. Of course, at the time, it was a given that she would be the next president. Everyone knew the job was hers. No one was going to challenge her place. Ainsley was simply going to hand the gavel over when the time came.

Now, out of nowhere, she had to deal with Nina and this absurd bid to take over the PBA. If Lanie could go back in time and run last night's meeting differently, she would have. She would have taken control and nipped this whole Nina movement in the bud. And there was no mistaking the fact that it *was* a movement. The working moms had left the meeting with these foreboding looks of determination on their faces, sharing glances of solidarity. But unfortunately, there was no going back. So, today, she would move forward.

She was feeling antsy as the klatches of moms gathered around in the sun to await their progeny. She had a plan, of course, but she needed Paige Lancaster, of all people, to execute it. And Paige wasn't there yet.

Then Dayna came around the corner and joined her, and Lanie felt like she could writhe right out of her skin.

"Hey." Dayna's voice was hoarse.

"Hello," Lanie said coolly.

If Dayna clocked her attitude, Lanie couldn't tell. The woman was wearing huge, round sunglasses with lenses so dark they seemed opaque.

"Felicity's having people over before the wake," Dayna informed Lanie. She hugged her black jacket to her as she spoke. "We're going to do some pre-party drinking."

"It's not a party," Lanie said, drumming her fingers against her forearm.

How could you tell her? Lanie wanted to scream. *You swore on Maurice's life you'd never tell.*

Everyone knew that Dayna valued her husband, Maurice Goodman, more than anyone or anything else on the planet. Five short years ago he'd plucked her from a life grinding out fifteen classes a week at SoulCycle and living with five roommates in a basement in Queens, married her in St. Barths, and moved her into the six-bedroom colonial he'd formerly shared with his first (late) wife and their young daughter. Dayna had zero qualms about telling everyone where she'd come from and how she'd gotten the hell out—and that while sex with Maurice was dry and bland, and she'd never seen herself as the mothering type, her Amex Black made it all worth it.

"I know that," Dayna said. "Obviously. But Bee and I thought . . ." She blew out a long breath. "We're going to need some liquid courage to get through it."

"Whatever."

"Okay. What is up with you?" Dayna challenged.

Lanie gritted her teeth. A couple of other moms glanced over at Dayna's raised voice, which stuck out because everyone else was whispering as if they were already at the funeral.

"Well, let's see," Lanie said, turning to face Dayna for the first time. "Ainsley just died under mysterious circumstances, my husband is in D.C. and will miss the wake, I have to mount a campaign for a spot that is rightfully mine, and I feel like I have no idea who my real friends are."

Dayna pulled back as if she'd been stung. Good. She should feel stung. Lanie felt *gutted* by Dayna's betrayal. Then, from the corner of her eye she saw Paige hoofing it up the sidewalk from the front of the school.

"I've gotta go."

She strode purposefully down the blacktop walkway, putting on her widest, friendliest smile.

"Paige, hi! How are you?"

"You don't really want to talk to me right now."

Lanie froze. Who said things like that? She was so thrown she almost tripped herself.

"I'm sorry?" she said.

"Are you?" Paige said. "For what?"

Lanie glanced around, wondering if there was a hidden camera somewhere in the bushes. "Okay, can we start over?" She paused and noticed that Paige was out of breath and that her skin was blotchy. Maybe she was having a stroke? "Are you okay?"

"No. No, in fact, I'm not okay."

Paige pushed her hands through her curly hair and looked around at the gathered assembly of moms. Lanie noticed that many of them quickly looked away or flinched when Paige's eyes landed on them.

"I made the stupid, infantile mistake of looking at the *Hollywood Reporter* this morning, and you know what I found out?" Paige said.

The pause went on long enough that it seemed Lanie was expected to answer.

"Um . . . what?"

"I found out that Victoria Lane is going to be the showrunner for the new Shonda Rhimes mystery series on Netflix. Victoria Lane! The woman spent her entire tenure at her first job stealing *my* jokes and putting them in *her* scripts! But now she has a seven-figure job with Shonda freaking Rhimes! And . . . get this. This total asshat who was our intern last year just got a first-look deal with Disney based on his idiotic YouTube videos where he farts in strange places!"

"Ew. You're kidding."

"No! I am not kidding! Look at this!"

Paige brought up a YouTube page lightning fast and played a video wherein a sweaty, corpulent man walked into a Chinese tea-room and farted grotesquely, clearing the establishment of the innocent victims within.

Lanie felt sick. "Why would anyone, anywhere, want to watch such a thing?"

"Thank you!" Paige threw up her hands and shoved her phone away. Then she looked Lanie up and down shrewdly. "What did you want again?"

"Oh. I . . ." For half a second Lanie couldn't remember why she'd come over here. Paige had the oddest effect on her, throwing her off in a way few people ever did. "Right, I wanted to ask you a favor."

"A favor."

"Yes, I was hoping you could talk Nina Anand out of running for PBA president."

Paige snorted. "Seriously?"

"Yes. Seriously."

"Why me?"

"You seconded her nomination," Lanie said. "And the two of you seem to have hit it off."

"I barely know the woman. I barely know any of you."

Lanie took a breath. Maybe this would be easier than she thought. If Paige and Nina weren't friends, then Paige had no real motivation for backing Nina—or for turning down Lanie's request.

"Look, you're new here, so you don't really know how it works. But Ainsley wanted me to take over for her when she stepped down. It was supposed to happen at this week's meeting. Everyone knew it. Nina knew it. What she's doing now is just rocking the boat at the exact moment when what we need most is a smooth transition."

"But Ainsley *wasn't* going to step down this week," Paige said. Loudly.

Lanie froze. She had been hoping Paige wouldn't remember what she'd overheard at the party. Or that she wouldn't understand what she and Ainsley had been talking about. Or that she wouldn't have the guts to bring it up.

"Yes. She was. We've been planning the transfer of power for months."

Paige's eyes narrowed. "Maybe I misheard."

"Yes. I'm sure that's the case." Lanie grabbed onto the opening like a life preserver and plastered on a wide smile.

The school bell rang, a sound so piercing Lanie couldn't believe the teachers' union hadn't forced the school to change it yet. The kids were about to be released. She suddenly felt the pressure of a ticking clock on this conversation. "So, can I count on you? To talk to her?"

"Why don't you talk to her yourself?" Paige asked, stepping back as small children began to weave through the crowd, shouting when they found their mothers, shucking their backpacks, lifting art projects up for inspection.

Lanie forced a laugh. "How would that look to people? Me asking my only competition to back out?"

"It would probably look like you're worried you might lose."

Lanie glared at Paige. She couldn't believe she ever thought she could be friends with this woman. Maybe she *had* murdered Ainsley. Lanie could suddenly picture it quite clearly. Paige confronting Ainsley on the deck, telling her John belonged to her. Ainsley laughing in her face—which was absolutely what Ainsley would do—and Paige snapping. Just like she'd done on the security video. Just like she'd done in Ainsley's bathroom. All it would have taken was one hard shove.

"I'm not," she said, trying to shake the image of Ainsley's shocked face as she tumbled to her death.

"Not what? Worried? Sure looks that way to me."

At that moment, Haddix ran directly into Lanie's legs from the side, throwing her tiny arms around Lanie and knocking her off-balance. Lanie opened her mouth to say something. To level a denial or a threat or tell the woman to kiss her ass. But before the right retort could form in her mind, Nina Anand appeared as if from nowhere, grabbed Paige by the arm, and dragged her away.

"Mommy! Can Millie and me have a playdate?"

"Not today, honey."

Lanie's phone rang. She fished it out and saw the words PIERMONT PD on the screen. Heart suddenly hammering, she picked it up.

"Hello?"

"Lanie Chen-Katapodis? This is Officer Dominic Ramos of the Piermont Police Department."

Hot Cop, her brain supplied automatically. It was what all the moms in town called him.

"I'm hoping we can set up a time to sit down and talk."

Lanie's mouth went dry as Haddix raced off to join her friends on the hill.

"Talk? About what?" Lanie asked.

"About the night of Ainsley Aames's death."

paige

It wasn't lost on Paige that all eyes were on her and Nina as Nina pulled her up the short embankment next to the pickup area, toward the line of trees that separated the school from the playing fields. She could see the other women judging her, and even heard a few of their whispers as they went.

That's her? The woman John—

Nina Anand is so weird. Of course they're friends.

Yeah, she could totally murder someone.

What is with the acid-wash?

Okay, these jeans were the height of fashion back in L.A. It wasn't Paige's fault that this ass-backward town still thought Burberry was cool. And honestly, if they really believed Ainsley had been murdered, they should have been focusing on Lanie, who wanted to pretend that Ainsley hadn't been about to steal back the presidency. Or freaking Nina, whom Ainsley had accused of a felony mere hours before she died.

What was she even doing here? When Paige woke up this morning and saw the sun shining, felt the crisp fall air through the window screens, she'd been sure it was going to be a productive day. She'd been looking forward to getting some writing done and then coming to school to chat people up and see what she could learn about Ainsley and her potential enemies. But then she'd gone and fallen down the L.A. tabloid rabbit hole and ended up wasting the entire six hours Izzy was in school feeling sorry for herself. She should just go back to L.A. Beg her agent to find her something—anything. Paige hated feeling like her career was leaving her behind. And then she'd gone and missed her chance to get new info out of Lanie, all because she was whining about YouTube.

"You can let go of me now." Paige wrenched her arm from Nina's iron-like grip. "For a person who doesn't like being touched, you sure have no problem manhandling other people."

"Sorry. I don't have much time." Nina straightened her black jacket, which she wore over—shocker—a white shirt and black pants. "I have to get the kids to their enrichment programs and then get back to the office for a meeting at four, but I wasn't sure when I'd see you, and I need you to be my campaign manager."

"I'm sorry, what?"

"I need you to be my campaign manager," Nina repeated impatiently. She almost rolled her eyes, Paige could tell, but stopped herself. "And if you're going to be my campaign manager, you can't be seen talking to Lanie Chen-Katapodis."

Paige snorted a laugh. Should she tell Nina exactly what it was that she and Lanie had been talking about? No. She didn't want to give Nina the satisfaction of knowing that Lanie was unnerved by her.

"Okay, first of all, I'll talk to whomever I want to talk to. Secondly, you're running for president of a school parent organization. Isn't having a campaign manager sort of overkill?"

Nina took in a breath to reply, but Paige held up a finger to stop her.

"And thirdly, you don't want me as your campaign manager. In case you're living under a rock, you should know that half this town thinks I murdered Ainsley Aames. I am not the person you want handling your PR."

Paige gestured down the slight hill toward the rest of the moms. A couple dozen heads snapped in the other direction, as if they hadn't been watching. Paige was both offended and amused. They were so transparent they could have all been made of glass. If only they knew. Not only was she innocent, but the police had entrusted her with helping in their investigation. Well, their pseudo-investigation. Okay, one guy's pseudo-investigation.

She saw Izzy emerge from the back door and look around, her hands on the straps of her purple backpack. Paige waved, and her daughter's face lit up. She couldn't believe she had missed this for so long. Had let freaking Martha be the person who picked up her kid after school every day.

"Wait. Ainsley was *murdered*?" Nina whispered.

Nina looked legitimately shocked at the suggestion. Paige made a mental note. She'd have to tell Dominic.

"No. Maybe. I don't know. But that's what these women are saying."

Izzy had paused with a bunch of other little kids to look at a caterpillar on the wall of the school. Paige kept an eye on her as Nina took in the news.

"That's . . . interesting."

Not terrible. Not ridiculous. But interesting.

"Look. The thing is, I need help," Nina said. "I'm not good in crowds. I need someone with guts to advise me on what to do. And you clearly have guts. Also, you're a writer. You can come up with a slogan. Write my speech."

Paige narrowed her eyes. "How did you know I'm a writer?"

"I googled you," Nina said matter-of-factly. "I know you worked on that detective show for three years and recently left to pursue other creative endeavors back East. I know you're forty-two years old. I know you've never been married. I don't know who Izzy's father is, but I'm guessing it's that actor Harrison Stype you dated the year before she was born. And I know—"

"Stop."

Nina's mouth snapped closed. Paige's breath had gone shallow. "You're cyberstalking me?"

"Hardly." Nina drew herself up straight. "All of this information is readily available with a basic search."

"Okay, first of all? It wasn't Harrison. Secondly, you're a psycho and there's no way I'm working with you," Paige said. She turned to trudge down the hill and get her daughter, when Nina spoke again.

"If you don't help me, I'll tell everyone why you really had to leave L.A."

Paige stopped in her tracks, skidding down the steepest bit of the hill. Her mother didn't even know why she really had to leave L.A. And it wasn't, as far as Paige was aware, something one could find out with a basic internet search.

Ignore her, she told herself. *She's just trying to manipulate you.* She took another step.

"And if people around here really suspect that you murdered Ainsley Aames, I'm guessing it's something you'd rather keep quiet."

nina

As soon as the kids were planted in front of Nick Jr. with their water bottles and bowls of fruit, and Ravi was locked in his studio, Nina hurried to the basement game room. She closed the door quietly behind her, because if the kids knew she was in here they would come begging for her to play Foosball with them. (She always let them win, and each time her competitive soul died a bit more. She'd give it one more year and then they'd be old enough to learn how to be gracious losers.) The click of the game room door was like Pavlov's bell for those two little maniacs, and she couldn't deal with the effort it would take to put them off right now.

She knelt in front of the old toy chest that held all the things they no longer played with—Thomas & Friends train sets and plastic Lion King dioramas and puzzles with overly large pieces. Nina knew she should get around to donating these things—there was no third child in her future—but she hadn't been able to bring herself to do it. It was uncharacteristically sentimental of her, and she knew she'd get over it, but she hadn't yet. Luckily, that sentimentality came in handy now—

because there, under the wooden train station, was the hot-pink folder she'd stolen back from Ainsley. Nina pulled it out, hugged it to her chest, and took it back to her office.

Inside, she kept the overhead light dark, turning on only her desk lamp. Her fingers shook as she placed the folder on her desk.

"Shit," she muttered. Fingerprints. Could the police lift fingerprints off a paper folder?

Ainsley Aames. Murdered.

Could it be true? If it was, then this folder—*her* folder—might be evidence. It might very well contain a motive. But even if it wasn't evidence of murder, it was, as Ainsley had pointed out—as the note she'd found in her car implied—evidence that Nina had committed a felony.

Nina was sure the note had been from Bee. That must have been why the handwriting was so carefully disguised. Nina knew Bee's handwriting because Bee had handwritten the "syllabus" for Lita's art class. Plus, she was the only one left alive to whom Nina's knowledge of the PBA's accounts was a threat.

"*Shit*," she said again. What was she supposed to do? If she turned Bee in, she'd be turning in herself as well.

Nina had looked at the numbers. Of course she had. And she knew that there were a few things in there that didn't add up. But did it mean what she thought it meant? She had no idea. If the cops found out what she had done, though. If they questioned her . . .

Stupid. She was so stupid. She should never have hacked that website. Stupid, stupid, stupid.

Nina slapped herself. Hard. Her eyes stung. Then she did it again. And again. And once more for good measure. Only then could she breathe. One tear spilled over, and she whisked it away with her fingertips.

Her father would tell her to bury it. To burn it. To erase her internet history and dump her computer. So she knew what she had to do.

She had to study it. She had to sit down and figure out what was really going on here, and only then could she make an informed decision about her next steps. She could not be rash. Not again. Hacking the account had been rash. Telling Ainsley about it—rash. Getting Veronika to sneak her back inside while the catering crew was cleaning up after the party so she could retrieve the folder—rash.

This was what happened when Nina didn't think. When she acted emotionally.

She took a long, deep breath. She felt better now that she had a plan.

Still, something nagged at her. When Ainsley looked over these papers, her first reaction hadn't been anger. There had been something other than ire behind her eyes. Something Nina didn't think Ainsley Aames was capable of feeling.

There had been fear.

And a few hours later, Ainsley was dead. Nina wondered if Ainsley had already taken her last breath when she'd snuck into the office to grab the folder. Had Nina been mere yards away from Ainsley's dead body? She sat with that for a moment. Waited to feel something. But nothing came.

The office door opened and the light clicked on. Nina grabbed the folder and shoved it under her laptop.

"Hey!" Ravi said. "There you are."

"I thought you had a class," Nina said.

"The kid was a no-show. I still get paid, though, so win-win. That twelve-hour cancellation policy was one of the best ideas you ever had."

He grinned and dropped into the armchair near the wall. "So? How did it go?"

"How did what go?"

"You were going to talk to that Paige person after school, right?"

"Oh." She blew out a laugh. "Right."

"So?"

Nina remembered the expression on Paige's face when she'd turned around to look up at her on the hill. It had been enough to make Nina wonder if Paige *had* murdered Ainsley Aames. Izzy had run up behind Paige at just that moment and grabbed her hand, shouting, "Mommy! Hi! I had the best day!" And Paige had shifted on a dime, all bright smiles and joy. There was something off with that woman. The stories she'd found on the internet hadn't been *that* bad. Plenty of people had done worse. But she had the sense that Paige was capable of things.

Of course, Nina had been the one blackmailing another mom on the grassy knoll behind the school.

"She said yes," Nina told her husband. "She's going to be my campaign manager."

"That's great!" Ravi cheered. He got up and kissed her forehead, a long, firm, proud kiss—then he kissed her mouth for good measure. "See? Of course she said yes. You're a rock star."

"I'm not." Nina smiled, but looked away, because tears had sprung up in her eyes out of nowhere.

"Yes, you are. Which is why I'm going to go pour us some champagne and get out those strawberries you bought at the farmer's market. Meet me in the kitchen in five."

"'Kay," she said, not trusting herself with more than one syllable.

The second he was gone, Nina got up and went to the tall filing cabinet against the back wall. She pulled over the step stool, climbed up, and tugged forward the fake potted plant atop the cabinet. She just wanted to touch it. Make sure it was still there if she needed it.

She plucked out the plant, fake dirt and all, and pulled out the gun she kept hidden inside the pot. Its cold metal heft in her palm took away the last of her nerves. She was in control. She was in control. She was in control.

paige

Paige was so glad her mother had introduced her to Marie. For the first time all day she felt quasi-relaxed and semi-accomplished. She was sitting at a quiet corner booth at Aldo's, her laptop open to a document filled with actual words. She had no idea whether they were good words. Whether there was anything promising or even coherent on the screen. But there were words. In the past hour she'd put more thoughts down than she had in the past week. Which might have been due to the wine.

Marie was keeping her glass full with a lovely merlot that went down like butter.

"How's it going over here, Ephron?" Marie asked, topping her off once again.

"Mmmmm, I like that nickname." Paige lifted her glass. "You can call me Ephron any time." She put her glass down and folded her arms on the table next to her computer, squinting up at Marie, who was backlit by a dimmed pot light in the ceiling. Her thick dark hair was up in a ponytail with pretty pieces framing her face, but she looked tired. "Can I ask you a question?"

"Shoot." Marie leaned over to pluck a couple of water glasses off the next table, which had been recently vacated.

"Do you think Ainsley was murdered?"

Marie drew in a sharp breath.

"What?" Paige asked.

"I thought you were going to ask if the cannoli was made in-house."

Paige laughed. "Sorry. I guess it is a little morbid."

"Well, it's the scandal of the day," Marie said. She shrugged, one water glass in each hand. "Truth is, I don't know. Ainsley was super influential in this town. She threw all the big parties, donated crap-loads of money to the hospital and the animal shelter—and all that time to the PBA, of course."

"She sounds like a saint."

"Well, 'saint' isn't the word I'd use, but she certainly worked her ass off. She just . . . she could be kind of a dick, you know? She would act like your best friend until she didn't need anything from you any-more."

Paige took a long sip of merlot and thought of Lanie. "Do you think she was really going to step aside and let Lanie take over the PBA?"

Marie shrugged. "That was the plan. According to the bylaws, you can only be president if you have at least one kid at the elemen-tary school or in middle school. Her youngest is in sixth grade, but she told everyone at the end of last year she felt like she'd given all she could to the organization and would step down this year. New officers are always installed at the first meeting in October, and it was just sort of known that Lanie was next in line. Why do you ask?"

"I don't know. Just figuring out how it all works, I guess."

"You really screwed Lanie with that whole Nina thing, though," Marie said. "I hear a lot of people are thinking about voting for her."

"That's good," Paige said, even as her insides burned at the threat Nina had leveled at her earlier. "It would be nice if it were close. Or at least fair."

Marie snorted. "Ainsley just rolled over in her grave. Oh, wait. She's not buried yet."

"Marie, did something . . . happen between you and Ainsley?"

"What makes you say that?" Marie moved over to the nearest table and began straightening the flatware.

"It's just a hunch."

Marie stood up straight and sighed. "It's a long story. But yeah, we weren't really speaking when she died. She almost put me out of business. Still might."

"What? How?"

With a shrug, Marie turned away. "Like I said, long story. But let's just say, *fair*? Not a word in that woman's vocabulary. The only thing in this world that mattered to Ainsley was Ainsley."

"Hey, Paige. Marie."

Paige startled. "John!"

Marie froze, her eyes wide as she stared at Paige. Had he heard what she'd just said? Paige shook her head ever so slightly. She was pretty sure John had heard nothing, because the guy looked wrecked. His face was pale and covered with a five-o'clock shadow. There were bags under his watery red eyes and his blond hair had been gelled but was now mussed, so that pieces stuck out stiffly from one side of his head. He wore a dark suit, but his tie had been loosened, and he was carrying a few brown takeout bags stamped with the Aldo's logo.

"John! You're . . . here." Marie recovered first. "I'm so sorry I couldn't make the wake tonight, but I'll be there tomorrow."

"Of course. It's fine. The place was jammed anyway."

"Do you need anything?" Marie asked.

"No, I'm good." He lifted the two bags slightly at his sides. "I gotta get this back to the kids." He looked away from her and down at Paige. "Hey."

"Hi." Paige's heart was hammering. She had no idea what she was supposed to say to her ex-boyfriend whose wife had just died. Marie slunk away quietly, leaving the two of them to stare at each other over the glow of her laptop. "I'm so sorry, John."

Part of her felt like she should stand up and hug him, but she envisioned herself sliding awkwardly from the booth and him trying to hug her back with two hands full of Italian food, and decided to stay put.

"Thanks," he said. "It's just so surreal. I keep waiting for my phone to ping with a text from her asking if I remembered to get the white balsamic dressing instead of the dark."

Paige's throat felt tight. She knew how that felt. To this day, whenever the Yankees were on TV, she missed the play-by-play reactions from her dad. He used to text her every two minutes, the excited messages riddled with misspellings.

"Speaking of. You never texted me back last night."

"Right. Shit. I'm sorry. I was at a . . . thing when you texted, and I've been so busy." She gestured lamely at her computer, her face burning at the implied lie that she had work. The last thing she wanted to mention to him was the PBA. "But that's no excuse."

"It's fine. I just . . . I don't know how I'm supposed to get through this."

"You will," she said. "It's not going to be easy, but you will."

He nodded absently. "Are you coming to the reception tomorrow? After the burial?"

Paige's stomach turned, all that wine sloshing around. "I really don't think I should. I didn't know Ainsley for long and I . . . I don't think she liked me very much."

Again, he nodded absently. "I get it. Then maybe we can hang out when it's over? Grab coffee? My mom is taking the kids for a few days, and I just think . . . I don't know, I'd like to talk."

Talk? About what? What did that mean? *Talk about us?* He couldn't mean that. His wife had just died.

But what if that's what he did mean? Maybe their marriage had been unhappy. Maybe it had been dead for a long, long time. Maybe he was already ready to move on before this ever happened.

Maybe he murdered her.

Paige clenched her jaw against the random thought and focused on John's kind, tired eyes.

"You know, talk to someone who didn't know her. Talk about something other than . . . this."

Or maybe he just needed an escape.

"Sure." Paige gave him a small smile.

"Cool. Okay. I'll text you, I guess."

"Okay. This time I promise to reply. Try to get some rest."

John nodded. "Good luck with your work."

He trudged away and was barely out the door when her phone pinged.

The text was from Lanie.

PLAYDATE TOMORROW? SOUNDS LIKE DICKINSON AND IZZY
HAVE REALLY HIT IT OFF AT SCHOOL!

Paige took a deep breath. This was it. Her chance to talk to Lanie alone. Dominic would tell her to jump on it. Although Lanie had slipped below Nina on her list, what with all her cyberstalking and the blackmail. Still. She had a job to do. And Izzy would love a play-date with Dickinson.

She texted back.

WE'RE IN

nina

Nina stood on the edge of the crowd under the tent in Bee's backyard, trying to get an angle on the kitchen windows. No one was allowed inside the house other than Bee and the caterers, who were ostensibly using Bee's half-dismantled kitchen to warm food and clean dishes. Nina was dying to see what was going on in there. Had they gutted it completely, or were they only replacing countertops and fixtures? There was a big difference, budgetarily speaking.

She slowly walked around the perimeter of the tent, sipping her white wine, watching while people became increasingly loud, and laughter peppered in among the reverent whispers. The luncheon had started out hushed and sad, but, like most funeral receptions Nina had been to, it would probably be a drunken mess within the hour.

Near the front of the tent she paused, looking up at the house again. What she wouldn't give to get inside. To do a quick search. Bee was the type of person who would leave all her bills and important paperwork strewn about for anyone to see. It would probably take

Nina five seconds to find out how much she was spending on these renovations. To see if her niggling suspicions were correct.

She scanned the crowd. Cori Levin caught her eye and quickly looked away. No one had spoken to her this entire time. No one aside from John, to whom she had paid her condolences upon arrival. Nina may as well have been invisible. A ghost. She wished Ravi were here, but he had classes to teach this afternoon and he'd barely ever said two words to Ainsley.

Nina kept moving. At the back of the tent, the greenhouse Bee used as her art studio came into view. It was tucked behind a hedgerow and, it occurred to Nina with an excited leap of her heart, there was an office attached.

Why hadn't she thought of this before? That tiny, closet-like office where she and Bee had argued about Lita's class fee. There had been a small, unkempt desk and piles of folders and canvases. Nina swigged the rest of her wine, placed her glass on a table, and slipped behind the hedges. There, she paused for half a second and listened to hear if anyone was following her. But of course they weren't. She was invisible.

Inside the unlocked greenhouse, the air was warm and smelled of paint and turpentine. Ignoring the paintings in progress set up on easels throughout the room, Nina moved toward the office. The light coming through the one window was wan, but she didn't dare flick on the lights. She grabbed the first stack of papers she saw and brought them back to the greenhouse so she could see in the sunlight streaming through the glass ceiling.

It was a pile of invoices for art classes. Apparently, Bee's rates had only gone up since her and Nina's standoff. Nina scoffed and replaced the stack, grabbing the next one.

Old letters and receipts from various organizations in the city.

Thank you for your generous donation . . .
We request the pleasure of your company at our charity gala . . .

Your reservation for our annual Dinner Under the Stars is confirmed . . .

Some of these were years old. Had Bee claimed these donations and event tickets on her taxes? Or did she not even know that was a thing?

Groaning, Nina put the stack back. She sifted through other random scraps of paper, little drawings and musings, shopping lists and to-dos, feeling more desperate by the moment. Then she pulled on the bottom drawer of the desk, which only opened half an inch before jamming. Nina pulled again. Nothing. She crouched down to see what was stopping the drawer and saw it was full of old paint jars and crusty brushes. She slammed it and opened the one above.

Bank registers. Finally.

Nina took out the top one, which was of course not dated or numbered, and opened it. Pages and pages of incoherent chicken scratch. Bee didn't even use the lines on the register consistently, sometimes scrawling a transaction across three rows.

Cash for supplies

Or

Cat food

Or

Vacation!!!

Revolting. Nina's skin crawled at the level of disorganization. The lack of care. There were no balances. Just random numbers. Nina was willing to bet that Bee had never tallied her check register against her bank statement in her life. A task Nina looked forward to every month as a moment of zen reflection.

She looked back into the drawer. Below the registers was a pile of bank statements. Those would definitely be much more helpful. At least they had a shot at being accurate, though Nina had found mistakes on her own bank statements in the past—always a thrill. She yanked the statements out, and at that moment, the door to the greenhouse opened.

Nina shoved the bank statements into her bag and closed the flap.

Lanie. She hadn't spotted Nina yet. Nina stepped out of the office doorway and over to the nearest painting. It was a depiction of a horse in garish pink, the proportions totally wrong.

"What're you doing in here?"

Lanie stalked right over to Nina's side. She was wearing a slim, black, sleeveless dress, her star necklace proudly displayed by the V-neck cut.

"Just taking in some artwork." Nina's voice sounded strained, even to her. She cleared her throat. Lanie's eyes trailed over to the open office door and she looked Nina up and down. The drawer. Nina hadn't closed the drawer. But that whole office was a disaster. One open drawer proved nothing.

"No, you were in the office."

"I wasn't. I just needed a break from all the mourning, so I slipped in here. My daughter used to take classes with Bee."

Lanie's mouth made a thin, straight line. Nina realized that this was the most unkempt she'd ever seen Lanie. The woman wasn't even wearing lipstick.

"I think you should go."

Suddenly, out of nowhere, Nina wanted to cry. Everyone hated her. Everyone would always hate her. But even more disconcerting than this thought was the fact that it suddenly seemed to matter to her.

"Fine," she said.

She'd gotten what she'd come for anyway.

lanie

MY DAILY SCHEDULE

8:40: Drop off kids

10:00: Ainsley's burial

11:00: Home/change clothes

11:30: Arrange fruit plate (text Paige to make sure no
      allergies!!!)

12:30–2:30: Reception @Bee's (bring lemon squares)

2:45: Pick up kids

3:00: Home/change clothes

3:30–5:00: Playdate with Paige and Izzy

6:00: Kids dinner

7:00: Baths

8:00: Story time

8:30: Brush teeth/bed

9:00: L & M (?) dinner—M home when??? Tell M about call
      from PPD???

* * *

IT HAD BEEN a strange day. Too sunny. Too quiet. Too normal in spots. Like school drop-off when the crossing guard shouted at a teenaged driver who had ignored his stop sign. Or the moment at Bee's house when the caterer dropped a pile of clean plates and, after a moment of silence, everyone had laughed. How could they all stand there and laugh when they were all milling around wearing black on a Wednesday afternoon and Ainsley Aames Anderson was dead? Nothing made sense.

At least she had gotten that cop to put off their meeting until tomorrow, claiming that she needed the day to mourn. She wondered what Officer Dominic Ramos would think if he knew she intended to spend the next two hours entertaining, not mourning.

What the hell did he want to talk to her about anyway? She'd thought Ainsley's death had officially been ruled an accident. Why were the police talking to *anyone*, let alone her? Had someone seen her driving through Ainsley's neighborhood late that night, her headlights off, furtively watching the house? Had a neighbor noticed Michael's car in the driveway even after everyone else had gone home? Every time Lanie thought about it, she found herself fighting a panic attack.

But for the moment, she had to shake it off. This playdate had to go perfectly. She had to get Paige on her side. As wealthy as the people in this town were, and as much time as they spent playing golf and tennis and jetting off to vacation homes on the Cape or in the Caribbean or the South of France, they were also bored and hungry for something to talk about. And the second Paige Lancaster stepped foot in this town, she had become the thing to talk about this season. She was intriguing. A former resident! Daughter of that police chief everyone loved whom Piermont had a parade for! A TV writer! John Anderson's high school girlfriend! (First love? First everything?)

And, okay, *maybe* a murderer. But really? A murderer?

All Nina Anand needed was for some of that intrigue to rub off on her and the game would change. Nina herself wasn't without her interesting qualities. She was the youngest mom at the school, as far as anyone could tell, and there was a rumor that she'd graduated from high school at twelve and college at sixteen, then gone on to business school. Plus she was married to that hottie musician dad who always looked as if he'd just rolled out of bed all sexily rumpled.

And then there had been that whole thing in the greenhouse today. Nina had obviously been snooping around, and when Lanie told Bee about it, she hadn't even seemed surprised. Lanie, though, had been unnerved. There was something dangerous about Nina. She couldn't let her get ahold of their beloved PBA.

Lanie had to get Paige to call Nina off. It was the only way. But today she would take a different tack. She was going to impress the crap out of Paige and become her new best friend so that Paige would have no choice but to do what she wanted. After this playdate, Lanie wouldn't even have to ask Paige to do it. She'd do it out of newfound loyalty.

She just really did hope that Paige was not, in fact, a murderer, because if she was, it was probably a bad idea to invite the woman over to her house.

As Lanie pulled from the fridge the fruit salad she'd so carefully assembled after Ainsley's burial, she wondered what kind of sex life Nina and Ravi had. She was so buttoned up and frigid, and he was so . . . *not*. Did Nina play schoolmarm? Sexy librarian? Did Ravi serenade her to turn her on?

"Mom!"

Lanie dropped the ceramic platter on the countertop with a horrible clatter. Luckily, Dickinson didn't seem to notice.

"They're here!"

As Paige and Izzy walked into the kitchen, Paige glanced at Lanie with concern. "You okay?"

"Fine. The platter slipped. Sorry. I didn't even hear the bell ring."

"Dickinson opened it before we had the chance," Paige explained.

"Well, she's just so excited to have you here. We both are!" Lanie quickly wiped her hands on her apron, then untied it and flung it over the back of the nearest chair. "Hi! Welcome. Hello, Izzy!"

"Hi," Izzy said shyly.

"Can we go outside and play soccer?" Dickinson asked. "I want to show Izzy my new nets!"

"Sure, as long as that's what Izzy wants to do."

Paige squatted down to Izzy's level. "You love soccer, right, Izzy?"

"Okay," Izzy said.

Dickinson opened the sliding glass door and the girls ran out, giggling.

"Where are your other kids?" Paige asked.

"Austen and Haddix are with their grandmother for the afternoon and Marcus is at lacrosse." Lanie pulled the plastic wrap off the salad—melons balled, pineapple cut into stars—and placed a serving spoon next to it, then went for the water pitcher.

"Would you like some?"

Paige slid into a chair at the island and dropped her massive bag atop the counter. Lanie tried not to scrunch her nose, thinking of the news report she'd seen about the germs all over the bottom of women's purses. She could always Lysol later, and the cleaning crew came tomorrow.

"No thanks. I just ate."

"Oh." Lanie poured them each a glass of water, and gulped hers.

"You go ahead, though," Paige said after thanking her for the water. "It's really okay."

"No, no. We can wait."

Paige rolled her eyes. "You're obviously, hungry. Please, just eat." Paige reached over, took a melamine bowl off the stack Lanie had set out and held it out over the island. Lanie was half-appalled by her audaciousness and half-grateful. She took the bowl, against her better judgment, and filled it with fruit.

"Thanks."

"How was the . . . funeral? The reception?" Paige asked. She wandered over to the glass doors.

"It was . . . fine. Exhausting. You know." Lanie stared at the colorful bowl in front of her and saw Ainsley's coffin being lowered into the ground. Her fingers automatically went up to touch her necklace. "It's all going to take some getting used to."

"I'm sorry. Let's talk about something else. I can be your distraction for the afternoon." She smiled, and Lanie did, too. It felt like a peace offering of sorts. Paige looked out the window again, lifting up onto her toes. "I can't see the girls."

"The soccer field is up the hill," Lanie said, taking a bite of watermelon.

"How big is this property, anyway?"

"We have fifteen acres."

Paige whistled.

"It's not that big. My husband grew up on a farm and he's always saying this is like a postage stamp."

Paige snorted. "I guess it's all relative. Back in L.A., I could see my neighbor's toilet from my kitchen."

Lanie laughed a genuine laugh.

Paige bent at the waist and looked west. "What is that over there? Those tall telephone pole–type things."

"Oh, that's my obstacle course."

"Your *what*?"

Lanie got up, taking her water glass with her. "You know *American Ninja Warrior*?"

"Uh, yeah! I'm obsessed."

Lanie smiled. There it was: something in common. Everything was going to be fine. "Then you have to come see."

* * *

"THIS. IS. INSANE."

Paige's head was tipped back as she took in the spiderweb netting, the swinging gauntlet, the balance beam, and the rock wall.

"You really use this?" she asked.

"Yep." Lanie walked over to the climbing wall and tugged on a pair of mesh gloves, pleased she'd put on her Lululemons after school pickup. "My husband had it built for my thirty-fifth birthday. I can't stand traditional exercise, but I always loved a good obstacle course as a kid, and I participated in some Tough Mudder races in college. I won the Panhellenic obstacle challenge two years running. Michael says it was watching me throw myself over the top of the climbing wall while covered in mud and bleeding from my knee that made him fall in love." She felt a pang, remembering the look on Michael's face when she'd slugged beer out of her trophy that night in the basement at Chi Phi. When was the last time he'd looked at her that way? She held out a pair of gloves to Paige. "Wanna try?"

"Uh . . . we should check on the girls."

"You're right." Lanie pulled out her phone, clicked open the security app, and tapped on the icon for the field camera. There they were, in full Technicolor, shooting soccer balls into the net on the north side. She turned her phone to show Paige. "They seem fine."

"Holy . . . How many cameras do you have in this place?"

"A few dozen. Michael travels for work a lot and he wants to make sure we're safe. Everyone in town should have a security system now, what with all the car robberies that have been going on."

Lanie still couldn't believe that Dayna and Maurice had been hit. If these burglars were venturing up to palaces like Dayna's, no one was safe.

"Your husband sounds like a dream."

Lanie grinned, though her throat was tight. "That's my Michael. So . . . climb?"

Paige hesitated. "I don't know. I'll probably fall on my ass."

"That's what the harnesses are for."

"You don't really take no for an answer, do you?"

"Never. It's one of my more endearing qualities."

They were halfway up the wall, Lanie lagging behind her usual time, to stay even with Paige, when Paige said, "I have a hard time picturing you covered in mud."

Lanie laughed. "Me too, these days."

"What happened?"

"What, like I'm not cool anymore?"

Paige went green around the gills. "No, I mean—"

"I'm joking. I know. I guess I just . . . outgrew it?" She looked up at the bell at the top of the wall. She could have been there ten times over by now. "I don't know. Sometimes I think about signing up for a race. I do miss how fearless I was. I think that's the main thing."

Paige reached for the next handhold and pulled herself up with a grunt. "That's the thing about getting older that no one tells you. You lose all that fearlessness."

"Not you, though," Lanie said. She pulled herself up another foot, forcing Paige to look up at her.

"What do you mean?"

"You picked up and moved yourself and your daughter across the country. That takes guts."

"That wasn't guts," Paige muttered.

"What do you mean?" Lanie crooked her neck to look down. She was now a few feet above Paige.

"Nothing. You were pretty brave the other night, though. When you confronted Ainsley at the party. From what I've heard, no one ever contradicted her."

"Yeah, well, it was much safer not to."

"What do you mean?" Paige asked.

"Just, she was one of those people, you know? She always had to be in control of everyone and everything, no matter what it took.

Some people she could just push around because they're weak, but with me . . ."

Lanie paused. Why was she saying all of this?

"You're not weak."

Lanie snorted a laugh and tears sprang to her eyes. "Not around Ainsley I wasn't. I honestly think she kept me close because she knew I wouldn't bow to her bullshit, and on some level, that scared her. But some people couldn't help themselves. They'd do anything to get on her good side. Including telling her everyone else's secrets, apparently."

"People like who?"

"Nothing. Never mind. Forget I said anything."

She quickly climbed the last couple of feet, rang the bell, and zipped back down to the ground.

"Lanie?" Paige said, dangling above her.

"Come down. I think the kids should eat something."

Lanie's heart was pounding and her palms were sweaty. She ripped off her climbing gloves and shook out her fingers. Just as Paige was starting her painfully slow descent, there was a scream—long and loud and anguished. Lanie looked up.

"What was that?" Paige croaked.

Lanie fumbled for her phone. Checked the camera. The kids were gone. She could check the other cameras, but her hands were shaking. She dropped the phone and ran.

"Lanie! Wait!"

But the kids were still screaming. Both of them now. Lanie ran up the stone steps two at a time and saw them, running toward her. There was something running after them.

"Mom!"

"Shit!"

It was a coyote. A mangy, pissed-off, probably rabid coyote.

"Lanie!?"

The thing was gaining on the kids. Lanie turned and jumped back down to the ground, ignoring the pain in her knees as she connected with the turf. She lunged for the storage trunk, which she and Paige had left unlocked, reached in, and grabbed the canvas bag that held her pistol. Paige had just made it to the ground.

"Is that a *gun?*"

Lanie didn't answer. She couldn't. She sprinted back up the stairs. The screaming was louder. More intense. She half expected to see Dickinson on the ground getting mauled. But the coyote was still a couple of feet behind them. Lanie cocked the pistol, shoved her arm straight above her head, and fired.

"Lanie!"

The kids hit the ground, face-first, covering the backs of their heads with both hands. The coyote turned and fled, whimpering, back into the woods. Paige arrived at Lanie's side, panting, hands on her knees.

"Holy shit. What happened?"

Lanie shoved the gun in her waistband and ran for the kids. Paige at her heels.

"Are you okay? Kids! Are you okay?"

The girls flung themselves at their mothers. Paige was on her knees, hugging a sobbing Izzy, when she looked up at Lanie, wide-eyed.

"What was that thing?"

"Coyote. We've had a problem around here lately."

"It ate my neighbor's rabbit." Dickinson sniffled.

Izzy sobbed louder.

"What's with the gun?"

Lanie had forgotten all about it, but now she felt the barrel of the pistol pressed against her tailbone.

"It's just a starter pistol," she said. "For the obstacle race. It's totally harmless."

paige

Lanie had just saved Izzy's life. Which made what Paige was doing so reprehensible she wanted to stab her own eyes out with a plastic fork. But did that stop her? No. No, it did not.

With Lanie and the girls safely ensconced in the theater room watching the latest incarnation of Mary Poppins, Lanie slipped upstairs and straight to the crafting room/office that was clearly Lanie's favorite room in the house. After everyone had recovered from The Coyote Incident, which was how she was already mentally referring to what had happened, and which might make a good title for a screenplay, Lanie and Dickinson had given Paige and Izzy a tour of the house, along with Marcus, who had just been dropped off after practice. Said tour had revealed two things to Paige: One, the home was way too big for her to ever find anything that might be useful to her investigation, and two, if there was anything useful to be found, it was in this room.

As soon as it was clear that Izzy was fully distracted, Paige told

Lanie she had to call her agent, and now, here she was, rifling through Lanie's things.

The room was meticulously organized. There was a wall of ribbon shelved by color that would have made rainbow-obsessed childhood Paige weep with pleasure. Adult Paige took her phone out and placed it on the desk next to the laptop so that she could pretend she'd just hung up if anyone found her here, and then tackled the drawers.

In the first, clear organizers divided the shallow space into smaller sections for pens, pushpins, paper clips, Post-its, and charger wires. Not so much as a wayward staple out of place. In the second were piles of stationery in seasonal colors, along with a set of gold and silver pens and a book bound in floral-print cloth.

Paige grabbed the book, set it on the desk, said a quick prayer that it was what she thought it was, and opened to the ribbon book marker.

A diary. Bingo.

> *I invited Paige and her daughter Izzy over for a playdate. It has to go well. It sounds obnoxious, but I've never had such a hard time getting someone to like me. Or even smile at me. It's not just the election. I can't describe it. I feel wrong when I'm around her. Like I'm trying too hard. Even though she might be a psycho.*

Wait. What?

> *God, am I one of those people who needs everyone to like her? I don't want to be that person. Fuck those people. I have to talk to Frida about this. Note: Book next appointment for when she's back from Cabo.*

Yes, of course you're one of those people who needs everyone to like her, Lanie. Kind of like I'm clearly an adrenaline junkie with little to no moral compass. Be a little self-aware.

Heart pounding, Paige glanced at the door and flipped back a few pages. She saw Ainsley's name quite a few times and paused at each mention, but it was mostly about wishing she'd stayed later at the party because maybe she could have done something, about feeling badly for John and *those poor kids*. Then, her eyes landed on a word that made her blood seize up in her veins.

Affair.

It was from the night of the Parents and Pinot Party.

It's after 12 and he's still not home. What if he's with her? Ugh, I can't even think about it. My stomach cramps every time I do. Just the idea of Michael touching Ainsley. Looking at Ainsley the way he used to look at me. What if they're together? What if she told? Is that why he's been so distant lately? Does he know about Dr. Canton?

She wouldn't. Would she? She knows my life would be over. But if she wants him, maybe she would. Maybe that's the whole point. Maybe that's even why she wouldn't give up the presidency— because she couldn't stand to see me happy. God, I hate this. I HATE her!

Paige bit her bottom lip. This was what they called "pay dirt." Lanie suspected her husband of having an affair with Ainsley, and he hadn't come home until late on the night of the party. Had he still been there at the time of death? Maybe the woman really was murdered. And maybe this Michael person had done it.

Or maybe Lanie had done it. It was right here in her own handwriting. She hated Ainsley. Ainsley knew things about her that she didn't want Michael to know. Secrets Lanie had shared with someone else, who had gone and told Lanie because they were, in Lanie's own words, "weak" and "willing to do anything to get on Ainsley's good side."

I know a few things, darling. About what you did during quarantine? I will destroy you.

Maybe that threat had caused Lanie to snap. Maybe Paige was standing in the craft room of a brutal murderer.

What the hell did you do during quarantine? Paige wondered.

The semi-ajar door behind her pushed open and a man walked in. "Hey, Lane. Listen, we have to talk."

Michael. Her new murder suspect. Paige froze. He took off his suit jacket and tossed it over the back of the nearest chair. Something fell out of a pocket and rolled right over to Paige. It hit the toe of her boot and fell flat. Paige quickly shoved the book back in the drawer and picked up her phone. That was when Michael noticed she was not his wife.

"Who the hell are you?"

Paige bent to pick up the item at her feet. It was a casino chip. Blue. Three *A*s intertwined at its center. She held it out to him.

"I'm Paige Lancaster."

Blank stare. He stepped forward, took the chip from her and shoved it deep into his pants pockets.

"I'm new in town? Moved here a couple of weeks ago. My daughter, Izzy, is here on a playdate with Dickinson. Lanie must have mentioned it."

Silence. Paige's nerves sizzled. She didn't like people who didn't engage. After twenty years in L.A. she was used to men talking over her, talking over one another, talking, talking, talking. Everyone always trying to be the most important dick in the room.

"I should go back down."

She made a move toward the door, but Michael stood his ground, blocking her exit. She couldn't help noticing how large he was. Broad shoulders, biceps that strained against his white shirt. And tall. At least six foot four.

"What were you doing in here?" he asked.

She lifted her phone. "I had a call with my agent."

"Your agent."

"I'm a writer."

He studied her. He had arresting, green eyes that stood out, thanks to his dark eyebrows and hair. Were they the eyes of a killer? There was something about the look of him that made Paige think he'd be more at home in a T-shirt and jeans and biker boots than the multi-thousand-dollar suit he was currently sporting. Attractive. But even attractive men could snap, as Paige knew all too well.

"What do you write?" he asked, still not moving.

"TV. Crime shows." She wanted to see if he would react. He did. By relaxing. He crossed his arms over his chest.

"Oh yeah? Anything I would've seen?"

"I've been on *Chance Encounters* for the last few years," she said.

He frowned; shook his head. "I don't know that one."

"You're not exactly our target demographic," she told him. His brow knit and Paige stifled a chuckle. "I should get back downstairs before my kid gets worried I disappeared."

Michael finally stepped sideways so she could slide out the door. "You mind letting my wife know I'm home?" he asked.

"Sure," she said.

Don't look back, she told herself as she walked down the hall, deliberately measuring her steps. *Don't look back or you'll look guilty.*

But she couldn't help it. When she reached the top of the stairs, she did look back. Michael stood at the door of the craft room, arms still crossed over his intimidating chest, watching her.

lanie

"She was in the craft room?"

It was after dark. The kids were asleep. Michael was home at a normal hour, and she'd thought that maybe they'd have a chance to catch up. She could tell him about the funeral. Talk about the night of the party. But now this. Lanie swung herself out of bed and stormed down to the craft room. Michael followed.

She flicked on the light and looked around. Nothing seemed out of place.

"What are you so worried about?" Michael asked as she moved to her desk and opened her computer. Locked. "Are you keeping state secrets in here?"

Secrets.

Lanie opened the drawer where she stashed her journals. The breath completely left her.

"She read my journal." The book was facedown in the drawer, the spine facing right. That was not how she left it. Lanie always kept her journals in two neat stacks in the drawer, oldest on the bottom left, newest on the top right, all of them faceup. "Oh my God. She read my journal."

How far had Paige gotten? Where had she started? The beginning of this journal was far less damning than the end. Had she read the whole thing? Or just a part? And *which damn part?*

"How long was she in here?"

"I have no idea."

"Well, did you see her with this in her hand?" Lanie held up the journal. "Did she read it?"

"Lanie, I don't know. What are you so afraid of, huh? What's in that journal that you don't want anyone to know?"

"Why are you yelling at me? I was the one who was violated."

Michael gave a short laugh. "That's rich."

It was at that moment that Lanie knew she'd just walked into a trap. But she kept going, pretending like it wasn't true. "What do you mean by that?"

"Lanie, were you ever going to tell me?"

Shit. Shit shit shit. Lanie's arm dropped to her side, the journal heavy in her hand. "Tell you what?"

He knew about the rehab. Dayna must have told him. Or Dayna had told Ainsley, and Ainsley had told him. They had told her husband the one thing she never wanted him to know. Well. One of two things.

"God, this is insane. I am your husband. I've been waiting for months . . . years . . . for you to just tell me. Just *tell* me what you did. But you can't even give me the courtesy of saying it to my face."

"Michael, I don't—"

He stepped over to her and grabbed the journal out of her hand. She made a reach for it, but he held out an arm, holding her back so easily it was as if she were made of feathers.

"I *know*, Lanie. I know about the baby. I know about the operation."

"What?"

And even though Lanie had read dozens of Victorian novels in which women fainted dead away at the utterance of shocking news, she never believed, until that very moment, that it was actually possible. But that was exactly what she did.

WHEN SHE WOKE up, she was lying on her bed, and Michael was kneeling at her side as if in prayer.

"Are you all right?" he said, the second her eyes fluttered open.

"What happened?"

"I think you fainted. Did you eat anything today?"

"Not really."

"Can you sit up?"

He propped the pillows up behind her and she shimmied back until she was sitting against them. Her head throbbed and her eyes were dry. He handed her a glass of water and held his hand over hers, warm and large and comforting, until she was able to get a sip.

"Ainsley told you."

What she couldn't figure out was how Ainsley had known. Lanie had told Dayna about going to rehab. About getting sober. About using Ainsley as her cover story. And she assumed that was what Ainsley was talking about when she'd said she knew what Lanie had done during quarantine. But the baby? The operation? Lanie had never told anyone about that. Maybe *all* her friends were reading her diary.

Michael's face screwed up in confusion. "What? About the baby? No. Why would you think that?"

Lanie looked away. She couldn't look him in the eye. She'd lied to him for so long, and now it was out and she couldn't bear to see what he thought of her.

"Because you two . . . I mean . . . you seemed to be spending a lot of time together."

Michael stood up abruptly. "What's that supposed to mean?"

"It means what it means." Lanie was exhausted. She felt attacked and violated and sad and sorry. This felt like the end of her marriage. Might as well get it all out.

"You think me and Ainsley . . ." Michael laughed. It was an amused, somehow sorrowful laugh. Then he went to his closet and popped open the suitcase that was still there from his trip. He dumped it out and started repacking.

"What're you doing?"

"I'm going to go stay at the firm's apartment in the city for a little while. I don't think I can be here."

"Michael. We need to deal with this."

"I can't, Lanie. I can't right now."

"But Ainsley knew. She told me she knew. She—"

Michael stormed out of the closet, the tendons in his neck straining. "Did you not hear what I said in there?" He threw his hand out in the direction of the hallway. "I've known about this *for years*. You want to know how I found out, Lanie? I took a Friday off that summer, during the pandemic, remember? So that you and Dayna and Bee could go over to Ainsley's for that outdoor spa experience. I hung out with the kids all day so that you could go get some time away."

Gee, one day, Lanie thought sarcastically. *Father and husband of the year right here, ladies and gentlemen.*

"And while we were playing out back, the phone rang, and I went inside and answered it and it was your doctor. And she said she wanted to follow up to see if you were in any pain. Having any side effects from the procedure."

Tears filled Lanie's eyes. She stared straight ahead.

"They can do that, you know, because you have me down as someone the doctors can talk to about things. Because I'm a person you *trust*."

His voice cracked and Lanie's tears spilled over.

"So I asked a few questions, pretending as if I knew what was going on with my own wife. I remember I had Haddix in my arms and she was falling asleep, so I had to whisper while I was trying to figure out what the hell this woman was talking about. But I did figure it out. You were pregnant and you never told me. You had a miscarriage and you never told me. And then you went in and got your tubes tied so we could never have another kid, and you *never told me.*"

Lanie covered her face and cried, her body racked with sobs.

"And you know what, Lanie, it's not even that these things happened, but that you felt like you needed to keep it all a secret from me. Was I that big a monster? I thought we were in love. I thought we told each other everything."

"No."

"What?"

"No. I've never told you everything. Or maybe you just didn't want to see it."

"Oh, so now you're accusing me of something?"

"Michael, I was so depressed after Haddix, don't you remember? The postpartum, the pandemic . . . I've never experienced anything like that. Don't you remember me in here crying at all hours? Not showering, not feeding myself, barely moving unless someone needed something from me, which, by the way, was *all the time.* I had four kids under ten, and there was no school and no activities and no *relief,* and you were *always* working. I couldn't have another baby. I wasn't sure I could survive it."

"It wasn't that bad."

The laugh that came out of her was so low and guttural she didn't even recognize the sound. "It was that bad, Michael. I was drinking way too much to try to numb the fear, and when that didn't work, I'd take a Xanax to top it off."

"No. No, that I would have noticed."

"But you *didn't.*"

Michael huffed, frustrated. "Well, why didn't you say something?"

"Because! I was scared. And ashamed. I don't know. You didn't seem fazed by any of it, but I was . . . I was falling apart."

"So what does this have to do with the baby?"

"I'm getting to that." Lanie stood up and pushed her sweaty palms into her thighs, leaving marks on her leggings. "There was this one day . . . one of the first warm days . . . when I was outside playing with the kids and I sat down at the patio table for one minute. One minute to rest my eyes. And when I woke up, it was dark. The automatic lights had come on. And Haddix . . ."

She squeezed her eyes closed. There was no way she could say it out loud. She could barely think it.

"Haddix what?" Michael's voice was strained.

"She was sitting under the hydrangea eating dirt."

"What?"

Lanie could still see it so clearly. Her baby. Her little girl. Sitting there with mud spilling out of her mouth and down her dress, fists full of it in her lap. There could have been fertilizer in the soil. One week later and there would have been.

"She could have died, Michael. Right there next to me."

"Oh my God."

"So I checked myself into a rehab. I told you Ainsley and I were going to Bermuda, but I went to Arizona and got sober instead."

"Holy shit, Lanie. How many lies have you fed me these last few years?"

"Too many." Lanie rubbed her forehead with her fingertips. "But *that's* how bad it was. I couldn't put myself through it again with another baby. I couldn't put the *kids* through it. But then I miscarried, and I knew it was a sign. That I shouldn't have any more kids. So I booked the appointment."

"This is unbelievable." He went back into the closet and started throwing things into the suitcase at random. Within seconds he'd slapped it closed and clicked the latch. "I'm gonna go. I need some time on my own to . . . to think. As long as you're sure you're all right."

She blinked. He meant after the fainting. She'd almost forgotten about the fainting. She'd fainted at his feet, and he was packing a bag.

"I'm fine," Lanie said through her teeth, forcing herself to look him dead in the eye. "It's not like you're ever here anyway."

paige

She kept waiting for a call or a text from Lanie accusing her of searching her personal things, but her phone was silent all evening until John texted.

KIDS OUT. YOU STILL COMING OVER?

They'd decided to grab takeout instead of going for coffee, because John didn't want to bump into anyone he knew—and he and Ainsley knew everyone. He'd spent the entire day with people mourning, crying, offering condolences, and he was done. She texted back.

WILL PICK UP FOOD AND BE THERE IN 20.

Now she was pulling up the driveway of his immaculate home with a bag of delicious-smelling Indian food on her passenger seat, her palms sweating.

This was her ex-boyfriend's house. The house of her first true love. Who had just lost his wife. Whose wife might have been having an affair and may have been murdered because of it.

Should she tell him what she'd read in Lanie's diary? But then she'd have to confess the fact that she'd read another woman's personal thoughts. She still couldn't believe that she'd violated Lanie's privacy that way—right when she was starting to like the woman. But what was this big secret Ainsley was holding over her? Who the hell was Dr. Canton? She'd tried to google the name earlier, but there were so many hits, she'd given up.

She wondered how John would react if she told him about Lanie's suspicions about Ainsley and Michael. Although it was quite possible he already knew. John wasn't an idiot. He'd always been weirdly perceptive, even as a teenaged boy when he should have been blinded by hormones. If his wife was sleeping around, he'd at least have to suspect something was going on. Maybe she could get him to talk about it without bringing up the diary. Coax it out of him.

But if John confessed that his marriage was a mess and his wife had been sleeping around, she couldn't take that confidence back to Dominic. It would make John look culpable. What was she even doing here?

After leaving Lanie's, she'd dropped off Izzy at home with her mom and driven to the police station, intent on telling Dominic about Lanie's suspicions regarding Michael and Ainsley, though maybe not about how she'd found out about them. But when she'd looked Dominic in the eye, she hadn't been able to do it. She didn't know these people very well, but God help her, she was starting to like them. Even Michael, though she was self-aware enough to know that was only because he was so good-looking. And Lanie had *saved Izzy's life*. Every time Paige thought about her daughter's face as she ran from a rabid animal, her heart began to pound. Paige had completely frozen, and Lanie had been so badass.

Of course, Lanie also thought Paige was potentially a psycho, though Paige had no idea why. Unless Nina had somehow shared what she'd learned on Google, but the two of them never spoke to each other, as far as Paige could tell.

Maybe Dominic's investigation was just a wild goose chase. A mad and ill-advised grab for power. And if it was, did she want to play an integral role in having all these people dragged down to the station for questioning? She could just imagine the scandal—the gossiping. Bee and Dayna and the rest of them standing around, talking about the murder suspects, pretending that they were horrified, when they were really just entertained.

Maybe she should ask John about his money problems instead. Those rumors seemed a bit less sordid. She could find a way to work that into conversation. Bring up her own issues with cash flow at the moment, and maybe he'd spill. It could be that Ainsley had borrowed money from the wrong person and that was what had gotten her killed.

She glanced at her own eyes in the rearview mirror. This wasn't her. She needed to call Dominic and tell him she was out.

It was at that moment that the front door opened and John stepped out, lifting his hand in a wave.

Shit, even from the driveway he looked gorgeous.

Paige killed the engine, grabbed the food, and got out.

The walk to the door seemed a mile long. Past the perfectly squared-off hedges, the subtle landscape lighting, the almost ludicrously green, freshly watered lawn. John didn't move the entire time. He just stood there and watched her. His gaze was intense. All she could hear were crickets and the beating of her own heart.

You are not here to hook up. You are not here to hook up. You are not here to hook up.

But God, it had been so long since anyone had touched her. The Dickhead had stopped initiating sex six months ago and had barely responded the last few times she'd tried, claiming exhaustion from the rigors of his new job. Now she knew the real reason. Big boobs, big hair, big scream.

She gave her head the slightest of shakes to clear the unsavory memory.

"Hey," John said when she arrived on the step just below where he was standing. His blond hair was mussed, his skin wan, his eyes desperate and questioning.

"Hey," she said.

And then he grabbed her face and kissed her.

Paige was so surprised she dropped the food, but neither of them stopped to do anything about it. John tasted like whiskey and mint and his lips were rough and dry and his hands were all up in her hair, and it was John, John, John.

She was kissing John Anderson. John Anderson who had first held her hand on the teeter-totter in the playground on the hill when the rest of their friends were trying out schnapps for the first time. John Anderson who had picked her up for their prom in a top hat and tails and brought flowers for her mom. John Anderson was kissing *her*.

You can't go back again, a voice in her head told her. *This is so, so stupid and you promised yourself no more stupid.*

And then John dragged her inside the house, and the word "stupid" lost all meaning.

WHEN SHE WOKE up, the first thing she smelled was coffee. The scent was so strong she wondered if she'd slept in the kitchen, but when she pried one eye open, she found herself in John's bed.

Shit, she thought. *Why am I still here?*

Last night had been . . . weird. At first it had been sensory overload in the best possible way. Kissing. Touching. Tongues, hands, fingers. It had been so long, and this was *John*. It was all incredibly familiar and wildly, bizarrely different from what she remembered. But then, of course it *was* wildly different. They had been each other's first. What they'd done together back then had barely been sex. They were just kids, fumbling around, embarrassed and full of hormones.

John had learned a lot since then. This was her first thought when he'd thrown her half-naked over the arm of the couch. Ainsley's couch. He'd learned a lot, possibly from Ainsley. At that point, she'd wanted to stop. Because Ainsley was dead. Because Ainsley was everywhere. Because he was Ainsley's. But then he'd entered her, and she'd really *not* wanted to stop. The second time they'd had sex it had been in this bed. And John had cried. And that was when Paige decided this was definitely a mistake and she would go home the second he fell asleep, and they'd never speak of this again.

And yet.

Damn her deep-sleeper genetics.

Paige's gaze drifted to the silver-framed family photo on the bedside table, Ainsley smiling her pearly white smile with her arms around two of her three kids, while John had his hands on the shoulders of the third.

She shuddered and rolled over, swinging her legs out of bed. Problem one, her clothes were downstairs. She pulled a throw from the settee in the corner and wrapped it around herself. Out the sliding glass doors to the bedroom's veranda she saw the sunlight winking on the ocean, highlighting the waves all the way to the horizon.

"This view does not suck," Paige said to herself.

The house was silent. But then again, it was so big that if John was in the kitchen, he wouldn't have heard her scream.

She walked over to the door, wondering if she could find her way to the living room and her clothing, and then out the door without him noticing. Probably. There were those back stairs she'd ruined with her wine spatter a few nights ago. But could she even locate them? The two times she'd come upstairs in this place she'd either been traumatized and pissed, or naked and throbbing.

She glanced into the hall. Nothing and no one. No indication of where the stairs were. Maybe she should attempt to find a T-shirt of John's. A pair of boxers. There were no dressers in the vast room, so she went to the closet, her heart giving a nervous skip at another intrusion, and pulled open the door. She expected rows of dresses and gowns, shelves full of Jimmy Choos, a display case of bags that could each have bought a family enough food for a year. And maybe a corner for John.

Instead she saw boxes. Dozens of them. The pile closest to the door was four high. There was a shipping label affixed to the one on the top.

Classic Couture, LLC. A New York address.

Paige glanced around the closet. Clearly this space had belonged only to Ainsley. It was larger than her childhood bedroom, with clothing rods set at all heights and ample shelving, as well as a vanity table at the back, complete with a mauve velvet chair. But most of the shelves and racks were empty save for some in the back. Curious, Paige stepped inside, skirting around the boxes. The room contained a heady scent of lavender and lemon—it must have been Ainsley's perfume—and there was an elaborate gold filigree chandelier overhead. The remaining clothing was mostly folded on shelves and consisted of cozy-looking winter sweaters, a few college sweatshirts, and some well-worn, but carefully organized sneakers. Clearly everyday, hanging-around-home clothing—which Paige was surprised Ainsley owned. She turned and eyed the boxes again.

John was selling off his dead wife's clothing merely days after she'd died. He'd already boxed it up and found a buyer. Or hired someone who had.

On an empty shelf clearly built for shoes sat a pile of papers. Feeling almost greedy for information, Paige lunged for it.

It was an itemized list. Gowns. Bags. Shoes. Scarves. Hats. She flipped to the last page. The total that Classic Couture was paying John was in the mid–six figures. Paige whistled to herself.

Maybe John and Ainsley really were having money troubles.

She had to tell Dominic about this. But she definitely couldn't tell Dominic about this.

Paige gulped down a lump of guilt and fear and confusion and self-hatred. She'd officially gotten too close. She put the documents back on the shelf and stepped out of the closet. John walked into the room with a big smile and a tray of coffee and pastries just as she was clicking the door closed. He had her clothes folded over one arm like a waiter would fold a towel or napkin.

His face instantly fell. He looked at her, then at the closet, then back at her.

"Yeah, I can explain."

There was nothing he could have said that would have made him look guiltier than that line. Except, maybe *It's not what it looks like.* It was so perfect, in fact, that she almost laughed. She could picture her writers' room back in L.A., the wall of windows overlooking the lot and the mountains beyond, the sunlight backlighting her under-washed, overtired colleagues. Jerry Michaels making pyramids out of Froot Loops atop the wood-grain table and saying, "I've got it! He's already packed up all her expensive fucking shoes and dresses and shit! He already *knew* he was going to be selling them. Had a buyer lined up and everything!"

This was straight out of Screenwriting 101, the chapter on how to make your culprit look guilty—the closet, the invoice, the fact that she was here, wrapped in a cashmere throw, four days after his wife had "accidentally" died.

Paige waved a hand. "There's nothing to explain. I shouldn't have gone in there and it's your house, your things. None of my business."

His shoulders relaxed. And what shoulders they were. The man was shirtless, his golden skin gleaming in the sunlight streaming through the room's many windows. Paige felt that telltale tightness down below just looking at him.

"I should go," she said.

And against his many protestations, she wrangled her clothes from him and went.

lanie

"No. No. She does this every year! The Trunk or Treat is in *two days*. It's too late to sign up for a slot. We have the whole parking lot mapped out already," Lanie said into her earpiece in the car on Thursday morning. "Just text Calista and tell her thank you, but maybe next year."

She felt this morning as if she were playing a role in some ridiculous play and that everyone in the audience could see right through her performance, but she just kept saying her lines, because she didn't know what else to do.

"Are you sure there's nothing we can give her?" Lauren said. She expected Lanie to save the day. Everyone always expected Lanie to save the day. She stifled a groan.

There was, of course, the Andersons' space. But Lanie had planned to leave it empty. A sort of tribute to Ainsley. It seemed gauche to fill it with another car. And there also existed the infinitesimal possibility that John would want to use it. Ainsley had had her theme all planned out, and Lanie was sure she'd already purchased the goodies she was planning to distribute. John was the type of guy to make it happen in his wife's honor. Unless he was just too wrecked to get out of bed that morning. Which she would totally understand.

It was also prime Trunk or Treat real estate. As president, Ainsley always got the best spot in the parking lot, and Lanie wasn't about to hand that over to someone who couldn't be bothered to sign up until two days before. So she could, what? Pass out bargain-basement Dum Dums from an unthemed trunk? No. Just. No.

"There's really not."

"Well, she wants to schedule a call. A Zoom call, no less," Lauren said, the eye roll clear in her voice. "You know how she is. She's going to browbeat me into submission and then she's going to bring those awful caramel apples that make everyone's teeth basically jump right out of their heads."

Lanie sighed as she turned the corner. The traffic was backed up all the way to Palm Avenue. There was no way they were going to make it before the bell.

"Are you okay, Mama?" asked Haddix, in her adorable anxious voice.

"I'm fine, baby, but I think we're going to need to walk."

"Yay!" Austen cheered.

He loved it when Lanie bailed out of the line and then he got to walk alongside it, waving to everyone waiting in their cars. It made him feel like a mini celebrity. And like he was getting away with something. He was free to skip and dance and strike poses while everyone else was stuck in line, seat belts fastened. Lanie glanced in her side-view mirror and flipped a quick, illegal U-turn, hoping there were no cops around.

She was already meeting with them later today. She didn't need to have a precursor run-in this morning.

"Tell her she can share a slot with someone else," Lanie told Lauren. "But the spots in the lot are full. If we add any more, there won't be any room for the activities."

Lauren sighed a mighty sigh. "Fine. I'll tell her. But you owe me a drink."

Lanie saw a spot up ahead on Palm and pulled in quickly, slamming on the brakes to avoid a squirrel. The kids in the back squealed.

"It's fine. Everything's fine," she said into the rearview. And then, into her phone, "Lauren, I gotta go."

Three minutes later, with everyone's backpacks situated and Austen's diorama of the ancient Grecian aqueduct system safely in her arms, Lanie ushered her kids across the street and along the sidewalk toward school. She was sweating, her bangs plastered to her forehead, and she attempted to detach them with a shake of her head. Nothing doing. It was an oddly humid October morning, threatening rain, and she was just going to have to deal.

As Austen waved to friends, performed TikTok dances and jumped up and down like a maniac, Marcus texted on his phone, and Dickinson dutifully held Haddix's hand, Lanie took a deep, cleansing breath. She had barely slept, what with the argument with Michael, the impending meeting with Officer Ramos, and Paige's violation of her personal thoughts. It was bad enough that Ramos had refused to tell her exactly *what* about Ainsley's death needed to be discussed. She knew she had done nothing wrong, but what about Michael? It was entirely possible that the police had learned that he'd stayed later than the other guests. Was she supposed to lie and claim she had no idea where he'd been that night? Or lie and say he'd been home with her and the kids? Or tell the truth and say she'd driven back over there and seen his car in the driveway? He'd never denied that he and Ainsley had something going on between them. Why hadn't he denied it?

Maybe she *should* tell Ramos the truth. Part of her thought Michael deserved to have some random cop show up at his office to question him.

And then there was Paige. *Why* had she been snooping through Lanie's things? Lanie had assumed she would take her all-important work call in the kitchen. Or in any one of the number of rooms she could have popped into before arriving at the craft room. What the hell was she doing in there?

Lanie must have fallen asleep at some point, because she'd woken up far too late to get the kids fed and ready and out the door, trying the whole while to compose a text to Michael that would make him talk to her, and another to Paige that would somehow accuse her of snooping without outright accusing her of snooping. She'd finally given up and gotten in the car.

Was Paige just a curious person, or had she been looking for something specific? Maybe she was a drug addict. Or a petty thief. The woman *had* moved back in with her mother at the age of . . . forty-something. Maybe she was broke and looking for something to sell. Lanie already knew the woman had a violent temper. It was possible she was unhinged in more ways than one.

Maybe she really had killed Ainsley.

Lanie finally got her kids to the front door of the school, kissed each of them atop the head, handed Austen's project off to him, and waved them through the doorway. She was about to go home for a second shower and a deep dive into the Trunk or Treat parking lot map, which she was most certainly going to have to rejigger once Lauren failed to talk Calista out of having her own spot, when she saw a tight group of women standing off to the side of the door, Dayna included. She didn't at all feel like talking to Dayna, but she could tell something was up. The heady scent of fresh gossip was in the air.

"What's going on, ladies?" she said as she approached.

"You haven't heard?" Rebecca said, eyes gleaming. "Caroline told Indira that Paige Lancaster's car was parked at Ainsley's house last night."

Lanie's heart thunked. She could almost hear the next words before they were said by someone at the back of the crowd.

"*All* night."

Lanie's vision went fuzzy for a split second, then sharpened into focus right on the face of Nina Anand. Which was odd. Nina wasn't normally part of these little gossip klatches. She sometimes lingered at afternoon pickup, but in the mornings she was a drop-and-run mom. Work beckoned. Lanie wondered what that would be like, to have someplace she needed to be by a certain time each and every morning. She had to admit the idea intrigued her. She'd never regretted her decision to give up working and focus on the kids. But now she could picture herself in a chic pencil skirt and crop jacket, a coffee in one hand and an iPad in the other as she chatted into her AirPods with some fellow senior staff member, some upbeat music playing in the background.

Lanie looked away quickly, still put off by the way Nina had reacted when Lanie found her in Bee's studio the day before. Nina had lied right to her face without even blinking. It was unnerving. Lanie had told Bee to check the office and make sure nothing was missing, but she hadn't followed up yet. One more thing she'd need to do when she got home.

"She totally did it," someone said. "She moved here, wanted John back, and murdered Ainsley."

Lanie could *feel* Dayna trying to make eye contact with her from the other side of the circle, but flat-out refused to look her way.

You betrayed me, she thought. *We're not sharing any private glances.*

"You people have no shame. Ainsley's death was an accident," someone said.

"Besides, Paige left the party before any of us," Lanie added. "She wasn't even there."

"Who's to say she didn't circle back?" Rebecca said. "Had a good look around that palatial estate and decided she wanted it for herself?"

"Not to mention her hot ex."

Lanie was having what could only be defined as a hot flash. Paige? Really? Paige, who had been in her house—in her *craft room*— just the day before? It was one thing to have the random thought herself, but to know that others were starting to talk about it like it was truly plausible . . .

What was she doing in my private space?

Her own children weren't allowed in the craft room.

"What do any of us really know about her?" Rebecca said. "So her dad used to be chief of police. So what? Does that make her trustworthy?"

"You know, I remember when Chief Lancaster died, some people thought the circumstances were suspicious."

"That's right! I remember that too! He'd just gotten a clean bill of health or something and then, *boom.* Dead."

"I don't think—"

"Or maybe she didn't kill him. Maybe she's working undercover for the police to find out who did," Caroline spoke up.

Everyone stopped talking and looked around. The idea clearly intrigued every last one of them.

"I did see her chatting with Hot Cop the other morning before school," Dayna said.

"And she wrote for that detective show, didn't she? The one about the female cop who always *goes undercover.*"

Everyone glanced at everyone else, and then they all cracked up laughing. All except for Lanie, who felt as if she might faint. Again.

The late bell pealed and the group started to break up as people headed off to their yoga classes or mindfulness classes or shopping appointments. Lanie turned on her heel to head back to her car, but Dayna stepped in her path.

"Can I help you?" Lanie said.

"Yeah, you can tell me why you've been avoiding me. You barely even looked at me at the funeral yesterday."

"I don't want to talk about it." Lanie made a move to go around Dayna, but Dayna wasn't having it. She grabbed Lanie's arm and held tight. "Let go of me."

"Lanie, we just lost Ainsley. I don't understand why you're shutting me out like this."

"Because I know, all right?" Lanie said through gritted teeth. "I know you told her."

Dayna let go of Lanie's arm. "Told who what?"

Lanie rolled her eyes so hard it hurt. "Ainsley." She glanced around at the other moms still loitering. "And you *know* what."

Behind her dark sunglasses, Dayna paled. "I did not tell her, Lanie. I would never. You know I would never."

"Well, you are literally the only person on earth who knew, and yet somehow, Ainsley found out. So, you do the math."

"When did she tell you this?"

"The night she died," Lanie replied, her voice a croak. "It was one of the last things she said to me, come to think of it, so thanks for that."

"Lanie, I swear to you—"

"Just stop, Dayna, okay? This is all hard enough without you lying to my face. I have to go."

She started to walk away.

"Do you think she was really murdered?" Dayna asked.

An odd, choking laugh emitted from Lanie's throat. "I really hope not, Dayna. Because if she was, I'd probably be a prime suspect."

As she strode off, Lanie held back tears. She had to get it together before she met with Hot Cop that afternoon. Because it suddenly all made sense to her. Paige chatting up Officer Ramos. Paige snooping around in her space. Reading her diary. The diary in which she spilled every last one of her secrets and suspicions.

Including the ones she'd told Dayna.

And the ones Michael had apparently known for years.

And the ones about Michael and Ainsley.

nina

Nina had gone over it and over it and over it. There was no doubt in her mind now that Bee Dolan had been stealing from the PBA. Stealing for quite some time and getting away with it for quite some time. There had to be repercussions for that sort of thing. A person couldn't just smile in everyone's faces while baldly stealing money that was meant for their kids and the betterment of their schools. Nina had to tell the police. It was the only responsible thing to do.

The withdrawals from the PBA account didn't perfectly line up, dollar for dollar, with the deposits into Bee's bank account, but there were some. Enough to warrant someone official looking into it. How else would Bee have the funds to pay for her renovations? She had to have been funneling the money through an account at Oceanside Bank. Depositing it there, taking it out as cash, and then slowly depositing the cash into her own account in smaller chunks.

It was diabolical, really. Nina honestly couldn't believe Bee was capable of such forethought.

Unfortunately, there was no way for her to tell the police without implicating herself. Ainsley had been right. What she'd done was a felony. If she gave her evidence to the police, there was nothing to stop them from accusing her of the crime. She'd hacked into the account. She could have easily stolen all that money and now, in a panic, be trying to pin it on someone else.

They would eventually have to requisition her bank records, which would show she was blameless of the crime, but how long would that take? And did she really want random cops sifting through her personal files?

No. No she did not.

But she also couldn't stomach the idea that Bee might get away with this. That her and Ravi's money and Felicity Klein's money and even Caroline effing Roday's money had paid for those Carrara marble countertops and that wine fridge and that Viking six-burner stove.

And then there was all this talk of murder. What if Ainsley had confronted Bee about the account and Bee had murdered Ainsley to shut her up? Stranger things had happened.

So. She'd come up with a plan. Which was what brought her here on this sunny Thursday afternoon, to the parking lot of the Piermont PD. On her seat was one of those awful hot-pink folders. In it were the PBA bank records printed out on crappy recycled paper from Staples, as well as copies of Bee's bank statements. On top of it was a stack of flyers for this weekend's PBA Trunk or Treat. On her hands were a pair of purple latex gloves left over from the supply she'd stockpiled during the pandemic.

Her plan was to go inside, replenish the front desk's supply of flyers, and leave the folder beneath them. By the time someone found the evidence, no one would remember that she had been there. That was the benefit of being plain and forgettable. Nina often found that people didn't even notice her when she was standing right in front of them.

She killed the engine. Across the street at the park, a young mom jogged by pushing a sleek stroller, and a Brownie troop searched for litter. So innocent. Such life ahead of them. By the time she was that age, she'd already been acutely aware that her life would never be rosy.

Nina knew the police were a necessary entity that gave most people a sense of security. But she had been raised with a serious distrust of the legal system, from judge and jury all the way down to the downtrodden crossing guard. Once Nina's older brother, Nathan, who was ten years her senior, had been arrested for the third time at the age of seventeen and finally thrown in jail, Nina's father had spent the rest of her young life pointing out all the ways in which the U.S. justice system was "a fucking joke." He'd maintained that people needed to take care of their own business. And that was when he'd started collecting guns. And teaching Nina to shoot them. She'd hated him, but she'd loved the guns. A fact which had always surprised her and made her feel simultaneously ashamed and proud of herself. Holding a gun, though, hitting a bull's-eye on a target dead-on, it made her feel powerful, which was something she hardly ever felt in her family, or in the world, what with her diminutive size.

Every day, though, her father seemed to grow more paranoid. That something would happen to them. To her. He started to lock her room at night. To track her every move. Nina knew she needed to get away from him or it would only get worse. So she'd become a straight-A student. A role model. She didn't get detention. She didn't speak out of turn. She did everything by the book. She skipped a grade and started college at sixteen. She'd merged her genius IQ with her incredible work ethic and gotten out of that house as quickly as humanly possible. Everything was going to be fine. She had taken charge of her life.

And then life proved her father right.

Nina shook the awful memories from her head, got out of the car and shouldered her bag, clutching the folder and the flyers. She took one step and then froze.

Lanie Chen-Katapodis had just walked out of the station.

Nina backed up, nearly tripping herself, and fumbled her way back into the car. She watched as Lanie shook hands with a uniformed officer. They exchanged a few words, their expressions grave. The officer checked his notebook quickly and posed a question. Lanie nodded and spoke a few words.

Shit. *Shit.*

Why was Lanie CK here? What was she telling the police? She couldn't have been reporting Nina for sneaking into the greenhouse at the reception yesterday, could she? It wasn't as if Nina had trespassed. Or stolen anything. At least, not that Lanie knew of.

Nina's brain whirred. Maybe Lanie somehow had figured out what Nina knew about the PBA account and was preemptively blaming her for the missing funds in an effort to protect Bee. Or perhaps Ainsley had tipped off her and Bee and Dayna before she'd died. God, how perfect for her. If Lanie could get Nina arrested, or even have her brought under suspicion for stealing from the PBA, Nina would have no chance of winning the presidency.

She tossed the folder and flyers back onto the passenger seat and started her car. Clearly, she had underestimated Lanie and her little cadre of friends.

It was time for a new plan.

paige

The sun shone down on a perfect autumn day on the morning of the Piermont Elementary School PBA's Trunk or Treat celebration, and it all sort of made Paige want to scream. There was no parking within a mile of the school, so she and her mother walked Izzy—dressed as a pirate—up the street toward the crossing guard.

"Did this town make a pact with the devil or something?" she asked.

"What do you mean?" her mother asked.

"Look around. It's too perfect. It's like straight out of the Amy Sherman-Palladino playbook."

"So maybe we made a pact with Amy Sherman-Palladino."

Paige rolled her eyes, but her mother laughed and gave her a sideways squeeze. Leaves in joyous hues were whisked from the trees to dance around the hordes of perfectly turned-out trick-or-treaters and their parents, grandparents, and nannies. Some parents had even dressed up. Paige thought it was a bizarre specimen of adult who would go to the lengths some of these people had with their costumes. One woman had dressed up as Ahsoka Tano, with her body and face fully painted green. A dad wore an inflatable poop emoji costume with a sign pinned to his back that read, FLUSH ME. And there was a dude standing near the wall of the school in full black with a long leather coat, sunglasses, and a fedora. Either a Blues Brother or a mafioso, no doubt.

Does anyone ever grow up? she wondered.

And then she remembered that she'd just had sex with her high school boyfriend a few nights ago and was currently living with her mother, and clearly she was in no position to judge.

"I can't wait to meet all your new PBA friends!" Elizabeth said with an alarming sincerity.

"Yeah. That'll be great," said Paige.

The Trunk or Treat took up the entire front parking lot at PES and was full of gleeful squeals, joyous shouts, and the shrieks of toddlers overdue for naps. Each trunk had a theme, and each theme was more elaborate than the last. SUV doors yawned open to reveal caves fashioned of crepe paper and witch's cauldrons overflowing with treats. One parent had decked out her car like a haunted circus, complete with a red-and-white-striped tent over top and a scary clown that lurched out from the innards of the vehicle every time a child reached for the popcorn buckets on offer inside. There were games and activities, too. Guess How Many M&M's in the Glass Pumpkin! Corn Hole Harvest Style! Bob for Apples! (In your own individual bucket, of course, because germs.) For the little ones there was a coloring station, a face-painting station, and a temporary tattoo station with adorable glitter spider tattoos.

"Mom! They have shaved ice!"

Izzy's face lit up as she pointed out a food truck at the far end of the lot with a long line winding away from it.

"Can I?"

"Paige!"

She looked up to see Nina Anand weaving toward her through the crowd. At least she was pretty sure it was Nina Anand. The woman had painted her face with a perfect, white skull, surrounded by black paint around the edges, and wore a full black robe with tattered sleeves. It all had the effect of making her eyes seem bulbous and bloodshot. Izzy staggered back a step. Elizabeth smiled, however. Clearly, she thought Nina was one of her daughter's new "friends."

"Mom could you take Izzy for shaved ice?"

"What? But I—"

"Please?" Paige said through her teeth.

"Sure." Her mother shot her a concerned look, then put her hands lightly on Izzy's shoulders to steer her away. "Come on, Iz! Let's see if they have pineapple!"

"I need to talk to you," Nina said, arriving in front of her finally.

"Nice costume. Are you death?"

"Obviously." Nina rolled her eyes. "I left my sickle by the car."

"Of course. What do you want, Nina?"

Nina glanced around. "Over here."

Before Paige could protest, Nina shoved back through the throngs of children and between two SUVs, stopping near a large oak tree at the front of the property. When she looked back and saw that Paige hadn't followed her, she waved her forward with a scowl.

Death beckons.

Against her better judgment, Paige followed. As she slipped between two cars—their owners handing out giant KitKat bars from the one, and cider and donuts from the local organic farm from the other—Paige noticed a couple of moms tracking her with their eyes. She wanted to knock their heads together, Three Stooges–style. People around here really needed to get a life.

"Okay, what?" she asked Nina.

"I need to know whether you're an informant or a murderer."

The word "informant" sent a slight chill down Paige's spine. Was she made? Already? She'd barely done anything. Suddenly she felt as if she and Nina were being watched. When she looked up, the Blues Brother dude was walking across the parking lot, not toward them, but with his gaze trained on Paige. Though it was difficult to tell for sure with his dark sunglasses. She shook herself and focused.

"Not you too," she said to Nina.

"Are you in love with John Anderson? Is that why you did it? Everyone knows you two slept together the other night. I really hope it wasn't in Ainsley's bed."

Paige's face burned.

"Okay, first of all, that's none of your business, and secondly, how do I know *you* didn't kill Ainsley?" Paige said, louder than she intended. "I saw the two of you, you know. At the party? You were fighting and she seemed pretty pissed."

Nina's head pulled back. "You *saw* us?"

"Yep, and she mentioned you committing a felony. So, who looks guilty now?"

There was a slight commotion in the parking lot, and Lanie neared them, wearing an oversized cashmere sweater, an ankle-length plaid skirt, heeled boots, and a pair of cat ears that perfectly matched the sweater. She had whiskers painted on her face, and her nose had been colored pink.

"Can you two please pin the conspiracy theory conversation?" she whispered, glancing around. "People are starting to talk!" She crossed her arms over her chest, the sleeves of her sweater nearly covering her hands.

"No, we cannot pin the conspiracy theory conversation!" Nina shot back under her breath now. "She just accused me of murder."

"You accused me first!" Paige said.

"Oh my God, you two!" Lanie grabbed both their arms in a painful grip. "This is an event for the *children*!"

They fell quiet and looked over at the parking lot. A few people *were* staring. Most of them went back to what they'd been doing when they saw the three of them look. The Blues Brother dude was definitely staring.

"I wouldn't go around accusing people, Paige," Lanie whispered. "Not when you've got more motive than anyone. Not to mention being responsible for all the destruction of property."

"I don't know what you're talking about."

"The potpourri? Ainsley's bathroom?"

"What did you do in Ainsley's bathroom?" Nina asked.

"Nothing! It was an accident!" Paige's face burned as she glared at Lanie. "And you're one to talk about motives, Miss Maybe My Husband Is Having an Affair!"

"You *did* read my diary!" Lanie accused.

"There's no way Lanie killed Ainsley!" Nina said. "She worshipped the ground she walked on just like everyone else did!"

Lanie scoffed.

"What?" Nina said. "It's true."

"You have no idea what you're talking about," said Lanie. "Half this town had a motive to kill Ainsley."

"No one killed Ainsley!" Paige shouted at the top of her lungs. "The woman got drunk and fell down the stairs. End of story! It was an accident! You're all just a bunch of bored housewives with nothing better to do than make shit up!"

She was mostly just saying it because it seemed like the right thing to say. As far as she was concerned, murder was definitely a possibility.

"Says the woman who actually tried to kill someone!" Nina countered.

"What?" Lanie gasped.

"Don't," Paige warned, her jaw clenching.

"Why not? Shouldn't Lanie know why you're really here in town?" She turned to look squarely at Lanie. "She attacked her boyfriend with a tire iron! That's why she had to move home to mommy!"

Paige's fingers twitched. She wanted to slap Nina so badly she could already feel the woman's skin beneath her hand, could see all that grease paint stuck up under her fingernails. But Izzy was here somewhere. And her mother. And she wasn't going to hit someone on the off chance that they'd see her do it.

"Uh, excuse me, Lanie?"

Bee was stepping over a pile of empty KitKat boxes to get to them, her long, hippie skirt snagging on the cardboard. Her eyes darted left as she grabbed Lanie's hand, her other hand fingering her star necklace. Paige's heart was pounding from trying to keep her composure, and her breath was shallow as she turned.

John Anderson stood not ten feet away with his son, Bradley, who was wearing some sort of *Assassin's Creed* outfit and looking pale, exhausted, and stunned. Paige's entire stomach turned inside out. It was clear that the two of them had heard everything.

A whoop of a police siren split the silence. Three police cars pulled up along the curb, zooming to a stop as if responding to a bomb threat. Six uniformed officers spilled out from various doors, including Dominic, who studiously avoided Paige's questioning gaze.

She half expected them to walk over and arrest her, Nina, and Lanie for disturbing the peace. This sort of thing did not happen in Sherman-Palladino-Ville. Instead, they approached John.

"Mr. Anderson? You're needed down at the station," one of the cops said, laying a beefy hand on John's shoulder. It wasn't Dominic, at least, Paige noted with relief.

"I'm here with my son," John said tremulously.

"I can take him," Lanie offered. "We . . . he can hang out with the boys, right, Bee?"

Bee nodded mutely.

"What's going on?" John asked.

"We just have a few more questions for you."

"Dad?"

The sound of Bradley's voice broke Paige's heart.

"Is this really necessary?" she said, stepping up to Dominic. "Look around."

John was already getting in the third car. Telling Bradley it would be all right and he'd pick him up at Lanie's later. To have fun. Not to worry.

"I know, but it has to be now," Dominic told her.

"Why?" Paige asked. "What's the sudden urgency?"

She felt Lanie and Nina stepping closer, listening in.

"The coroner's report came back." There was an odd, excited look in Dominic's eyes. "It was definitely murder."

paige

Paige sat in her car outside the Piermont Police Station, playing *Tetris* on her cell to distract herself while keeping one eye on the door. She and John used to play *Tetris* on their Game Boys while gabbing on the phone at night before bed and avoiding their homework. Try as she might, she'd never been able to beat his high score. She'd come close, but John had been a mastermind at anything related to math or puzzles or spatial awareness. He'd wanted to be an architect. That was his dream. But instead he got to be a millionaire hedge fund guy. And a murder suspect with a dead wife.

She shouldn't be here. It didn't look good, what with everyone talking about her overnight stay at the Andersons' on the night of Ainsley's burial—she'd overheard a bit of chatter at pickup on Thursday afternoon and had sent her mom to pick up Izzy on Friday—and Nina's outburst at Trunk or Treat earlier. She hadn't had a chance to talk to her mom about it yet—wasn't sure whether she and Izzy had heard or whether they'd been far enough across the parking lot to have missed it—and she didn't want to. Part of her reason for being in this car right now was avoidance. She knew that. She owned it.

She was also kind of proud of herself for not googling Nina Anand, finding out where she lived and throwing eggs at her probably very clean, very monochromatic house.

The door to the station finally opened and a haggard-looking John stepped out, his jaw set, as the lawyer next to him ranted into his cell phone. The lawyer wore a crisp suit with a pocket square, his silver hair slicked back from his face, his tan fresh. John looked like he could collapse into bed at the snap of his fingers. Paige wanted to get out of the car right away, but instead she gripped the steering wheel and waited. The lawyer hung up. The two men said a few words to each other, and then John was alone. He wandered toward the corner of the building, tapping away on his phone. She went to him.

"Hey."

John nearly jumped out of his skin. "Paige! Jesus!"

"Shit. Sorry." She tried for levity. "I didn't know I was that stealthy."

"What are you doing here?" John glanced around as if expecting her to be tailed by a camera crew.

"I wanted to make sure you were okay. I felt so badly about earlier and I . . . God, John, what happened? Are they really sure Ainsley was—"

He nodded, then looked away. "They found skin cells under her fingernails. And they said they analyzed where she fell and she . . . they think she was pushed."

"Oh my God." She hadn't allowed herself to believe it, but hearing it aloud—hearing it from John—made it real. "I don't know what to say."

"I don't even really understand it," John said. "How can they know something like that? From where she fell, I mean?"

Paige eyed him as he paced in front of her. It was an odd thing to say, dialogue-wise. Not *who would have done this* or *I wish I had been there . . . seen something*. But *how can they know*.

She shook her head slightly. This was John. Squirrel-loving John. He was just confused and exhausted and angry and grieving.

"But they let you go."

"They have no evidence," John explained. "Nothing against me except a wonky alibi."

"You have a wonky alibi?"

John sighed. "I left the party right after you did. Didn't come back until seven in the morning." He shot her a rueful look.

"So where were you?"

"Sleeping one off down at Benny's."

Benny's. Why did that sound so familiar? It took half a second for the memory to click into place and when it did, her face scrunched up. "That fisherman's bar?"

It was a tiny, smelly, hole-in-the-wall shack down on the old docks where working fishermen still brought in huge hauls of flounder and sea bass each day. Back in high school, kids used to dare one another to go into Benny's and order upscale drinks like dry dirty Martinis or Stoli on the rocks. Only one person she knew of had ever been brave enough to do it—Felix McIntyer, the kid who starred in all the school plays and musicals and seemed to have been born without fear or even a sense of embarrassment. Paige hadn't been there to see it, but legend had it that he'd literally been kicked out the door by a Hemingway-esque man with an eye patch.

"Benny's son Joe runs it now. Decent guy. Has a comfortable couch in his back room. But no security cameras."

"Ah," Paige said.

"There are cameras at the docks, of course, but the various owners are apparently being reticent about handing over the tapes."

"But they'll get them eventually," Paige assured him. "Someone will clear you."

"Yeah, and in the meantime this entire town thinks I killed my wife. And my kids . . ."

"God, John. I really am sorry about this." She reached for him, but he didn't move toward her, so she let her arm drop awkwardly.

"I have to go," he said.

"Do you even have a car here? I could drive you. We could talk . . ."

"No."

Paige startled at the fierceness in his voice. His eyes were sharp.

"I was just trying to help."

John covered his face with both hands and rubbed his skin like he was trying to take it all off. "You're not working with the police, are you?"

Paige had the oddest sensation. As if the world had just flipped on its head and then quickly righted itself, leaving her dizzy and off-kilter, her heart pounding in her temples. "What?"

"Just . . . people are talking. The wives apparently think you're an informant?" He gave her an apologetic look at the word "informant." Like it was so insane he suddenly couldn't believe he was saying it.

"John, that's ridiculous."

But also, why did he care? If he was innocent, what would it matter?

"I know. I'm sorry. It's just . . . I don't know which way is up any-more. I have to go talk to the kids. They're going to be staying at my parents' for a while because, you know, their house is now officially a crime scene."

Paige swallowed hard. "What about you?"

"What about me?"

"Where are you staying?"

"Oh, there's an apartment above the garage. They said it was okay if I stayed there, provided I didn't go into the house until they say it's clear. Which should take about a month, considering the size of the fucking place."

"Sounds like you don't like it there."

He looked out across the parking lot. "I hate it."

Paige hesitated. "Are you sure you don't want me to come over? We don't have to . . . you know. We can just talk."

"I kind of just want to be alone," he told her. "Besides—" They both looked up as a pair of uniformed officers emerged from the police station, laughing and chatting as if this were just any other day. A muscle in John's jaw worked as he stared them down. Neither of them even glanced their way.

"Besides?" Paige said, still feeling a little light-headed.

John's eyes were still on the officers. "The cops are going to be watching my house."

lanie

It was easy enough for Lanie to burn her diary. The fire pit out back was large, with wood and kindling and matches ready to go. There was nothing in the book she wanted to remember anyway. It was mostly whining, theorizing, desperate babbling. Nothing, really, about her kids. She documented their lives on Instagram.

She dropped the book in the center of the pit, built a pyramid of small logs around it, and burned it to ash.

The kids and Michael were asleep when she did it. The night sky winking with stars. Lanie sat on an Adirondack chair and watched the flames lick at the logs and blacken their edges.

She had no idea where her husband was at the time that Ainsley had died.

But she did know a few things. About Ainsley. About John. About their marriage.

She didn't believe that John Anderson could have murdered his wife.

But then what did that say about the fact that she could sort of believe that her own husband could have murdered John's wife?

She would tell the police what she knew. It was the responsible thing. The civically minded thing.

Lanie closed her eyes, pulling her fleece blanket closely around her, and let the fire burn.

paige

Marie lived in one of the newer developments on the outskirts of town. It had a name proclaimed in elegant script on a faux-antique wooden sign: *Miller's Hill*, and from what Paige could tell, was composed of about a hundred houses, each constructed from one of three models. Owners had clearly been allowed to choose from five exterior colors, brick or stone accents, and various shades for their shutters, but the houses were close together and the driveways short. It was nice, but the neighborhood seemed sad in its newness, when compared with the more established neighborhoods of Piermont. The trees were babies, recently planted, and looked like they were trying too hard. Nothing had any character.

Paige pulled up at the front of a line of cars parked along the curb in front of Marie's—her house was blue with stone accents and black shutters—just as the sun was starting to turn the sky pink. She let out a heaving sigh.

When Paige volunteered to help out with the Thankful Dinner, she'd done so because she liked Marie, and Marie had volunteered to be in charge, so she thought it might even be fun. And also because of her promise to Dominic to spend as much time with these women as possible. But that was before John had been hauled downtown for murder. Before she'd slept with him: the current prime suspect. Before the two PBA president wannabes had accused *her* of also having motives.

She wondered whether Lanie and Nina were here, and wished she'd paid attention to what sort of cars they drove. Either way, this was going to be interesting.

Paige rang the bell and heard Marie shouting instructions to someone before she opened it, cell phone in hand. She looked stressed but managed a smile.

"Hey! Hey! Come on in!"

There was a pile of shoes near the door, so Paige kicked off her boots, and by the time she did, Marie was in the open kitchen area. Down the hall Paige saw a group of women sitting around on a couch and armchairs and floor cushions, sipping wine. She was, as ever, late to the party, and the party fell silent when she arrived.

"Do you want red or white?" Marie asked her.

She gestured at the island, which not only displayed an array of wine bottles, but was absolutely covered with hors d'oeuvres. Bacon-wrapped scallions, bruschetta with a variety of toppings, and tons of colorful salads. Dayna appeared from behind the open door of the fridge with a bottle of beer. She used the countertop to pop it open.

"I'll have one of those, if that's okay."

Dayna was a person Paige was definitely interested in getting to know better. She was clearly one of Ainsley's best friends. And besides, she seemed vaguely normal, if brusque. She could imagine a world in which she and Dayna were friends. Especially now that the world didn't contain Ainsley.

"On it." Dayna went back in and got her one. Paige twisted it open with her hand, trying not to wince. Dayna smirked, either amused or impressed.

"Great," Marie said. "Both of you grab some snacks and join us." She slipped back to the living room, as Paige and Dayna surveyed the options.

"She calls this 'snacks'?" Paige said.

"You should see what she calls 'brunch'." Dayna began to fill a clear plastic plate with food, so Paige did the same.

"I haven't had the chance to say I'm sorry for your loss," Paige said.

"Thanks. I haven't had the chance to say I'm sorry for this town."

Their eyes met over the island. "I think you said that the day we met," said Paige.

"And you were offended." Dayna raised one eyebrow.

Paige snorted.

"Seriously, though. People around here suck and what they're saying about you . . . it's just stupid. I mean, I know you know that, but I thought you should know that *I* know that. That someone's got your back."

"Thanks," Paige said, touched.

"And for the record, Ainsley and John hadn't slept together in, like, a year. So, ya know, good for him for getting some."

They had maneuvered their way into the living room when Marie spoke up. "All right, everyone, we all know how the Thankful Dinner works, and I don't think this is the year to be changing things up, so let's keep it simple." She opened up a notebook on her lap and kept her phone faceup next to her on the chair. "We'll have it at the country club, as always, and they'll be providing the food, but I'm going to need someone to deal with Louie on the menu because if I have to tell that guy one more time why you have to salt the pasta water, my brain will literally explode."

There were a few chuckles, and then someone Paige hadn't met yet volunteered for Louie duty. They went around assigning other responsibilities: the invites, the place cards, the fundraising, the emcee. Paige didn't like the sound of any of the tasks, and occupied herself with stuffing her face and avoiding eye contact.

She wondered whether these women really thought they were sitting with a murderer. Which made her wonder if *she* was sitting with a murderer. Did any of them have a big enough grudge against Ainsley?

"We should dedicate the night to Ainsley, shouldn't we?" someone volunteered. "Do it in her honor?"

Marie froze and there was a slight, irritated glint in her eye—so quick anyone who wasn't paying close attention might have missed it.

"I love that idea," Dayna said. "In fact, I think we should rename it in perpetuity. The Ainsley Ames Thankful Dinner."

"If you all think that's best," Marie said, and glanced down at her phone.

"All in favor?" one of the other moms asked.

Everyone raised their hand, including Paige. She couldn't see why not to do it, other than Marie was clearly perturbed. But Marie voted yes, too, and the motion carried unanimously.

"Speaking of favors," Marie said, looking down at her list, then up again. "Paige, do you think you can handle putting together the swag bags?"

Paige brightened a bit. This was something she could actually do. Over the years she'd received dozens of gift bags at Hollywood events, and she knew what was useful and fun and what was plain crap. "Sure, I'm in."

"I'll help," Dayna volunteered.

"Oh, you don't have to," Paige said automatically. She was so accustomed to doing everything by herself.

"Yes, I do. Trust me." Dayna took a swig from her beer bottle. "Swag bags are always a nightmare."

"Oh my God, there was a whole thing last year where the watchbands weren't adjustable?" one of the women said.

"Watchbands?" Paige asked.

"Longines. A lot of the husbands have, shall we say, more effeminate wrists?" Dayna loud-whispered.

"Not effeminate," said a woman with short red hair. "Are we even allowed to use that word anymore?"

"Fine. They're *not fat*. How's that?" Dayna said. "Unlike my husband, who couldn't even clasp the thing."

There were a few snorts and twitters. Paige was still wrapping her mind around the fact that these gift bags contained Longines watches. She had been to a few Emmy parties that offered over-the-top parting gifts, but that was Hollywood. This was a public school fundraiser.

"We'll get Lanie and Bee to help us, too," Dayna told Marie.

There was an odd ripple through the room. Paige wasn't sure where she stood with Lanie at the moment, but if Lanie hated her, wouldn't Dayna—one of her best friends—know to steer clear? Maybe they were, somehow, okay. Though if Lanie really did suspect that Paige had read through her diary, there was no way she wasn't enemy number one.

Still. If Paige could get some alone time with these women, she was sure she'd get more dirt for Dominic. It had taken her five seconds in Dayna's presence to learn about John and Ainsley's sex life. What other inside information did each of them have?

Marie made a note in her book. "Favors, Paige and Dayna," she said aloud as she wrote. Her cell phone rang and she grabbed it so fast she almost dropped it. "I have to take this." She tossed her notebook onto the coffee table, where it nearly knocked over a wineglass, and hoofed it out of the room. A few of the guests exchanged wary glances, but then they got right back to gossiping, leaning their heads together in little groups.

"So. What the hell was all that commotion about at the Trunk or Treat?" Dayna asked, cocking her head and leaning back on one hand.

"Lanie didn't tell you?"

"We haven't had a chance to catch up yet."

"Oh." Paige glanced around at the other moms, seven in total, who were busy comparing notes about homework and report cards. "I don't really think now is the time."

"Okay, but wasn't it weird, spending the night in Ainsley's house?"

A few of the other women fell silent. Paige's throat closed over. Then there was a shout from the other room and Paige shoved herself to her feet.

"I'm just going to check on Marie."

Down the hall, away from the others, Paige shook out her fingers and tried to get a grip on herself. She knew that Dayna was blunt, but that was a bit much. She paused for a breath and then heard Marie's raised voice.

"No. You can't do this to me. Not right now."

Paige stepped toward a door that had been left open a mere inch and pushed it slightly wider. Inside, Marie paced at the end of an un-made queen-sized bed. There were two laundry baskets overflowing with clothes in the corner, a pile of dishes and mugs on one bedside table, and an empty metal rack for a flat-screen on the wall across from the bed. For the first time Paige wondered where Marie's kids were. Or her husband, for that matter.

"Paul, come on. You know I'm good for it. I just need two more months. Three, tops. The holiday season is always our best—"

She paused, listening, and squeezed her eyes closed.

"Fine. *Fine!* I'll figure it out."

She hung up, threw the phone into one of the laundry bins, and then screamed into a pillow so desperately that Paige's own vocal cords hurt.

"Marie?" she said timidly.

Marie dropped the pillow and stared at Paige.

"Are you okay?"

"Fuck Ainsley Aames," Marie said. "She's dead and she's still ru-ining my life."

nina

She knew something was wrong as soon as she stepped into her house on Sunday evening, sweaty after a long walk. Ravi had texted to tell her he was taking the kids over to his mom's to carve pumpkins, Halloween being just two days away now, and she'd been looking forward to a little quiet time—a long soak in the bath with some Adele on in the background. But the silence was too silent. Too heavy. And the house too cold. She hesitated with her hand on the door, wondering if she should just back out.

Then she saw the broken glass.

"Hello?" Nina shouted. "Is anyone here?"

She pulled the door open again in case she needed to make a quick getaway, and slipped her phone from her pocket. Her thumb hovered over the emergency button.

Silence.

Nina took a soundless, sideways step toward the living room. The glass came from the top of the side table that used to display her collection of stained-glass vases. Used to, because the table was no more, and the vases had been smashed all over the floor.

"Shit," Nina said, tears filling her eyes. "If you're still here, I'm calling nine-one-one! I suggest you get the fuck out of my house before I get to my gun!"

Nina ran for the office, crunching over glass and taking in the destruction as she went. The couch had been pulled apart. The good china was smashed all over the dining room floor. Cabinet doors yawned open, one broken and hanging on by a single hinge. The window blinds were bent and tattered. A painting was missing from one wall.

"Nine-one-one. What's your emergency?"

"Someone's broken into my house. I think we've been robbed."

She made it to the office while on the phone with the dispatcher. "No! No no no."

The filing cabinets were open. Papers and file folders were strewn everywhere. Her spare laptop was gone, the charger cord hanging off the desk.

"Ma'am, are you all right?"

"I'm fine! It's just . . . everything's a mess."

She put the phone on speaker and tossed it on her desk.

"What's your name, ma'am?"

"Nina Anand," she said.

"And your location, Ms. Anand?"

"Fifteen Fifteen Beach Lane in Piermont."

Nina lunged for the fake plant, pulled out her gun, and cocked it.

"Are the intruders still in the house, ma'am?"

"No. I don't think so."

She held her breath and listened. There was nothing. Not a footfall or a breath or a whisper.

"All right, we're sending someone out to you. We suggest you wait outside your house. Do you have a car?"

"Yes." She'd just now picked it up from the dealership with its brand-new window.

"We suggest you get in the car and drive a safe distance from the location."

"Why?"

"Just in case the intruders are still in the house, ma'am."

"Fine. Yes. Okay."

"Do you need me to stay on the phone with you, ma'am?"

"No. It's fine. They're definitely coming?"

"ETA fifteen minutes."

"Fine," she said again, and she hung up the call.

Her mind was pinging in a hundred different directions. Who would do this? Why? She had to call Ravi, but she didn't want to alarm him. He would come right home and she didn't want to ruin his night with his parents and the kids. What were these people looking for? What else had they taken?

She went for the safe, in a cabinet under the bookshelf, and quickly opened it. The cash was still there. Their passports. The kids' birth certificates. She shut it and locked it again, then pulled her fingers back. Maybe she shouldn't touch anything else in case they needed to dust for fingerprints.

Fingerprints. Someone had been inside her house. She felt violated. How dare they? Why her? Why them? What did they have that the rest of the wealthy assholes in this town didn't have?

And just like that, she knew.

Nina shoved the gun in the back of her waistband and ran for the game room in the basement. The space was pristine, aside from the new Lego set the kids had opened over the weekend, its colorful pieces spewed all over the floor. Nina kicked off her shoes at the door in case they had any glass imbedded in their soles—she didn't want to leave any shards behind on the kids' carpet—and rushed to the old toy cabinet.

The hot-pink folder was exactly where she had left it.

If Bee had broken in here searching for Nina's evidence, she hadn't found it. Her spare laptop would reveal nothing. It was the one she kept on her at all times that would have proven she'd gotten into the PBA's accounts.

Nina walked out of the room, put her shoes back on, and went back upstairs to wait for the police.

For the next twelve minutes she sat in her car in the driveway and turned over the options in her mind. The police would definitely ask her if she had any idea who had done this. She could simply hand over the paperwork, tell the cops her suspicions, and let the chips fall where they may. She could tell them she suspected Bee without giving them any evidence and just hope they found something. Or she could keep her mouth completely shut and deal with this on her own.

Every five seconds she was certain she knew what to do and every five seconds her absolute decision changed completely.

This was why people had friends. So they had someone to call when things like this happened. Nina glanced at her phone. She could call Paige. But Paige probably hated her after the Trunk or Treat debacle. Had Paige ever really liked her? Or had she just stuck up for the underdog? An underdog who had then attempted to black-mail her.

A laugh burbled up in Nina's throat. She thought of all the awards and accolades that had been heaped on her over the years. Thought of her mother and father who used to look at her like she was some sort of alien, whose only response to her success over the years had been to tell her not to get too big for her britches and to call her a bitch and a snob.

You think you're too good for us, they'd said. *It doesn't matter where you go or what you do, you'll always be a Slater, and that means you're shit outta luck.*

Now, here she was, her beautiful home destroyed, sitting in her car with her gun pressing against her spine and evidence in her lap that could most definitely put her in jail. She couldn't go to jail. Nina could handle a lot, but not that.

Quickly, Nina shoved the gun into her glove compartment and the folder into her bag. Five seconds later, four police cruisers pulled into the circular driveway, lights flashing.

paige

Paige sat at a picnic table at the playground after school, ostensibly writing while her mother pushed Izzy on the swings and watched her climb all over some rope structure that looked like a geodesic dome. When Paige was a kid, this same park had been made out of old tires. Tire swings, a tire castle, even a tire pyramid. Now it looked like a modern sculpture display out of the Guggenheim.

What she was really doing was studying the range of fitness trackers that Dayna had sent to her, Laine, and Bee as potential additions to the Thankful Dinner gift bag. If they bought in bulk, Dayna knew a guy who could get them a discount. Still, the pricing made Paige's eyes bulge. What was the point of getting everyone to spend five hundred dollars a plate if the money was just going to go back into the parting gifts?

She didn't notice Dominic approaching until his shadow fell over her screen. She turned her head and looked up.

"Hey." Damn, he could really rock that uniform.

"We need to talk," Dominic said, his hands on his hips. Or was that one hand on his gun?

"Are we breaking up?" she said, a lame attempt at humor.

"Really? That's what you're going with?" It was the fact that he didn't even attempt to crack a smile that told her this was serious. She closed her laptop.

"Have a seat."

"No, I think I'll stand." He crossed his arms over his chest and looked across the playground to where her mom and Izzy were playing, oblivious to his presence, thank goodness. "When were you going to tell me that your relationship with John Anderson was not so much in the past as it is current and ongoing?"

"Oh," she said. "That."

"So you don't deny there's a relationship," he said, finally looking her in the eye. "Currently."

"I don't deny there was a blip. Recently."

Dominic's jaw worked. He was pissed. Not just pissed, he was jealous. The very idea gave Paige a little thrill down her spine.

"You're going to have to come with me down to the station."

Paige glanced toward the parking lot and saw that he had another cop with him—a woman. Tall, broad, and stern.

"Wait, am I a suspect?" she asked.

"I need to confirm your alibi," he told her, and slipped on a pair of sunglasses. "And you might want to call a lawyer."

He walked away from her, back toward his partner, leaving her behind with sweating palms. She pulled her phone out and brought up the contact information she'd been hoping she wouldn't need.

Halfway across the verdant, freshly mown grass Dominic turned back to her and said, "Oh, and we have a warrant for the bear."

"McFancyPants?" she said.

Dominic almost, *almost*, broke. If he had, she would have known everything was going to be okay. She would have known that, at the very least, *he* didn't think she was guilty. But he contained the smile at the very last second. "Yeah," he said. "That's the one."

THE LAWYER'S NAME was Terrence Pfeiffer, and he had this whole Morgan Freeman thing going on that Paige found endlessly comforting. His voice was the kind of low, calm tenor that could put a girl to sleep on a rainy day, but piss him off, and it contained the same sort of authority Morgan might have commanded playing an army general on some big-budget Bruckheimer dick fest in the eighties.

Dominic appeared suitably intimidated. But the plainclothes detective they had brought in to question her did not.

"Have you reviewed the nanny cam tapes?" Pfeiffer asked, casually sitting back in his chair with one ankle crossed over the other knee. He wore a custom charcoal suit and a white shirt with a dark purple tie, but his socks were lavender, and he had no problem showing them to the world.

"Our team is going through them now," said Detective Lawrence. Her suit was undoubtedly off the rack at Ann Taylor—a little too big in the shoulders, a little too tight in the rear. But her hair was cut in a sleek, platinum-blond bob and her skin was flawless. Paige was sort of dying to ask what products she used. "So, let's talk about what happened in L.A."

"I don't see how that's relevant in this matter," said the defense lawyer.

Paige and Terrence had already discussed "what happened in L.A.," and he'd advised her to tell them the truth, since it was all part of the police record anyway. But he was going to stall first, so that when she did tell them, it would look as if they were playing ball. She was fine talking about it. In her more self-righteous moments, she felt justified in what she'd done. She wasn't about to show remorse for it, that was for damn sure.

Though she wasn't sure she'd ever have a chance with Dominic after he heard all the details. Of course, since he now knew about her one night with John, she probably had no shot anyway. Even if he had seemed jealous at the park.

"You don't think that a recent arrest and a restraining order are relevant in a violent murder case?"

Paige's eyes trailed along the metal tabletop and up to Dominic, who stood in the corner like a sentry. He stared back at her, his eyes curious. She wondered whether he'd already read the reports, and if so, when.

Terrence leaned toward Paige and whispered in her ear. "Give them the broad strokes. Stay calm. Don't show emotion."

Paige nodded, but she felt so shaky, she wasn't sure she could make that promise.

"What do you want to know?" she said, looking at the detective. "You've already read about what happened."

"Why don't you start at the beginning?" the detective said, and then sat back as if ready for story time. "What happened at work that morning?"

Oh. That beginning.

"Right, so I was passed over for a promotion on the show I'd worked on for three years and I kind of—"

Terrence put his hand on her arm, and she paused before saying *lost it.*

"Took it out on my laptop," she finished instead.

"Passed over?"

"Right, well, it was between me and this guy named Dan Buchanan for the showrunner position, and they gave it to Dan. Even though he'd been there half the time I had, and the show is about a woman."

Detective Lawrence shook her head. "That must have royally pissed you off."

"Yeah. It did."

"I don't blame you. Do you have any idea how long it took me to make detective?"

Paige's glance flicked to Dominic, and he looked at his shoes.

"Too long," Lawrence said. "Go on. You said something about your laptop?"

"Right. Well. I chucked my laptop at the window in my boss's office—which didn't break, by the way, because earthquake grade—but they said in the report that it shattered and they held me responsible for paying this ridiculous amount in damages, and I—"

Again, the hand to the arm.

"I also tried to knock over a potted palm tree, but that didn't quite work, so then I quit and stormed out."

"Quit trying to knock over the palm tree?"

"No. Quit my job."

"Your boss says he fired you."

"He's only saying that to save face. If he fired me, they'd be paying me severance, and if you have a look at my bank balance, you'll see that is definitely not happening."

"My client is not granting the authorities consent to requisition her bank records," said Pfeiffer, hand outstretched, palm down. "Just so we're clear."

"Okay, so you quit and stormed out. What happened next?"

"I drove home," Paige said, stone-faced.

"How long did that take?"

"An hour and fifteen, give or take."

Dominic whistled. They all looked at him. "Sorry. That's a long commute."

"That's a short commute in L.A.," Paige said. "Anyway, I tried to calm down on my way home, you know? Deep breathing and all that shit. But it's hard with people cutting you off and laying on the horn and shouting obscenities. Plus, I think I deserved to be a little pissed off. I put in all that time, and that character . . . Frankie Chance? She's me. At least, all her good lines are me. I can't wait to see what she sounds like when the new episodes start rolling out. The only women left on that writing team were still in diapers when Frankie Chance was taking the oath."

Lawrence's eyebrows rose. "You certainly take your job seriously."

"You have no idea what we put into what we do," Paige said. "Everyone thinks it's all glamour and spa days and parties out there, but when we're in season, we're on the lot. I've slept on that stupid writers' room couch more times than I can count. I used to drink Diet Coke and eat stale gummy worms for breakfast on the reg. Missed my daughter's kindergarten graduation. All so they could fucking pass me over."

Hand on the arm. Paige took one of those deep, cleansing breaths.

"Okay. So, you got home and then what happened?"

Paige could feel her inner temperature rising. She clenched her fists under the table and stared at the bridge of Lawrence's glasses.

"I found my boyfriend of four years fucking our teenaged babysitter in my hot tub."

"Teenaged?" said Detective Lawrence. "I thought she was twenty."

"Close enough."

"Where was your daughter at the time?"

"She was at school. Our nanny was picking her up."

"I'm sorry, I thought your boyfriend was fucking your nanny."

Paige shook her head. "Two different people. Martha Goedecker, our nanny, is a saint and I wish I could have brought her with us to Connecticut. *She* was at my daughter's kindergarten graduation. Took tons of pictures. Cried when they handed my kid her fake diploma."

"So this woman in the hot tub was—"

"Kenzie Levi. She babysat for Izzy some nights when Martha had off and I couldn't get out of work."

"Got it. So you found these two in your hot tub and you snapped."

"You're putting words in my client's mouth."

Lawrence showed her palms by way of apology or concession. "What happened next?"

"I went back to the driveway, picked up a tire iron and smashed the shit out of Trevor's Harley."

"A tire iron?"

"Yeah, he was working on the Harley at the time. Not at that *moment*, but at the time. There were a lot of tools lying around."

"And once you were done with the motorcycle, you went after this Trevor."

"No. No, I did *not* go after him. He came at me."

Dominic shifted on his feet.

"He came at you."

"Yeah. He came running around from the backyard holding a towel around his waist—one of Izzy's towels, by the way, with My Little Ponies all over it. So disgusting. He took a swipe at me and then basically threw himself in front of the motorcycle."

"And you hit him."

"Not on purpose."

"Not on purpose."

"I was trying to hit the odometer."

"Then how did his hand end up shattered?"

"He put it on top of the odometer."

She could still remember the way it had felt to break through his bones. That odd sensation of smacking a large, hard-boiled egg with a hammer. There was this sickening crunch, and then the screaming. So much screaming. Kenzie had come around the corner half-naked and puked on the pink flamingo lawn ornament Paige had put up as a joke. Thank God Izzy hadn't been there. To see three of the most influential adults in her life behaving like common trash.

Paige hazarded a glance at Dominic. His hand was over his mouth in a fist. She couldn't tell if he was stifling a laugh or trying not to puke himself.

"But you didn't do it on purpose."

"I told you, I was already swinging at the odometer when he put his hand there. I couldn't stop it."

"Are you sure about that?"

No.

"One hundred percent."

"All right, you know the rest," Pfeiffer cut in. "He takes out a restraining order, she pays for the damage to the bike *and* the damage to the office and moves out here to live with her mom. Whose husband was the most decorated police chief this department has ever seen, I might add."

"I'm aware," said Lawrence.

There was a quick knock on the door and the other officer from the playground stuck her head in. "Detective? Can I see you for a moment?"

The detective excused herself and was gone for all of two minutes. Two minutes of total silence in which Dominic didn't move, Pfeiffer checked his phone, and Paige wondered what her mother was telling her daughter right now. She wondered what Dominic was thinking. Finally, Lawrence rejoined them. She left the door yawning open.

"You're free to go. Your nanny cam has you singing to your daughter at the time of death." She glanced at the detective. "Girl had a nightmare."

"I can just go?" Paige asked, standing.

"Yes. We'll call you if we have any further questions Thank you for your cooperation."

"Unless you have any new information you'd like to share with us," Dominic said, surprising all of them. "About John Anderson."

Paige's heart thunked. She still hadn't told Dominic what she'd read in Lanie's diary. Or what Dayna had said at Marie's the other night. Or about the clothes all packed up in John's closet. But she sure as hell didn't want to tell him now. She might still find the guy attractive, but she wasn't currently in the mood to help him. Not after he'd driven her away from the park in a police car with lights flashing, for all the world, including her daughter and mother, to see. Not now that the chatter around her was going to go from friendly fire to nuclear bomb.

"Officer Ramos," Lawrence said in a warning tone.

"I have nothing else to say," Paige told them.

Pfeiffer held the door and ushered her out.

nina

"I don't know why you're showing me all these mug shots," Nina said to the aging detective. On the computer screen in front of her were eight male faces, one of thirty pages of faces they were making her click through. "I told you I didn't see anyone, and I know who did it."

She had told. She had finally told. And if Oblivious Bee thought she was going to take Nina down with her, she was sorely mistaken. Nina had already lined up calls with the top five criminal attorneys in the state. She was in what her brother would have called "fuck it mode."

"Mrs. Anand, we talked to Bee Dolan. She was at a dance class with her daughter at the time of the crime. There are dozens of witnesses. It couldn't have been her."

"You're wrong. She's getting her little friends to cover for her. She did this. I know she did."

The man sat down across from her, coming down to her level. His blue eyes were watery and pleading.

"Mrs. Anand, we have had a series of car thefts and break-ins in the township over the last few months."

"I'm aware," Nina said. "But this isn't that."

"Some of these guys are guys we're already looking at for those earlier crimes," he continued as if she hadn't spoken, and gestured toward the screen. "So, what do you think is more plausible, that these losers have escalated to big-ticket items, like your artwork and computer, or that some township housewife randomly decided to ransack your house?"

Nina wondered if Bee had known this was the tack the police would take. That they would blame it on the same kids who'd been committing grand theft auto and petty thievery. If she did, then she was smarter than Nina had given her credit for. But it was the things that were taken that convinced her Bee was the culprit. The computer Bee thought contained the PBA account evidence, and, as an artist herself, she would have known the value of the paintings she'd taken.

"It wasn't random," she insisted.

"You keep saying that, but you've yet to give me a real reason. Why do you think she would have done this?"

"Because. She has it out for me," Nina said. She knew it sounded thin. It *was* thin. She wasn't even certain that Bee Dolan, with her flighty attitude and general obliviousness, could have picked her out of a lineup three weeks ago. But now, Bee definitely knew who she was. Clearly Ainsley had told her about Nina's investigation, about the evidence she had on her computer. But Nina couldn't tell this man that. That didn't mean, though, that she didn't want to see Bee punished for her crime. "She's upset I'm running for president of the PBA because she knows I'll fire her from her treasurer position."

The detective gave an exhausted sigh.

"Are you sure you don't recognize anyone from these photos?"

Nina stood up and walked out. She should have known better than to think the police would help her.

lanie

Lanie felt dirty somehow. And not because the Piermont Police Station was grungy. Quite the opposite, in fact. The place was as antiseptic as a hospital. No. She felt dirty because she'd just told some random police officer what she knew about Paige Lancaster. How she'd smashed a glass jar on the street for no good reason. How she'd somehow yanked a towel bar clear off the wall at Ainsley's house. How, when Dayna had asked if she'd slept with John on the night of Ainsley's funeral, she hadn't denied it.

She and Dayna were talking again. In a perfunctory way, thanks to Dayna volunteering Lanie for Thankful Dinner gift bag duty without her permission. It wasn't until she'd checked her texts this morning that she'd found out Dayna had signed her up to help Paige. Along with Bee. Except that Bee was never any help with anything. She'd received this text about five minutes after she'd agreed to come down here and spill about the woman she was now supposed to stuff gift bags with.

All in the name of civic duty, she thought. Besides, it wasn't like she could ignore a direct request from the police. She'd been surprised, though, at the vehemence of their questions, asking about the scene at the Trunk or Treat and what she'd meant when she'd mentioned Paige's violent temper. They'd tried to make it out as if Paige had hurt her, or Izzy, or someone else, and Lanie had to make it 100 percent clear that none of that was true. Instead, she'd told the truth. That was it, and that was all. Except for the fact that Paige had snooped around her house and maybe, possibly read her diary. She didn't want to touch that with a ten-foot pole. Because then they'd ask why Paige was so interested in her diary. Which didn't exist anymore.

But she still felt dirty.

As she stepped out of the interview room, she held her trench coat tightly to her waist and checked her phone. There were a ton of messages, but none from Michael. She shoved it away and headed for the door, walking right into someone's side.

"Lanie."

"Paige!"

"Ms. Lancaster, I've got to hit the road, but I'll be following up with the detective to make sure we're all squared away here," said a handsome black man with a gorgeous leather briefcase. He had the comforting demeanor of a wise college professor—someone who would sit back and guide you through your dissertation like it was as simple as writing a grocery list. "You did great in there. I want you to get some rest. Call me if you need anything."

"Thanks so much for coming last-minute," Paige said.

He lifted a hand and slid through the automatic door.

"Detective?" Lanie asked.

"I just had to solidify my alibi," Paige said in a sardonic tone. "That was my lawyer, in fact. What are you doing here?"

Lanie thought about lying, but she was suddenly sick of lying.

"They called me down here to ask about what happened at the Trunk or Treat."

"Fab," said Paige.

"Hey, listen, I'm sorry about all that. I was just exhausted and upset and . . . paranoid."

"Yeah, well, you had good reason to be."

Lanie clutched herself a bit tighter. Paige clearly had something to say. She was about to ask what she meant by that when Nina Anand suddenly stormed out of a nearby office and barreled right toward them.

"Looks like the gang's all here," Paige said.

Nina glowered. "What are you two doing here?"

"Being dragged over the coals," Paige said.

"Same," Lanie added. "You?"

"Someone broke into my house," Nina said, staring Lanie down as if she expected her to confess. "Tore the place to shreds."

"What?" Lanie said, her hand flying up to her chest. "Nina, oh my God! Are you okay? Are the kids—"

"They're fine. No one was home. But they're staying with my in-laws for a few nights while we get everything cleaned up."

Nina seemed to deflate, and Lanie reached out to squeeze her arm. "I'm so sorry. Did they get anything of value?"

"Yes, in fact, they did," Nina said. And then, suddenly, she started to cry. Her hands flew up to cover her face, and Paige and Lanie locked eyes. Lanie honestly couldn't believe Nina Anand was capable of showing emotion.

"I think this little crew needs a drink. Yeah?"

"I'm in," Lanie said. "Nina?"

Nina just nodded behind her hands.

"I know just the place," Paige said.

paige

It was clear by the way that Lanie and Nina surveyed the bar with wide eyes and scrunched noses that they'd never been to Benny's in their lives—not that Paige had, either. But they had probably never even heard of the place. Which was exactly why Paige had chosen it. She, for one, did not want to be interrupted by any of the other moms from town, and after their encounters with the police, she was pretty sure Lanie and Nina didn't either. Besides, if Paige could get some alcohol in them, she might just be able to get to the bottom of their relationships with Ainsley.

There were five men at the bar, two more shooting pool in the corner, and four empty booths. The bartender, less Hemingway and more Julia Roberts, gave them a nod, and Paige led her group to the largest booth.

The place definitely played up the fisherman's bar vibe, with casts of various creatures of the sea mounted and displayed on the walls, and buoys and trawling nets hanging from the ceiling. The floor was silty and the vinyl of the booth tacky to the touch. Rather than remove her coat, Lanie belted it tighter, seemingly trying to make herself as small as possible. Nina sat and checked her phone, then laid it on the table in front of her.

"You ladies from out of town?" the bartender asked, hands on her curvy hips as she approached the table. She had long, wavy red hair that hung down over one shoulder and wore a low-cut V-neck T-shirt that exposed the very edge of a red tattoo.

"No, we all live in Piermont," Lanie said. "How long has this place been here?"

"Since the dawn of time." The woman smirked. "What can I get ya?"

"White wine?" Lanie said, as if she suspected the woman had never heard of it.

"I'll have a Corona," said Paige.

"Whatever whiskey you have is fine. Make it a double," said Nina. Paige's eyebrows rose. "What? My kids are away, remember?"

The bartender laughed. "You got it."

The woman walked away, and Paige looked at her two companions. Lanie was stiff as a board and Nina looked broken.

"So, Nina, tell us what happened," Paige said gently.

"I came home from a walk yesterday and the place was destroyed." Her eyes trailed over to Lanie as if she was waiting for Lanie to say something. To apologize. Like it was somehow her fault. "Ravi had the kids over at his mom's, carving pumpkins. They still don't know what happened. At least they're excited about trick-or-treating there tomorrow.

"Ravi's parents live in a condo complex," she explained to Lanie's questioning look. "Less walking; more candy."

"Ah. Smart kids."

"I stayed with them over there last night because I didn't want to be alone, but I have to clean up. The place is . . ." She got a far-off look in her eye and took a sip of her whiskey.

"I've never understood why people have to destroy everything when they break into someone's house," Lanie said. "It seems so unnecessary. Why not just grab the valuables and go?" Paige shot her a look, and Lanie shrugged. "What?"

"What did they take?" Paige asked Nina.

"A few paintings and my laptop," Nina said.

"Ugh, if I lost my laptop I'd be screwed," Paige said as their drinks were delivered. "I never back up anything."

"You have to back up your files!" Lanie said, scandalized.

"I know, I know. It's a character flaw." Paige took a swig of beer. "Do they have any leads?" she asked, knowing there was no way they had leads. Breaking-and-entering cases were usually impossible to close, unless the home had a zillion and one cameras. There had been a rash of break-ins during her father's tenure, and the fact that they'd never caught anyone had been one of his bigger frustrations.

"They think it has something to do with all the car thefts," Nina said, turning her whiskey glass around on the table. "That it was gang activity."

Lanie turned a bit green. "I can't believe we have gangs now."

"It wasn't a gang. I know who it was." Nina picked up her glass and tossed its entire contents down her throat. "It was Bee Dolan."

Lanie laughed. It was a big, genuine belly laugh, so contagious that it made Paige snort. But she got it. She couldn't imagine Bee performing a smash-and-grab either. Unless it was some sort of living art installation. Nina, however, glowered until Lanie fell silent.

"Oh. You're serious."

"Yes, I'm serious."

"Nina, first of all, that's insane. Bee wouldn't hurt a gnat, let alone break into someone's house. Secondly, don't you think you accusing her is a little . . . I don't know . . . transparent?"

"What do you mean?"

"You've been stalking her for months."

Nina went still.

"Wait a minute," Paige said. "You've what?"

Nina didn't respond. She looked as if she wasn't breathing.

"It's true. She has," said Lanie, then turned back to Nina. "I mean, you're lucky *she* hasn't filed a criminal complaint about *you*."

"It's not a crime to drive down a public street."

"It is a crime to follow someone around town," Lanie said. "To grill the people working on her house. To go snooping around her private things—"

She stopped talking and glanced across the table at Paige. Shit. So she definitely knew about the craft room.

"It hasn't been months," Nina snapped. "And I told you I wasn't snooping."

"Fine. Weeks. Does it matter? The only reason she hasn't reported you or confronted you is because she has such a big heart. Dayna keeps telling her to, but she says as long as you're not hurting anyone . . ." Lanie shrugged. "That's just the way Bee is. She would never break into your house and destroy your things."

Nina slid out of the booth and stood up abruptly. "I have to go."

"Nina, wait. Why do you think it was Bee?" Paige asked, trying to validate her conviction. She seemed so shaken.

Nina fumbled some cash out of her bag and threw it on the table. "Forget I said anything," she told them.

"Nina, stop."

But the woman was already on her way out the door.

"Well." Lanie took a sip of her wine. "That was interesting."

"She's really been stalking Bee?"

Lanie nodded. "It's pretty disturbing. Mostly it's just been the drive-bys. Bee has noticed her car in the rearview a few times. But then I found her in Bee's studio on the day of Ainsley's burial and she was clearly going through Bee's private paperwork. She acted like she was just admiring the artwork, but—"

"I read your diary," Paige said, then winced. The elephant in the room had gotten too big to handle.

There was a long moment of silence. One of the men at the pool table cheered over a good shot.

"Yeah," Lanie said finally. "I figured."

"How?"

"It was in the drawer facedown. I never do that."

Paige swallowed hard. "I didn't read the whole thing. I only skimmed the last few pages."

"Did you tell the police what you . . . skimmed?"

"No."

Lanie gave her a dubious look.

"I swear, I didn't. I'm still sort of processing it, to be honest. I'm really sorry. I shouldn't have done it."

"It's fine. I burned it anyway, so even if you did tell them, it would be your word against mine."

"What? Lanie! You can't do that! That's evidence."

"It's only evidence if Michael or I did something wrong, and we didn't."

Lanie sipped her wine and looked toward the pool table, as if the game were suddenly riveting to her.

"But you have your suspicions. About Ainsley and Michael."

Lanie gave a false laugh. "Just the paranoia of a bored housewife."

"Lanie, you have to tell the police. You can't let them keep going after John for this," Paige said. "He just lost his wife. And his kids . . . they can't lose their dad, too."

"What about *my* kids?" Lanie was suddenly vehement. "They're just babies. What about *me*?"

"Lanie . . . do you know where Michael was when she was killed?"

Lanie blinked. She stared at nothing. "No."

"Then . . . what if he did do it? What if something happened and he snapped? Do you really want to live with a murderer? Do you want your kids living with him?"

Lanie began to tremble. She closed her eyes. Her fingers shook as she toyed with her necklace, pressing each glittering star against her collarbone, one by one. "Ainsley was going to leave John."

"What?" Paige blurted.

"That was why she wasn't running for PBA president again. Her plan was just to get through the holidays and then she was going to file for divorce. She wanted to start over. Talked about selling all her jewelry and couture and moving to the Caribbean."

Paige sat with that for a moment. The boxes in the closet. Was it possible Ainsley had done all of that herself? She couldn't imagine a woman like Ainsley giving it all up and going off the grid. She'd seemed to adore her position as queen bee, the person who lived in a castle on the hill and ran everyone else's lives. It was what defined her.

But maybe that was the problem. Maybe it was all too much. Or maybe that definition simply no longer appealed to her.

"Were she and Michael—"

"No!" Lanie glared at Paige. "I mean, I don't know. But no. Not that I know of. I just know she was going to leave John. She told Bee one night when the two of them had too much wine watching *The Bachelorette*. Ainsley used to really let loose on *Bachelorette* night."

Paige sipped her beer, everything she thought she knew, rearranging itself in her mind.

"Does anyone else know? Does *John* know?"

"I have no idea, but Ainsley thought he was going to give her a hard time about it because his image is so important to him. To his job. Something about his clients wanting someone stable and upright managing their money. A divorce would not have been ideal for him."

Not ideal. "Are you implying . . ."

"If John did find out, then he definitely has a motive," Lanie said. "And if I tell the police that I thought she and Michael were having an affair, that's even more of a motive."

"So why don't you tell them? At least that you knew she was leaving?"

"Honestly? Because I *like* John. I don't want him to have done this. I don't want anyone to have done this. I just want it all to go away."

Paige sat back. The idea that John might kill someone, might kill the mother of his kids, because a divorce would reflect badly on him . . . It just didn't track. Not with the person she knew. The kind, humble, thoughtful John who had been her boyfriend all those years ago.

But now.

She thought of his house. His cars. His view. The photos of all the vacations he and his family had taken over the years. He claimed to hate the house, but what if that was only because the life he lived inside of it was so unhappy? What if the status mattered?

His life was different now. He was different now.

She got up and walked over to the bar.

"Need another?" the bartender asked.

"No, I just have a question."

"Shoot."

"Does this place have any other rooms? Like an office or an apartment or anything?"

The bartender shrugged. "What you see is what you get. We got a small kitchen for bar snacks, but the office is a desk in the corner next to the garbage cans."

"There's not a couch back there or something?"

The woman gave a short laugh. "Nope. Why do you ask? You looking to buy? Because we don't own the property, but I could put you in touch with our landlord. He was talking about dumping the place anyway."

"Who's your landlord?" Paige asked.

"His name's John Anderson."

lanie

After paying for their drinks, Lanie said good night to Paige and speed-walked to her car. She didn't like this part of town. Most of her friends kept their boats in the marina on the north side, where handsome young men in white slacks and colorful polo shirts were there to help carry supplies from car to galley and lend a hand up if one were wearing unsensible shoes. Down here everyone seemed disgruntled and grimy, like the gunk under their fingernails needed to be dug out with a shovel.

Also, it was gate night. Not that anyone in Piermont ever really did anything on gate night, what with the curfew and the general neighborliness. But someone had broken into and trashed Nina's house, and she lived in one of the nicest neighborhoods in town. Lanie's heart rate picked up as she neared her SUV. Ridiculous, of course, but she felt as if she was being watched, and Paige had already gone.

She clicked the remote to disengage the locks, thinking about how stupid it was to even come here. Nina and her insane claim about

Bee. Paige and her weird obsession with figuring out who killed Ainsley. The more she thought about it, the more certain she was that Ainsley had misstepped and fallen. Paige was innocent. John was innocent. Michael was innocent.

At her car door, she paused. Something was off. It took her a second to realize there was something on her windshield. A ticket? No. She was in a parking lot. She edged around to the front of the vehicle, half expecting to see a bloody fish carcass (definitely too many late nights with Netflix), and paused. It was a folder. Hot pink. Secured to the windshield by the wiper.

paige

It was starting to drizzle, and the air was rapidly moving from cold to frigid as Paige pulled into John's driveway. The chill brought back Halloweens with costumes hidden under down coats, and winters with snow so high it made it over the shaft of her snow boots to melt down her ankles and soak her toes. She regretted making that crack about Amy Sherman-Palladino.

The driveway curled around the front of the house to a car park along the side where the four-car garage sat detached from the house, a perfect little mini mansion in and of itself. The lights were on in the apartment above, and Paige could see someone moving around up there. The back hatch on John's Range Rover was open and the truck was pulled back toward the bottom of the outdoor stairs.

Paige's palms were slick as the shadowy figure moved back and forth in front of the windows. She didn't really think John was capable of murder. But why had he lied to her about crashing at Benny's?

She got out of the car and held the keys in her right hand, key between her knuckles like her father always taught her, just in case. It wasn't that she was afraid of John. Not exactly. But better safe than sorry. On her way up the stairs, she heard a crash, and then someone cursed. The door was propped open with a cardboard box. She jogged the rest of the way.

John was inside on his hands and knees, shoving the flaps of a box up and underneath each other. Paige took stock of the room, which was being cleared out. There were rolls of what looked like green carpeting leaned up against one wall and an octagonal table in the center that brought to mind high-stakes Vegas tables. The cabinets in the open kitchen beyond had been emptied and the counters were lined with glassware of all shapes and sizes, along with half-empty bottles of alcohol. Down the hallway behind the kitchen a door was open to a bedroom, and there was a closed door to what was probably a bathroom. There were a couple of couches and not much else. Most of whatever had been here had already been packed up.

Paige cleared her throat. John fell back on his hands, startled.

"Sorry. Didn't meant to scare you," she said.

"No. It's okay." John stood up awkwardly. "Just didn't expect to see anyone."

"What're you up to?"

John looked around guiltily, like maybe she'd walked in on something she wasn't supposed to see. "I'm just packing up. I'm going to put the house on the market and figured I'd get a head start up here."

Paige felt like the floor had dropped out from under her. "You're moving?"

"Yeah, well . . . once I'm cleared of Ainsley's . . . death." He picked up the box he'd been wrestling with and put it on the table behind him.

"Where're you gonna go?" she asked.

"California, in fact. San Francisco." He gave her an apologetic shrug. "I think it's time for a new start. Me and a few friends have been talking about starting up a new company for a while now. Michelle's in college, Danielle hates the high school here, so she's psyched, and Bradley, I think, needs the change."

"That's great." Paige wasn't sure what else to say. She felt . . . dumped. Not just dumped, but dumped by someone who didn't even register the fact that she might care that she was being dumped. Which was ridiculous. Did she really think she and John were going to start something up? His wife had just been murdered, and she wasn't even planning to stay here that long. Her feelings about all of this were stupid and lame and naïve and annoying. But they were still there.

"Even if—when—I do get my name cleared, no one around here is going to think of me as anything but a murderer anyway," John said.

Paige watched as he grabbed another box, placed it atop the first one, and picked them both up.

"I'll be right back."

She slid out of the way while he took the boxes outside and down the stairs. Paige walked over to the table and ran her fingers along its grooved edges. Definitely a poker table. There were even cutouts at each place to hold drinks. She wondered if John had some sort of weekly poker night with the guys—what the stakes in a game at a Palisades mansion might be like. She noticed a stray poker chip in the well of one of the drink holders and plucked it out. It was blue, with three gold *A*s entwined in the middle.

Michael had one just like it.

John rounded the corner and Paige instinctively shoved the chip into her pocket. He gave her a tight, questioning smile. "So . . . what's up?"

Right. She hadn't told him why she was here.

"I just wanted you to know that people are talking. About you and Ainsley."

"Not surprising."

"I mean about your marriage," she said. He remained placid. "They're saying she was going to leave you. In the new year. That she had a whole plan. And that she was worried you were going to fight it."

John gave a short laugh. "She told people that?"

"She told Bee Dolan, apparently."

"That's Ainsley for you."

He went over to the kitchen and grabbed some Bubble Wrap and a glass. Never had Paige seen anyone wrap up glassware so violently.

"What do you mean?"

"We were going to split up, but it was mutual. She wasn't leaving me. We were leaving each other."

He said it so matter-of-factly, Paige had to believe it was the truth.

"Knowing my dear, departed wife, she probably started telling her friends she was leaving me so she could make it look like she had the upper hand. That she had the power. That I was going to be heart-broken and would never have given her up because she was so damn perfect."

"Oooohkay."

"Sorry." He shoved a wrapped glass into a box and steadied himself with both hands on its sides. "Sorry. I'm just . . . it's been a lot." He picked up another glass and wrapped this one slowly, gently. "We hadn't been happy for a long time. We really just stayed together for the kids. But once Bradley seemed mature enough to understand it . . . we decided it was time."

"I see," Paige said. "So, what was the plan? Was she going to stay here, or . . . ?"

"No. She wanted a change. She was talking about the Caribbean or Arizona or New Mexico. That's where she was from originally— out West. She never could stand the humidity around here. Or the cold."

His gaze went distant, as if he was entertaining a fond memory. But as quickly as it came on, it was gone. He wrapped another glass.

"I was the one who was going to stay. At least until the kids finished out school. We were going to sell the house and I was going to buy something closer to town." He looked at her and smirked. "Maybe in the old neighborhood."

She smiled, hit with a sudden memory of sneaking into John's basement after some dance to play spin the bottle with a bunch of friends.

"John, can I ask you something?"

"Of course."

"Did you really sleep one off at Benny's the night Ainsley died?"

He paused. "Why do you ask?"

"I was just there and . . . they don't have a back room. Also, they said you own the building."

"So you're investigating me now, too? What are you, an amateur P.I.?" He said this without malice, but with a glint of amusement in his eye.

"No. I just went over there with some friends to have a drink in peace and . . . it came up."

"I'll bet." He put the latest glass in the box and looked at her. "Well, Sherlock, I'll tell you the same thing I told the police. I left the party and went to the bar to kill some time before I was supposed to get on an early morning flight to Dallas. I was supposed to go to the Giants–Cowboys game with some clients on Sunday, but I had too much to drink and passed out in a booth. Joe chucked me a blanket and let me stay there, which I did until the sun came up and I drove home to find the back door open and my wife at the bottom of our beach stairs."

Paige swallowed hard. "Oh."

"Yeah. Also, I missed my flight. And a really good football game."

"Why didn't you tell me the truth?"

"You really need to ask that?"

"Yes?"

"Because I didn't want you to see me as the kind of guy who gets so falling-down drunk that he passes out on a table."

She winced in recognition. "Been there. Done that."

John laughed. "I highly doubt that." He picked up another glass and started to wrap it, but then put it down to look her in the eye across the countertop. "I didn't kill my wife, Paige. It's really important to me that you believe that."

"I do," she said.

AS PAIGE WAS pulling out of the driveway, she spotted a dark gray sedan parked across the street, headlights off. Her heart lurched. The police. John had warned her they were watching the house. She thought about ducking or turning her head, but it was too late. The man behind the wheel was staring right at her.

Fantastic. Now Dominic was going to hear all about how Paige had spent an hour over at John Anderson's house.

Did she care?

That was something she was going to have to examine once her pulse stopped throbbing in her ears.

Making the split-second decision that it was better not to look guilty, Paige looked the man right in the eye as she drove past. He had a heavy brow and beady, dark eyes, and there was something familiar about him. Maybe she'd seen him at the station? But no. He didn't look like a cop. He looked like Tony Soprano.

But she wasn't exactly going to stop and give him the third degree. What did a cop look like, anyway, and who was she to judge?

She just kept driving, checking in her rearview mirror until she was around the corner and the car was out of sight.

nina

The second she walked through the door she started shoving things in garbage bags. Broken knickknacks, a shattered picture frame, the head from the mom figurine that she couldn't find the body for—the rest of the family was intact. Trying not to notice how hard her hands were shaking, she picked up the larger pieces of glass and wrapped them in newspaper. She pulled nails from the wall and tossed them. Then she got out the vacuum cleaner.

Once the living room was taken care of, Nina finally removed her jacket. She was sweating and breathless and could smell herself, but at least she felt better. Somewhat.

She wasn't going to think about what Lanie had said to her.

In the office, Nina made piles on the floor. Personal papers. Work papers. College papers. She tossed ripped folders and replaced folder tabs. Her hands shook even harder. She couldn't believe someone had gone through her things like this. The balance on the college accounts for the kids. The mortgage documents. The receipt from the headstone from when she buried her mother.

Bee Dolan knew she'd cheaped out on her mother's headstone.

Bee Dolan knew that Nina had been following her.

It was unfathomable. The woman was oblivious. Her head was in the clouds. Half the time, when she spoke, it was off topic from what everyone around her was discussing. She paid zero attention to anyone or anything. Nina had been so careful. How could Bee even have noticed her?

Nina sliced her finger with a file folder, a deep, stinging paper cut. She sat back on her heels and, much to her own surprise, screamed at the top of her lungs.

She needed some water. Or something stronger. She stood up from the floor where she'd been organizing, slammed her head into the underside of an open file drawer, and saw stars.

"Sonofabitch!"

Hand to the top of her head, she sat down again. She was not going to cry. She would *not* cry. Then, from the corner of her eye, she saw something glint, catching the light.

Nina's heart stopped beating.

Actual stars.

SHE SPOTTED PAIGE through the window at the coffee shop, legs pulled up story-style on the bench and a pencil clasped between her teeth. The woman looked like a college student, her laptop open in front of her and a cup steaming beside it on the table. Nina walked in and stood behind the opposite chair until Paige noticed her.

"Hi, Nina." Her look was questioning.

"Your mother said you'd be here. I'm not stalking you," she added.

"I didn't think you were."

"I need to talk to you, and I wanted to get you alone."

"Ooookay." Paige closed her laptop and put her feet on the floor. "Did you want to sit?"

"Yes," Nina said. "No."

Paige raised her eyebrows.

"Okay, fine."

She took the chair opposite Paige. "I just wanted to give this to you. In case something happens to me."

From her bag, she removed a folder—plain manilla this time—and placed it on the table.

"What is it?"

"It's evidence that Bee Dolan is stealing from the PBA. Her husband has been out of work for years and yet she's renovating her kitchen? Putting on a new roof? Throwing that luncheon for Ainsley's funeral? It doesn't add up."

"Okay . . ."

"That was what you overheard me and Ainsley talking about at the party. Actually, no. I didn't know then that someone was stealing. But I had the evidence. I just didn't know it at the time."

"I'm confused," said Paige, drawing the folder toward her.

"Just . . . just hold on to it for me. I feel like I can trust you with it."

"Why?"

"Because you listened to me last night. Because your dad was a good cop. Because I don't think you like these women any more than I do."

Paige smirked at Nina's bluntness. Nina got up and shouldered her bag.

"Wait, Nina. Do you really think you're in danger?"

"I don't know anymore. But I've got some evidence that proves Bee was in my house and I'm going to confront her with it. So."

"Alone?" Paige seemed alarmed.

"It's how I do most things."

"But don't you—"

Nina held up a hand. "Don't try to talk me out of it. I'll make sure we're in a public place. I just . . . I need to do this."

"Okay. If you're sure."

Nina thought of her kids who were, right now, getting ready for the Halloween parade at the school. This afternoon there would be trick-or-treating and pictures with their grandparents. Then they'd watch *It's the Great Pumpkin, Charlie Brown*—one of Ravi's traditions—and eat way too much sugar. She wanted things to be that simple. She wanted everything to be normal again. But they would be coming back to a house with missing furniture and bare walls. They were a long way from normal.

"Can you tell Lanie I'm withdrawing from the PBA entirely? She can have the presidency."

Nina turned away and Paige gasped. For half a second, Nina thought she was reacting to Nina's pronouncement, but when she looked back, Paige was staring at her phone, hand over her mouth.

"What's wrong?" Nina asked.

"It's from Lanie. She says John was attacked at his house. He's in the hospital."

paige

Halloween had always been Paige's favorite holiday as a kid. She'd loved dressing up, making her own costumes, trying to impress every adult who opened the door to find her standing there looking like a gumball machine or a flapper or a zombie cowgirl. There was something about the way kids completely let loose on this day, running around, screaming with joy, eyes wide as they took in the decorations and the colors and the candy. The giddiness of not only getting all those treats but of your parents sanctioning the whole thing was unlike any other holiday. They were all getting away with something, without even the minutest dread of eventual consequences.

"So, have you heard anything new?" her mother asked as they followed Izzy, who was dressed up as Jessie from *Toy Story 2* today—she'd shunned the pirate costume she'd loved mere days ago—down the sidewalk. Her mom's hands were in the pockets of her down jacket and Paige was cuddled into one of her dad's old coats, using a paper cup of latte to warm her hands. She had found the coat in the closet in her father's office this afternoon, when she'd gone in to put the clip back in his gun. Nina had seemed so spooked at the coffee shop, so sure she was in danger. Whatever was in that folder Nina had given her could put her in danger, too. So now, she had a loaded gun, which she'd shoved back onto the highest shelf in the closet, where she could reach it easily, but Izzy could not.

It was only temporary. Her father would want her to be able to protect herself and her mom and his granddaughter.

She reached into the deep pocket of his coat now, which still held one of his worn-into-softness leather gloves, and pulled out her phone.

"Nothing," Paige said. Lanie had told her she'd text if she heard anything about John's condition, but that had been hours ago. "I don't even know if he has, like, a broken leg or is fighting for his life."

"Mom! Look! A witch!"

On the porch of the next house, an elderly lady had gone all out with her costume. Tattered black dress, ratty green wig, prosthetic nose covered in warts. She held her bowl of candy and stood next to her door while a pack of kindergarteners hovered at the bottom of the stairs, afraid to go up.

"Do you want me to come with you?" Paige said.

"No. I got this."

Izzy traipsed up the walk, skirted the scaredy-cats, and went right over to the candy bowl to make her selection. That was her daughter. Terrified of kids her own age. No problem approaching a potentially homicidal witch.

"Brave little dearie," the woman said in a croaky voice.

"Happy Halloween! Thank you!" Izzy responded.

"She's pretty amazing," Elizabeth said to Paige.

"Against all odds."

"Don't do that." Her mother squeezed her arm. "I know you love to sell yourself short, but she's doing great. You're doing great."

"Thanks, Mom."

Izzy told the group of Power Rangers and Ninja Turtles and Jedis that there was nothing to be scared of and ran back over to Paige, who captured her wide smile with a picture.

"Can we go home soon? I want to hand out candy, too."

"Sure, kiddo. Let's just get to the end of this block and then we'll head back."

"Okay!"

Izzy jogged ahead, sidestepping a family with a dog dressed up in a bee costume heading to the next house. Paige checked her messages again.

"I'm sure he's going to be fine," her mother said.

It was at that moment that a police cruiser pulled up alongside them and parked at the curb. Dominic got out, gave some of the kids and families a nod, and walked over to join her and her mom.

"Hi, Mrs. Lancaster. How're you doing?"

Paige's heart hammered in her chest. He had an odd air about him. Like he was getting ready to deliver bad news. John. Something bad about John.

"I'm fine, Dominic," her mother said. "And you?"

"Fine, thanks. Happy Halloween." His eyes trailed uncertainly to Paige's face. "Can I borrow Paige for a second?"

"Of course." Paige's mother squeezed her arm. "I'll go catch up with Izzy."

"Thanks, Mom."

Paige squared off with Dominic as a stiff breeze sent a scattering of autumn leaves across their feet. The delighted squeals of the kindergarteners, who had finally approached the witch, faded into the background.

"What is it?"

"First of all, I wanted to say I'm sorry for how it all went down yesterday. The detective had to do her due diligence. She couldn't just not check your alibi because we're . . . friends."

"I'm not upset," Paige said, although she was, a little. She knew it was irrational, because she understood this was much bigger than her.

But part of her did sort of think Dominic could have done something to save her from that unpleasant experience. That he could have tried harder. Would have, if he'd wanted to.

"Okay. Good. Well, I also wanted to let you know John Anderson is in the hospital."

"I know."

"Of course, you do," he said, and gave a sarcastic laugh.

"Not like that," she said. "The mom network is powerful in this town."

Dominic nodded a few times, as if trying to decide whether or not to believe that was why and how she'd heard. "Well, I just got an update on his condition and I thought you might want to know."

"Okay."

"It was pretty bad," he said. "Whoever worked him over had something to prove."

Paige's stomach turned. "Just tell me."

"He has a concussion, a broken forearm, and severe bruising and lacerations to his face."

"Oh my God. Is he going to be okay?"

"They expect him to make a full recovery, but he's going to be uncomfortable for a while, for sure."

"Does he have any idea who it was?"

"He says the guy wore a mask, but he was big. At least six four, two-eighty. He says he's pretty sure he was white because he could see the skin around his eyes."

"Why would anyone do this?"

"Well, when one of the detectives from county found him, he was in the apartment above the garage and there were boxes overturned and poker chips and other gambling paraphernalia everywhere. It was like the guy was looking for something."

Paige felt dizzy suddenly. She'd been there just last night. How soon after she'd left had this happened?

"Looking for what?"

"We don't know, and John's not talking." Dominic looked her up and down quickly. "You don't have any idea, do you?"

Paige blew out a sigh. "No. Dominic, look, John and I barely even know each other. We were together a million years ago. As kids. And yes, we did something stupid one night, but that was all it was. A stupid thing. He's not my boyfriend or anything. He's not even my friend, really."

"Okay, okay, I get it." Dominic raised his hands, laughing. "You don't have to explain."

"No, but I do. I don't want you to think I'm carrying some weird torch for the guy."

"You don't?" Dominic's eyes sparked.

Paige blushed. "No. I really don't."

"Well. All right, then." Now Dominic was grinning. They held each other's gaze for a long moment and Paige could only imagine how doofy they looked. "Well, if you think of anything else . . ."

"Wait! Weren't the cops watching his house?"

Dominic had started to turn back toward his car, but paused and shook his head. "They took the detail off, citing lack of resources."

"But I saw . . . there was a man in a car, parked on the street outside John's last night."

"You were at John's last night?"

Paige sighed and waved a hand. "Yes, briefly. I just wanted to ask him something. But there was a guy."

"What time was this?" Dominic took out his notepad.

"Around eight o'clock," Paige said, grateful that it was an early enough time to not sound untoward.

"Okay. Can you describe this man? Or the car?"

Paige did, noting that she assumed the car was a plainclothes officer's police car because it was a boxy gray sedan. Definitely Connecticut license plates, but she hadn't gotten the number.

"Also, I found this poker chip," she added.

"Right, there were a lot of poker chips recovered. You saw them when you were over there?"

"I did, but I also saw them somewhere else. Michael Katapodis had one. Maybe Michael and John play poker together? This other guy could be part of their game or something. Maybe John owed him money."

Dominic laughed.

"What?"

"You really are a good writer."

Paige tried not to smile.

"I'll talk to the guy about the poker game," Dominic said. "Thanks for the tip."

"Thanks for coming down here with the update. I really appreciate it."

"Of course," he said. "I'll keep you posted. Have fun trick-or-treating. Try not to let all of this spoil the day."

"Thanks," she said. "I'll try."

nina

"Where're we going, Mama?" asked Liam from the back seat.

Nina forced a bright smile as she looked at her kids in the rear-view mirror. "Friday Fun Time at the library."

The kids cheered. Nina's fingers tightened on the steering wheel. She hated Friday Fun Time at the library. It turned what was a sacred, peaceful place of learning into a psychotic free-for-all. She had brought the kids exactly once, at the beginning of the previous school year, and Lita had ended up with glitter glue in her hair. And when Nina came back from washing it out in the bathroom, she discovered Liam eating colorful beads off the floor with two other kindergarten-ers. (Shockingly, it was Bee who was supposed to be keeping an eye on him.)

She had vowed never to return, but she knew that Lanie, Dayna, and Bee never missed one. It was an opportunity to gather and gossip and ignore their children for an hour. Half the town took part.

It was the perfect opportunity for Nina to confront Bee about the necklace she'd found in her house. She would do it in front of her friends, in a public place, and force a confession out of her. There would be a dozen eyewitnesses and—a bonus—the library was just across the municipal square from the police station. Nina could march Bee over there herself.

A laugh escaped her at the thought.

"What's funny, Mom?" Lita asked.

"Nothing," Nina said as she pulled into the jammed parking lot. "I'm just in a good mood."

She saw her kids exchange dubious glances and tried not to read too much into it.

Inside, the children's section of the library was chaos. It looked like today's craft had something to do with turkeys. Now that it was November, the jack-o-lanterns in the window would need to be switched out for colorful, doomed birds in pilgrim hats. Nina released her kids to the nearest craft table and looked around. Klatches of mothers stood along the window wall that looked out over the perfectly manicured soccer fields and baseball diamonds.

Her adrenaline was spiking as she scanned the faces. No sign of Lanie or Dayna or Bee. She checked the tables and saw Dayna's stepdaughter swirling glue onto brown paper. Totally ignoring the directions left out by the library, as well as the two youth librarians themselves, who were trying to get the kids' attention. Typical. Her own kids were sitting with their hands in their laps, listening intently.

Nina edged along the craft area, glancing down the rows of bookshelves. When she got to the windows, she looked out, and there they were, directly below on the sidewalk. Bee and Dayna, heads bent close together, eyes furtive. Nina wondered what they were talking about so intently. Maybe Bee had confessed to Dayna? But it didn't matter. Now was her chance.

"Lita, I'm going outside for just a minute. Keep an eye on your brother."

She kissed her daughter's head as she walked by and slipped quickly outside, skirting the book drop and turning the corner toward the fields.

Bee saw her first and nudged Dayna. Nina wrapped her fingers around the broken star necklace in her pocket as she approached.

"I know it was you and I know what you were looking for," Nina blurted, eyes trained on Bee.

So much for that carefully planned speech she'd rehearsed all morning.

"Hello, Nina. And how are you today?" Dayna said sarcastically.

"I'm not talking to you."

"You're not talking to anyone. You're talking *at* Bee, which, I have to say, I don't care for."

"I know you were stealing from the PBA and I know you think you can intimidate me into keeping my mouth shut, but that ship has already sailed."

"What are you talking about?" Bee asked. "Intimidate you?"

Dayna laughed. "You're out of your mind."

"You may have taken my laptop, but I printed everything out," Nina continued. "I have copies and I gave one to Lanie and one to Paige Lancaster, too. You know her dad used to be chief of police, right? I'm sure once she understands the gravity of what you've done, she'll be reporting what she knows."

"I have no idea what you're talking about," Bee said. "And I should get inside. I'm sure April is looking for me."

She started past Nina, but Nina couldn't let her go. She needed Bee to confess. She needed her to break down in tears and beg forgiveness and tell Nina that she'd been right all along. She reached out and grabbed Bee's arm, and when Bee turned, her colorful scarf slipped from her neck.

And there were her stars.

Nina froze.

No. Bee's necklace was in Nina's pocket right now. It had to be Bee's.

"Get your hands off her." Dayna stepped forward as if she was going to shove Nina, but Nina had already dropped Bee's arm. At that moment, Lanie pulled up next to the curb across the street. Leaving the engine running and her kids in the back seat, she jumped out of the car and jogged over.

"Nina? What're you doing?" she asked, wary.

Nina glanced at Dayna. Four twinkling stars.

The only other option was . . .

"Lanie?"

But no. Lanie's necklace was there, displayed across her perfect collarbone.

There was only one other of these necklaces in existence. And it belonged to Ainsley Aames.

lanie

At first Lanie didn't understand what she was looking at. She recognized it, certainly, as three years' worth of statements from the PBA's bank account, but she didn't understand why Nina had left them on her windshield—or how she'd gotten them. It had to have been Nina. No one else even remotely related to the PBA had been at Benny's that night, and Paige had left when Lanie had.

But as she sat at the desk in her craft room that blessedly quiet Friday afternoon, the kids all out at playdates after the Friday Fun Time at the library, her eyes caught on something odd. A payment to Aldo's restaurant in the amount of five thousand dollars. The last time Ainsley had deigned to use Aldo's restaurant for an event it had been the board's June Thank You dinner. There were only eight people on the board. There was no way they'd spent five thousand dollars on that dinner.

Lanie took a sip of her mango La Croix, which she'd poured into a champagne glass in an attempt to not feel like a hobo, and sat back. Even if everyone had gotten trashed that night, it could never have added up to five thousand. And, if she remembered correctly, that particular dinner had been rather tame. Cara Corcoran was pregnant with Sasha at the time, and the rest of the group had kept the wine-ordering to a minimum out of deference. Also, Marie likely would have given them a discount, being a member of the PBA and all. Ainsley and Marie's falling out had come later, as a result of that dinner, in fact. It was that night that Ainsley had suffered the food poisoning that had made her blackball Aldo's.

Why five thousand dollars?

Lanie wished she had access to the receipts, but Bee kept them all in a file at her house, and, if she was doing her job, scanned them into another private PBA cloud account. If Lanie had taken over the presidency like she was supposed to, Bee would have given her the access codes to the accounts, but as it was, she had no way of checking the actual receipt from that night.

"Eight people, say about a hundred dollars a person if everyone had an app, an entrée, and a dessert," Lanie muttered to herself. "Then there's coffee and guestimate four hundred for wine . . ." Really the most they could have spent was fifteen hundred, plus tip, so eighteen hundred. About par for what they normally budgeted for a dinner like it, with the group kicking in for the tip as necessary.

Lanie sat forward again, looking backward through the accounts. A couple of weeks prior to the event there was a deposit in the amount of three thousand dollars, cash. Lanie's face screwed up in confusion. Who would have deposited that much cash? Before the pandemic, the PBA held a lot of fundraisers that brought in actual paper money. The book fair, the holiday wreath sale, the spring festival. But ever since, their income had been mostly via Venmo or PayPal or direct credit card payments.

She flipped back further and found more cash deposits. Eighteen hundred, two thousand, five thousand. The back of her skull buzzed. Intrigued now, she dug a yellow highlighter out of a drawer and started to highlight these. As she was going through, she noticed other, odd expenditures. Multiple thousands to the craft store where they usually bought supplies for the Valentine's dance. A huge amount of money to something called AAA Supplies. It was about a month ahead of last year's Thankful Dinner, and the gift bags always cost a fortune, but Lanie had been the chair last year and she did not remember a company called AAA Supplies. She highlighted the expenditures in blue.

The only people who had direct access to this account were the president of the PBA and its treasurer. Ainsley and Bee. Had Bee been somehow using the PBA accounts for illegal activity?

Lanie paused. Then laughed out loud. It was an insane notion. As insane as the idea of Bee breaking into Nina's house. Bee, a criminal mastermind? It was absurd.

But something had clearly been going on. Had Ainsley . . . ? No. Not possible. She'd known Ainsley for years. She may have been a bitch, but she wasn't a thief. Lanie would have known if she were up to something illegal. Besides, she'd been the wealthiest woman in town. One of them, anyway. There was no reason for her to be screwing around with the PBA's accounts.

She thought back to that last dinner at Aldo's. Ainsley and Marie had spent an unusually long time in the office. Lanie remembered it clearly, because their voices had risen to near shouts at one point. And then the food poisoning had happened, and Marie had become persona non grata.

But Ainsley had been the only one who'd gotten sick. Lanie had always thought it was because Ainsley was the only one who'd ordered the sea bass. Nothing more.

But maybe it was something else. Maybe Marie had refused to take part in Ainsley's shady dealings anymore.

There was an uncomfortable feeling in the pit of Lanie's stomach now. She leaned forward and, starting at the beginning, went through the accounts again, line by line. She was so engrossed in her work that she didn't hear someone in the hallway until a creak sounded right outside the door.

Lanie's heart vaulted into her throat. She fumbled for her phone to check the security feeds, but it was locked. Another creak. She looked around for something heavy and was met with walls of ribbon and wrapping paper. Shit. Where was a golf club when she needed one? Her eyes fell on the table across the room. The three-hole punch. It was the best option. She lunged for it, then stood behind the door.

Please don't let me have to hit someone with this thing, she thought, holding her breath.

The door pushed open wider. There was a flash of black. Lanie jumped out, wielding her weapon.

"Lane?" Michael said.

Lanie screamed.

"Holy shit!" He dropped his briefcase and put his arms up defensively.

"Oh my God! Michael!"

She dropped the three-hole punch and threw her arms around him. "What are you doing here?!"

Michael hugged her back. "Were you going to kill me with office supplies?"

She pulled back and met his eyes. After a moment, they both laughed. She was so relieved it was him. It had been so long since she'd seen him. And now she knew he wasn't the psycho who had torn apart Nina's house. Or murdered Ainsley.

"Maybe. Sorry. There's a lot going on."

"That's an understatement."

The tone of his voice made Lanie pause. She pulled back farther. For the first time, she noticed how tired he looked—his skin almost gray. There was a five-o'clock shadow peeking out along his chin and cheeks. Lanie felt a thump of trepidation.

"Is everything okay?"

He sighed and rubbed one hand over his face. "No," he said. "No it's not." His eyes met hers and they were full of sorrow. "Lanie, we need to talk."

* * *

"I HAVEN'T BEEN completely honest with you either."

"Okay."

They were sitting on the small settee in her craft room now, the autumn sun streaming incongruously through the west-facing windows as it lowered toward the horizon. She had to pick up the kids soon. It was going to get dark. There was still dinner and bedtime to deal with, but all of that felt very far away.

"The night of the party, I stayed at the Andersons' after you left. For a couple hours."

Lanie held herself as still as possible. This was it. This was the moment she learned the truth about her marriage. About her husband. About Ainsley. She squeezed her eyes closed and tears pooled at their corners.

"But I wasn't doing what you think I was doing."

Her eyes popped open. "What?"

"I was playing poker," he said.

Michael stared down at his hands, clasped in front of him, forearms resting across his knees. His right leg jitterbugged beneath him.

"I was part of a regular poker game. We met once, sometimes twice a week in the room above the Andersons' garage. Ainsley . . . she thought it would be fun to hold one that night. A lot of the spouses bailed from the party early, and she took it as a sign." He gave a short laugh. "To be honest, I think she was offended that people had left, and wanted to hold the game as a sort of eff you."

Lanie had to shake her head in order to focus. "I'm sorry. Ainsley?"

Michael blew out a sigh. He reached into his breast pocket and pulled out a blue poker chip. It had a script *A* at its center, the tails entwined with two smaller *A*s in the background. Lanie knew immediately what it meant.

"Ainsley Aames . . . Anderson."

"She called it Triple A Casino."

Triple A. AAA. But it had to be a coincidence.

"Ainsley was running a regular poker game? When? For how long?" Ainsley hated gambling. She wouldn't even let Lanie throw a casino night fundraiser, even though Lanie had heard from friends in neighboring towns that they brought in piles of cash. Once, Dayna suggested a weekend trip to Vegas because she "had a hankering for some craps," and Ainsley had protested so vehemently that none of them had gone. Instead she, Dayna, and Bee had ended up slinking off to Mohegan Sun and had had an awful time. They'd spent a couple of hours eating their faces off at one of the buffets and had come home early.

"A long time. Over a year."

Michael ran his palms up and down his thighs. He looked like he was going to throw up. Lanie reached over to put a hand on his back, and he stood up, as if her touch had shocked him. He always hated being touched when he felt sick, but she was the exact opposite, so she was constantly forgetting.

"I was in debt to her deep, Lanie. Really deep. She . . . she took fifty grand off me last month alone."

"What?" Lanie blurted, standing. Heat pulsated up her neck and around her ears. "Fifty thousand dollars? Michael!"

"Yeah, but it's way more than that. The total is . . . I can't even say it, Lane. I just . . . I kept thinking I would make it back. Like I'd have one good night at the table and figure my luck had changed—that I'd go on a hot streak or something and I'd make it back. But there were way more bad nights than good nights."

Lanie couldn't process what he was saying. He wasn't having an affair. So that was a good thing. Yes. A very good thing. But this . . . was this even worse? All along, he *had* been lying to her about where he'd been, just not for the reason she'd thought. And instead of having mindless sex, he was . . . throwing away their money?

Plus, she was still having a hard time wrapping her mind around Ainsley as a casino boss. She had a sudden image of her in

a slinky red dress with a high slit, her golden hair styled into finger curls.

"Tell me. How bad is it?"

"It's bad. I still owed her money when she . . . when she died. If
the cops find out—"

"Michael, where *were* you when she died?"

"Driving," he said. "I left around one, one thirty, and just drove
aimlessly for a while. That night, before I left, I begged her for more
time to pay her back for some debts I'd accrued, and she said she'd
given me long enough. I was trying to clear my head. Figure out what
to do."

"What the hell does that mean, long enough? Did she *threaten*
you?" The idea was absurd. This whole thing was absurd. Suddenly
she wanted to punch Ainsley in the face. Except she couldn't. Because
Ainsley was dead.

"She had this guy, Lestor," he said. "A guy who would come after
you if you didn't pay up. Remember last year when Fred Carson broke
his arm building his kid's tree house?"

"Yes."

"That wasn't how he broke his arm."

"Holy shit, Michael."

"I know. The thing is, now that she's dead, I don't know if Lestor
still wants to collect. Or needs to. I have no idea if it was just Ainsley
or if she was, like, working for someone. What if he was employed by
the mob? What if that money was going somewhere else and that
person still wants it back?"

What if that money was going somewhere else?

"Oh my God."

"What?"

Lanie turned and half stumbled over to her desk, where the PBA
papers were still laid out and carefully highlighted. She arranged
them into a hasty pile and held them up to her husband.

"What do you know about money laundering?" she asked.

* * *

AN HOUR LATER, Michael was on his way to pick up the kids from their various playdates and Lanie was parking her car at Nina's. The kids were going to be so excited to see Michael, she almost wished she didn't have to miss it. But Lanie needed answers, and Nina was the only one who could give them to her.

She rang the bell. Twice. Finally, after what seemed like forever, Ravi answered. His long hair was piled atop his head in a floppy bun and he wore a long, hipster cardigan over a black T-shirt and jeans and bare feet. For the millionth time, Lanie wondered how he and the buttoned-up Nina had found each other.

"Hey," he said. "This isn't a good time."

He looked freaked.

"Is Nina okay?" she asked.

"No. No, she's not, so if you're here to debate about the presidency or whatever—"

"I'm not. I promise you. I just need to talk to her."

"I really don't think—"

"Ravi, listen, I know you don't know me very well, but I am extraordinarily good with people. Maybe I can help." It was a long shot, but worth a try. Ravi glanced back into the square, modern house and considered. Finally, he opened the door a touch wider and gestured for her to come inside.

"She locked herself in her office. She keeps telling me to take the kids to my parents. I know the whole break-in thing messed with her head, but we have a security company coming this weekend to upgrade everything and the police have told us a million times these people aren't coming back."

He walked her through the house as he talked. It was totally modern, but somehow still cozy. The furniture was expensive, and all clean lines, but the couches were piled with pillows and throws and there were framed family photos everywhere. Lanie could see the empty nails on the walls where artwork had been removed during the break-in, but otherwise, the place had obviously been cleaned and re-organized. Lanie's heart broke a little for Nina. What must it be like to have a stranger invade your family's space?

Ravi paused in front of a closed door in a back hallway and laced his fingers behind his head, his elbows sticking out like wings. "She's in here." He blew out a breath and knocked. "Nina? Lanie's here."

"Lanie?"

Ravi shot her a hopeful look. They could hear movement inside and then the lock clicked. He seemed to be restraining himself from lunging at the door. It opened a crack and Nina peeked out.

"What are you doing here?"

"I want to talk to you," Lanie said. "I believe you."

A crease appeared over Ravi's nose. "Believe her?"

Nina opened the door, but only slightly, allowing Lanie to slip in-side. It wasn't until she was in the room and the door was locked be-hind her, that she noticed the only light on was the desk light. And on the desk was a star necklace.

And a gun.

"Nina."

"Don't worry. I'm not going to shoot you." Nina walked back over to the desk. "This is in case Ainsley comes back."

"What?" Lanie tentatively approached her. "Nina, Ainsley is dead."

"I know. And yet somehow, she broke into my house and stole my laptop."

"I don't follow."

"I found her necklace when I was cleaning up. It was under a fil-ing cabinet."

Lanie's hand flew up to her own necklace. "That's Ainsley's?"

"Well, you have yours." Nina nodded. "And Dayna and Bee were both wearing theirs at the library today. Which leads me to believe that Ainsley is somehow not dead and is, instead, playing cat burglar."

She said all of this very lucidly, very matter-of-factly. Lanie got the sense that she didn't truly believe what she was saying but was drawing the only conclusions—logical or not—she could come up with.

"Can I . . .?" Lanie gestured at the necklace.

Nina shrugged and picked up the gun. Lanie flinched, but Nina shoved it into the back waistband of her black slacks. "Go for it."

Lanie stepped over to the desk. Holding her breath, she turned the necklace over, so that the stars were facedown.

"What're you doing?" Nina asked.

"Ainsley had each necklace inscribed with our first initial. Hers had an *A* on the back of the first star. Bee's has a *B* on the second. Mine has an *L* on the third. And Dayna's has a *D* on the fourth. It was for the order in which she became friends with each of us."

Nina stepped forward and leaned in. Lanie held the stars up to the light. On the fourth star was a tiny, capital *D*.

dayna

Dayna didn't want to hurt anyone. She just wanted to get the fuck out of Piermont.

Sometimes, she didn't know what she'd been thinking when she'd said yes to Maurice's proposal five years ago. It hadn't been *that* bad, living in a one-bedroom apartment with five other twentysomethings, eating ramen every day and splitting cans of Corona when they could scrape together enough cash to get drunk. It had been charming in a modern-day Dickensian kind of way. But the problem was, there was literally no way out. Dayna had no education to speak of. No prospects. The dream of being discovered by some modeling agent at SoulCycle had long since died. Sometimes, she lay awake at night on her mattress on the floor, listening to the mice scritch and scratch in the ceiling above her head and she imagined herself living like this at the age of forty. Forty-five. *Sixty.*

And that was why she'd said yes to that first date with Maurice. And the second. And the trip to St. Croix. And the ring. The ring, which could have bought and sold every last one of her roommates.

Maurice was charming in his own way. He could be funny. Mean funny, but funny. And he loved his daughter, which still sometimes touched Dayna's heart. Plus, he'd been attractive when they'd met. Before he'd gained all the weight and started randomly snorting like a pig when he ate—something to do with the resettling of his nasal passages.

These days, every time Maurice climbed on top of her in bed, she found herself remembering that scene from *Gone Girl* and wondering if she could get away with it.

She'd mentioned this to Ainsley once and Ainsley had scrunched her pretty little nose. "Way too messy."

She'd had a better way.

They'd spent two years creatively funneling money into the PBA account and out again. Half would go to Dayna, so she could leave Maurice, and half would go to Ainsley, so that she could pay down her gambling debt. But then fucking Nina Anand came along. And Ainsley got scared.

And then, well, shit happened.

But now. Now Dayna was so close. She'd already drained all the PBA funds and put the money in the secret account she and Ainsley had set up under her fake name. It was unfortunate that Nina had gotten into the PBA account. Even more unfortunate that she'd told Paige and Lanie about it. But all Dayna had to do was get rid of the evidence and it would be their word against hers, except it wouldn't matter, because she and her word would be long gone.

Brazil was the new plan. Warm. Full of beautiful people.

The authorities would undoubtedly look at Bee. For all they knew Bee was the only living person with access to the PBA funds. But once they figured out she didn't take the money, everyone would just have to move on. Part of her hated to put Bee through it. She was so delicate. But Dayna couldn't think about that now.

She lifted one hand off the steering wheel and touched the stars around her neck. Ainsley's stars. Dayna had pocketed them that night without thinking. She'd been wearing them since she lost her own—where and when, she had no idea. Wearing them felt a bit morbid, but she felt worse without them. Exposed.

When Ainsley had given her this necklace at Christmas three years ago, she'd felt accepted for the first time in her life. Powerful. Dayna had never been one of the popular girls. Not in grade school. Not in high school. Not even at SoulCycle, which was almost more like high school than high school was. But these stars. These stars proved she was one of the A crowd. Dayna had worshipped Ainsley from the moment she'd met her. Loved her, hated her, admired her, was appalled by her, wanted to *be* her. And now, Ainsley was gone.

Dayna gripped the steering wheel harder.

She was going to go to Paige's house. Find the papers, stuff them in her bag, and spend the rest of the night smiling and picking out expensive crap for the Thankful Dinner gift bags. Tomorrow, she'd do the same at Lanie's, and then . . .

Then she'd be gone.

nina

"Where are we going?" Nina asked.

"To Paige's. Dayna's on her way over there."

"Why are we running?"

Lanie stopped at the front door and turned to face Nina. Ravi, Lita, and Liam hovered in the entryway to the kitchen, watching them. Lita was eating an apple noisily, the juice running down her chin.

"Because, this is Dayna's necklace." Lanie held up the chain, which she clutched in her palm. "And as you pointed out, Dayna already *has* a necklace."

"She has Ainsley's necklace," Nina said, catching on.

"Which, according to John, the police couldn't find anywhere on or near Ainsley's body on the night she died." Lanie looked like she was going to throw up.

"Oh, shit."

"Mama cursed!" Liam shouted and giggled, pressing both hands over his mouth.

"Is that a gun?" Ravi said.

Nina paused. Her gun was still pressed against her back, held by her waistband. The kids were wide-eyed.

"Why do you have a gun?" Ravi asked.

Nina made sure the safety was on and carefully handed it to her husband. Her husband, who hated guns, who had marched against guns, who had called legislators and written letters to the editor and donated to anti-gun lobbies. She may as well have been handing him a live viper. "Hide it. Lock it up in one of the filing cabinets. We'll talk about it when I get home."

Then she and Lanie raced for the car.

"I just have one question," Nina said as she buckled herself into the passenger seat of Lanie's SUV.

"What?" Lanie rested her hands at her sides. She seemed like she needed a breath.

"If it wasn't Bee stealing the money, then how is she affording all these renovations? How did she throw that party?"

Lanie closed her eyes and shook her head slightly, summoning patience. "Her mom died, Nina. She left Bee a freaking fortune. She probably would have told you all about it if you'd just asked."

paige

She had all the supplies laid out on her mother's dining room table. Tasteful brown paper gift bags with gold stripes that looked like someone could have made them out of grocery bags, but that retailed for three dollars a pop. (They'd gotten a bulk discount.) There were reams of gold-flecked tissue paper, and gold raffia ribbon, which was going to be a bitch to tie into bows. Paige had a feeling they'd be lucky if that was all they accomplished tonight. Stacked along the walls were boxes full of goodies for the giveaway. Hundreds of thousands of dollars' worth of products that Paige had half a mind to donate to a local shelter. Not that homeless people needed the new iPhone, but if they sold these things on eBay, they could feed families for months. The people who were going to receive them would probably dump them in a drawer and forget about them.

"Thank you so much, Dayna. This is very sweet of you!"

Paige's mother and Izzy followed Dayna into the dining room. Her mom was holding some sort of coupon and had her jacket on.

"What's going on?" Paige asked.

Dayna put down the mug full of coffee she'd been pouring in the kitchen and shed her own leather jacket onto a dining room chair.

"I got these free coupons for that new build-your-own-ice-cream-sandwich place and I thought your mom might want to take Izzy."

"Oh, that's nice," Paige said. "But you haven't had dinner yet."

"Moom! Pleeeeease!" Izzy clasped her hands beneath her chin.

"Yeah, Mom. Pleeease!?" Elizabeth joked, mimicking her grand-daughter's pose. "We can get them now and put them in the freezer for after the steak."

"Okay, fine. That sounds like a plan."

"Do you want anything?" her mother asked.

"Sure. You guys know what I like. Dayna?"

Dayna gave a short laugh. "I don't eat ice cream. The vouchers were left over from my stepkid's cheerleading fundraiser."

"Got it. Okay. Well, you two go ahead," Paige said to her little family. "It's going to get dark soon."

Once they were gone, Paige started opening gift bags and standing them up along one side of the table. "I figured we could put tissue in all of them first and then open the boxes and start stuffing the bags. Shouldn't take long if we—"

"Hey, so I'm gonna need that information Nina gave you about the PBA account."

Paige paused. An awful, tingling feeling skittered down her spine. "I'm sorry . . . what?"

"Don't play stupid. It's beneath you."

Dayna's tone had completely shifted. It had gone from playful and generous to no-nonsense. Even threatening. Paige stood across the table from her and slowly finished opening the bag she'd already picked up. Had Bee told her about Nina's hacking of the PBA account? Was Dayna here to act as her friend's protector?

"I considered trying to search the place while you were distracted, but the very thought is just exhausting, and I want this all to be over with already."

Not *we. I.*

The room suddenly felt much smaller than it was. Boxes blocked one exit. The pile of stuff made it seem as if the walls were closing in. Dayna walked slowly around the table toward Paige. The woman had gotten rid of her mother and her daughter. She'd made sure there were no witnesses. Paige couldn't help noticing how strong Dayna looked. The muscles in her arms well-defined, her shoulders broad for her trim body. Could she have shoved Ainsley down the stairs? Easily.

But why? How was Bee stealing money from the PBA funds to renovate her kitchen connected to Dayna? And why would she have hurt Ainsley over it?

Paige had to stall. Bee and Lanie were supposed to be coming over to help. They had each made excuses for being late, but they should be here soon. Unless those excuses were fake. Were they both in on it? Did they know that Dayna was going to spend this time threatening Paige?

"I don't know what you're talking about," she said, standing her ground.

"Come on, Paige. I know you have it. It's a long list of numbers?" she said sarcastically. "Deposits and withdrawals? I know you're basically broke, but you probably remember what a bank account looks like."

"I don't understand what you need with a printout," Paige said, trying another tack. "You know there's a digital record of everything."

Dayna's eyes darkened. "Not anymore." Dayna reached up and fingered the star necklace she and her friends always wore. "Look, Paige. I have a black belt in karate and I taught spin and kickboxing classes for ten years. I don't want to hurt you. Just get. The. Folder."

"Okay! Okay, fine. Just . . . hang on a second."

Paige turned and walked the rest of the way around the table, wanting more than anything to just get away from this woman. She touched her back pocket, looking for her phone, but it wasn't there. Charging. Upstairs. In her room.

What the hell was she supposed to do? Maybe she could give Dayna a fake folder? Buy more time? It was so ironic, really. Nina had given her the information in case something happened to her, but now Dayna had come to her first. Unless . . . shit. Had Dayna already gotten to Nina? Was Nina okay?

Her dad's office. Paige skirted the living room couch and went for the office door.

"What's in there?" Dayna asked from across the room.

"My office," Paige lied, thinking of the gun on the shelf in the closet. "It's where I write. And where I keep all my . . . papers. I'll be right back."

She went inside and closed the door, not caring how it looked. So Dayna had killed Ainsley. But not to protect Bee. Clearly, she was the one stealing from the account. Paige had no idea why and she didn't care. All she knew was she was not going to be Dayna's next victim. Izzy needed her. And there was no way she was going to let some skinny bitch be the end of her.

Paige lunged for the closet to the right and slightly behind the desk, and pulled down the gun. Her hands shook as she double-checked the magazine, keeping the gun below the desk so that if Dayna walked in, she wouldn't see what she was doing. The magazine clicked back into place, and the door opened.

"Mama?"

"Izzy?" the word came out strangled.

"Gigi forgot her wallet and now she can't find it!"

Dayna walked in right behind Izzy. Paige stood up and Dayna's eyes zeroed in on the gun. Paige lifted her arm and trained the gun at Dayna's face, her father's wide desk between them.

"Izzy. Go to Grandma."

"Mom?"

Dayna grabbed Izzy by the scruff of the neck and Izzy screamed.

"Don't!" Paige snapped.

"Mommy?"

Dayna pulled Izzy in front of her and placed her other hand on Izzy's chin. "All it takes is one swift turn, Paige. A quick snap."

"Don't you dare hurt my kid."

"Then put down the gun and give me the folder. I swear to God, if you do, I'll just walk away. You'll never see me again." She clenched her jaw, pursing her lips. "Don't make me do it, Paige."

Her grip intensified. "Mommy," Izzy whimpered.

"What's going on? I heard Izzy scream." Elizabeth appeared at the door, clutching her wallet. She saw Paige with the gun drawn and backed up, her hand to her heart. "Paige? What're you doing?"

"Mom, just stay back."

Then the front door slammed. "Paige!? Dayna?"

It was Lanie. Dayna closed her eyes. Paige could see her starting to tremble. This was getting too complicated for her. More people. More witnesses. It might make her give up. Or it might make her crack.

"Back here!" Paige shouted.

Pounding footsteps, and then Lanie was there. And Nina. Together?

Lanie, to her credit, stepped right into the room and assessed the situation. "Dayna, what the hell are you doing? Let her go."

"I can't do that, Lanie. Not until I get what I want."

"And what is that, exactly? More money?" Lanie asked, lifting a sheaf of papers she held in one hand. Dayna's eyes widened. "What were you doing with it all, Dayna? What the hell were you and Ainsley up to?"

Dayna closed her eyes again and took a deep breath, but she still didn't release Izzy. Nina slipped into the room and stood near the corner. She shot Paige a bolstering look that Paige tried to appreciate, but this whole situation was out of control. And her arm was getting tired.

"It wasn't me! It was all Ainsley. At least that was how it started."

"Does it have to do with her poker game?" Lanie asked.

"What?" Paige said.

"She was running a weekly poker game."

"Oh, it was way more than weekly. Half this town was into her for over six figures a pop."

"Including Michael," Lanie said.

"Yeah, your husband has no poker face, Lane. No offense."

"I can't believe you two kept this a secret from me for so long," Lanie said. "All the committees we were on together. All the money we raised for the school. Dayna, you were my *friend*."

"You don't even know what that word means. No one does."

"Not even Ainsley?" Paige asked.

"Especially not Ainsley," Dayna spat. "She promised me that if I helped her figure out how to launder the money, she'd put money aside; she'd give me enough that I could get out. So that I could divorce my disgusting husband and move away from this bullshit town. But as soon as *she* caught us," Dayna said, throwing Nina a murderous look, "Ainsley balked."

"What do you mean?" Lanie asked.

"Nina hacked the account. She knew something was up. So that night at the party, Ainsley told me the deal was off. That we had to find a way to shore up the cash and then lay low for a while. She promised me I'd be out by Christmas and then she just shut it down. She even threatened to change the password on the account. Like she didn't trust me anymore."

"Holy shit," Paige said. "So that's why you killed her."

"Tell me you didn't, Dayna," Lanie said.

"Lanie." Dayna's voice was pleading. "You know what Maurice is like. You know I can't live like this anymore." But she never loosened her grip on Izzy, who was crying silently.

"Let go of my kid, or I swear to God I'll shoot."

"Everyone just calm down, okay?" said Elizabeth. "Calm down."

"You don't want to do this," Dayna said, shaking her head slightly. "If you put the gun down, we can all just walk away."

"Do you even know what you're doing with that thing?" asked Nina.

"Dayna," Lanie said coldly. "Where did you get that necklace? It's Ainsley's, isn't it? Did you think that we wouldn't find out? You know they're all monogrammed."

Dayna's hand released Izzy's chin and flew up to touch her collarbone.

"Mommy?"

Paige aimed at the window behind her daughter and fired. Izzy hit the floor. Nina, out of nowhere, kicked Dayna's legs out from under her. Paige grabbed her dad's handcuffs out of the top drawer, slid across the top of the desk on her ass, and cuffed Dayna while she was still down. She stood up and looked at Lanie. Nina's chest heaved and her hands were in fists. Izzy was clinging to Elizabeth in the doorway.

"Oh my God," Elizabeth breathed.

Nina stood up straight and grinned. "That was so Charlie's Angels."

*two
weeks
later*

lanie

"Thank you for coming out here to see us."

Lanie led Officer Ramos, whom she would never stop thinking of as Hot Cop, into the sunroom. Michael stood up to shake hands with him, and then they all sat. On the coffee table was a full spread of hot coffee, muffins, and pastries. No one touched it.

"You said you had an update for us?" Michael asked.

"Yes, well, thanks to the information you provided us with, we were able to track down most of the men and women who participated in Ainsley's poker games."

Lanie let out an involuntary snort. The men looked at her. "Sorry. It's still difficult to wrap my brain around."

Michael reached over and took her hand, resting it atop her knee. It was a kind, intimate gesture that she wasn't used to from him, and she tried not to smile.

"It was a larger number of people than you thought," Ramos continued, glancing at his phone when it beeped. "And with most of them cooperating, we were able to line up some withdrawals from various accounts Mrs. Anderson kept. It all checks out."

"What about Dayna?"

"She's confessed to helping Mrs. Anderson launder money through the PBA account as well as through several businesses in town. Apparently, they used intimidation to get certain small-business owners to comply."

"Intimidation?"

"As you know, you and your friends have a good deal of influence in this town, Mrs. Katapodis," Officer Ramos said. Was there a hint of judgment in his tone? "It seems that Mrs. Anderson and Mrs. Goodman threatened bad word-of-mouth and smear campaigns if these people didn't help." He sighed and looked out the window toward the backyard, where a stiff breeze tossed the fallen leaves into a small tornado. "And when that didn't work, they had a guy who sealed the deal for them."

"I told you," Michael said, gripping Lanie's hand a bit tighter. "I told you there was a guy."

"You know him?" Ramos refocused his attention.

"I never talked to him, but I did see him hanging around a few times. His name was Lestor something."

"Could you ID him in a lineup, you think?" Ramos asked, flipping open his notebook.

"Oh, definitely. He had one of those big, almost square faces, a wide nose, close-set eyes. Dark, thick eyebrows. And slicked black hair. Also, he wore a gold ring on his right pinky finger."

"Sounds like our guy."

"You've got him already?" Lanie asked.

"He's the one who roughed up John Anderson," Ramos said. "He somehow kept his face off the security cameras, but we did see the ring, and we got a description from another witness. If you could help us ID him, Mr. Katapodis, that would be big."

Michael puffed up a little. "Whatever I can do."

"Why did he come after John?" Lanie asked. John had been in the hospital for three days, and she was terrified the man would do the same to Michael.

"From what Mr. Anderson said, he was looking for money Mrs. Anderson owed him. Payment for services rendered."

Michael and Lanie exchanged a look. She thought of Fred Carson and his broken arm.

"So he's not mob?" Michael asked.

"We haven't found any connections, no," Ramos said. "Apparently the two of them have known each other since college."

"They're *college* friends?" Lanie asked.

"Yeah, it seems Mrs. Anderson's illegal activities go back quite a long way. But I probably shouldn't comment more as it's an ongoing investigation." He stood up and rolled his shoulders back. "If you could come down to the station this afternoon, Mr. Katapodis, I'd love to show you some pictures. See if you can ID our guy."

Michael stood up as well, bringing Lanie with him. "Yeah, of course."

"What about Ainsley's . . ." Lanie cleared her throat, tears prickling her eyes. "What about the . . . murder? Has Dayna—"

She couldn't finish the sentence. None of this seemed real. That Ainsley was dead. That she was a criminal. That Dayna had been in on it. *Dayna.*

"While Mrs. Goodman confessed to the lesser crimes, including breaking into the Anand residence and removing several items of value, she has denied any involvement with Mrs. Anderson's death."

"But she had the necklace," Michael said.

"She claims she found it earlier in the evening and intended to return it. She only started wearing it after she lost her own in the break-in."

"But she . . . she basically confessed in front of four people, including myself," Lanie said.

"Did she?" Officer Ramos asked. "According to my interviews with Mrs. Anand and with Paige . . . with Ms. Lancaster and her mother, she never outright said she hurt anyone."

Lanie's brow furrowed. Everything from that episode was already fuzzy, as if her brain were trying to protect her from the memory. No, Dayna hadn't outright said that she'd murdered Ainsley, but Lanie knew that she had. It was written all over her friend's face.

"I know it's not ideal, but even if we can't get her for the murder, she will be going away for a very long time."

As Ramos turned to go, Michael took a tentative step forward. "Officer, I have to ask . . . is there any chance of recouping any of our money?"

"I'm afraid not." Ramos appeared genuinely sympathetic. "The Andersons' accounts are going to be tied up in evidence for a good long while, and even then, the Feds aren't going to want to pay back a bunch of gamblers." He glanced at Lanie. "No offense."

"None taken," Michael said flatly.

They saw Ramos out and then returned to the sunroom. Slowly, Lanie lowered herself onto the couch again. She was shaking, more from anger than anything else. Dayna was going to get away with it. She had shoved Ainsley down her own stairs to her death, ripping off her beloved star necklace in the process, and she was going to get away with it.

"Are you okay?" Michael asked.

"I don't know," Lanie replied.

"Lane," he said. "About the money."

Right. The money. Shoving aside thoughts of Dayna and Ainsley, she slowly, carefully, filled two cups with coffee and added cream and sugar to hers. She took a sip and steeled herself.

"So," she said to her husband. "How bad is it?"

nina

It was almost midnight. The kids were fast asleep. And Nina and Ravi sat at the kitchen table with Nina's gun as the centerpiece between them. He had changed into his favorite, well-worn band T-shirt and flannel pajama pants but she'd chosen to remain in her work clothes.

"I don't even know where to start," Ravi said. His long guitarist's fingers were laced together on the tabletop in front of him, and rather than look his wife in the eye, he was staring at her weapon. As long as it was in his presence, he never took his eyes from it.

"Why don't you start with why you're so angry at me."

She said it mostly to force him to look at her. She knew why he was so angry at her. And her tactic worked.

"You know how I feel about guns," he said, leveling her with an accusatory glare.

"Yes."

"Then why do you have one in the house?" he asked. "Do you even know how to use that thing?"

"For protection, and yes."

He stared at her, incredulous at her businesslike tone. She didn't know why. She always took a businesslike tone in arguments. It was her go-to defensive setting.

"How long have you had it?"

"Since college." Now it was her turn to look at the gun. "My father gave it to me after I was attacked on campus freshman year and the police didn't do anything about it."

"What? You never told me this. Who attacked you? What did they—"

Nina lifted a hand. "I don't want to talk about it. I've never wanted to talk about it. That's why I never told you."

"But . . . we tell each other everything."

Nina sat with that for a moment. It was mostly true. She'd told him every important thing that had happened to her since they'd met. But most of the stuff that came before, she'd tried to forget.

"Look, my dad never trusted the cops."

"Because of your brother. I know."

"Right, so when this guy I knew tried to . . . hurt me." To this day she still could not say the word "rape" without gagging. "His solution was to give me a gun. Which I've never used outside of target practice, by the way. But it did make me feel safer."

His brow knit.

"I'm sorry, Ravi, but it did. It does."

He blew out a sigh and reached across the table for her hands, which were folded together in her lap. She lifted them and met his fingers halfway. They both squeezed.

"Are you ever going to tell me what this guy did to you?"

"Do you really need to know?" she asked. "I'm still the same person I was yesterday. Last week. Last year."

His head tilted as he considered. "And what about the gun? Do you still need it? Because I was kind of hoping *I* made you feel safer."

Nina's lips twitched. She got up, walked around the table and slid into his lap, resting her cheek against his shoulder. He held her tight against him. "The gun," she said, "we can talk about."

paige

It was a bright, crisp November morning when the last of the crime scene tape was removed from John Anderson's house and stuffed into a black garbage bag by the movers. Paige stood next to her idling car in the driveway. She didn't plan to stay long.

"You could come inside for a coffee," John suggested, turning up the collar of his expensive wool coat with his right hand. His left arm was still in a cast and sling.

"That's okay. I have a million things to do today. I just wanted to make sure I had a chance to say goodbye." She squinted one eye as she looked up at him, the sun winking at her from over the roof of the garage. The place where it all went down. The yellowish remnants of a bruise marred John's right cheek and there were stitches above his eye. He had already told her he'd thrown out all the gambling paraphernalia and sold the poker table, which was custom-made and worth a small fortune. "California, huh? I can't really picture you there."

"Neither can I, to be honest." He glanced over his shoulder at the house. "But we really do need a fresh start. I knew that Ainsley was running a weekly poker game, but I had no idea how many of my friends were involved, or how much money had changed hands. I definitely can't show my face around here anymore."

Paige thought of Lanie and how she and Michael had decided to put their house on the market. Downsize. Take stock. Lanie was even talking about getting a job. Part-time, of course.

"I can't believe no one told you in all that time."

"It's a pride thing, I think. It might be the two-thousand twenties, but men still don't want to admit that other men's wives are smarter than they are." He smirked and blew into his fist to warm his fingers. There was a pang of nostalgia and sadness behind his words. He missed Ainsley, even though they'd been planning to divorce. Relationships were so complicated. "Anyway, it wasn't just the poker. Ainsley had a massive gambling problem. She always did. It's something she was working on most of her adult life, and there were times she was good. Made progress. When I thought we weren't going to have any more back slides. But these last few years . . . Let's just say we would have had to sell the house eventually. Even if she hadn't been caught for her illegal activities."

"Wow." Paige took a deep breath. "I'm sorry you had to deal with all that."

"Yeah." He gave a wan smile. "Me too."

"Mr. Anderson?" one of the movers called out from the front door. "We need to know which of these boxes in the foyer are for the truck and which are for donation."

"Guess that's my cue," John said. "Thanks for everything, Paige. You've been a real friend these past few weeks."

"Of course," she said, blushing slightly as she tried to not remember tearing off his T-shirt. The whole thing seemed almost comical now. She knocked his arm with her fist, an awkward gesture. "Good luck with everything."

"Thanks. And if you ever move back out West, let me know."

"Will do."

He hesitated half a second, then pulled her into a warm, close one-armed hug. Then he released her and turned away.

lanie

"This autumn we have seen challenges we never could have predicted, and losses from which we will never completely recover."

Lanie paused to look out at the crowd of well-dressed people, the mothers and fathers of the PBA, elegant in their finest cocktail attire. The lights were low, except for the spotlight trained on her face, and the strong scent of cappuccino filled the room as waiters began to circulate with the dessert trays. Lanie still had a hard time believing that she was at a Thankful Dinner without Ainsley—that there could even *be* a Thankful Dinner without Ainsley. Yet here they all were, carrying on. She had to believe, in spite of everything, that it's what Ainsley would have wanted.

"I want to thank all of you for coming tonight, for volunteering your time, your talent, and your treasure all season long. We're certainly going to need more of that in the coming months."

There was an awkward titter of laughter. Most people knew that the PBA account had been drained. That the money wasn't coming back anytime soon, tied up as it was in the investigation into Dayna's activities. It was going to take a lot of hard work to replenish that money. Hard work Lanie was here for. Somehow it seemed appropriate that she'd finally taken over as president of the PBA right when everything was in shambles.

"But for now, let's all enjoy tonight, and if I may, dedicate this evening to my beautiful friend, Ainsley Aames Anderson." *Beautiful, lying, scheming, broken, criminal Ainsley.* Lanie lifted her glass. "To Ainsley."

"To Ainsley," the room chorused.

Lanie swigged her champagne and stepped off the dais to a round of applause. Various people swarmed up to congratulate her, to ask her questions, to say hello as she crossed the room to her husband. Since confessing about the poker game and the truth of their financial situation, Michael's entire demeanor had changed. He was standing taller now, more like his old, confident self, and his eyes were clear—even hopeful. The whole effect made him more handsome than ever as she approached, though the fitted cut of his Tom Ford suit didn't hurt.

"Care to dance, Madame President?"

"But of course, my first gentleman."

He took a quick sip of champagne and laughed. "They really need to come up with a better name for that."

Gently but firmly, Michael took her hand and led her out to the dance floor, joining several other couples who swayed to the band's rendition of an older Michel Bublé tune.

"Lanie! Michael! Are you coming to the after-party?" Caroline asked, laying her hands on their shoulders. Her hands were freezing and dry, but Lanie gave her a gracious smile.

"I'm sorry, Caroline, but we can't make it."

"Oh, really? Important plans?" Caroline said skeptically.

Lanie met Michael's gaze with her own. Part of the new deal of their marriage was spending more time alone together. Just talking or watching a movie or making dinner. Michael had explained, in one of their many state-of-their-union conversations, that part of the reason he'd been traveling so much the last two years was because he felt uncomfortable at home. Knowing that Lanie was lying to him. That he was lying to her. But now that everything was out, everything had changed. This week had been busy, so they'd decided that after the Thankful Dinner they would catch up on some of the Netflix shows they had only heard about for the past couple of years. Truthfully, they'd probably also get caught up on Realtor.com looking for houses to downsize to. Not paying their ridiculous mortgage seemed like the easiest way to start to recoup some of the money Michael had lost at Ainsley's poker games.

"Very important," Michael said.

The way he held her gaze made Lanie blush.

"Ugh. You two make me sick," Caroline joked. She turned away, twiddling her fingers. "Have fun!"

As Caroline moved on to her next unsuspecting couple, Lanie laughed and leaned into her husband.

paige

"What's with that big smile you've got on?" Paige asked Marie, sitting down next to her at the ballroom table after a quick trip to touch up her lipstick.

"Lanie just confirmed that I'll be catering at least three of the big PBA events next year. She wants to—quote—*right the wrongs of past leadership.*"

"Marie, that's fantastic!" Paige's mother lifted her champagne glass. "To Aldo's!"

"To Aldo's!" Paige and Marie echoed.

They clinked glasses and Paige sipped, giggling as the bubbles tickled her nose. Her cell vibrated atop the white linen tablecloth, and she put her glass down and pounced. She had been expecting a call from her agent all day, and even though it was now six o'clock on the West Coast, Paige knew that Farrin wasn't one to keep regular hours. Most people in L.A. weren't.

"Is it her?" Paige's mom asked.

Paige nodded, not trusting herself to speak. She got up from the table and squeezed her mother's shoulder before speed-walking out to the country club's ornate lobby. She had invited her mother to be her date to thank her for everything she'd done for her and Izzy over the past couple of months. Elizabeth had initially demurred, saying Paige should find herself a real date. Paige knew her mother was thinking of Dominic, but the two of them hadn't spoken since the day Dayna was arrested, and Paige felt awkward about calling him. She figured he'd assessed the weight of her baggage and decided that he didn't want to carry it.

"Hello," Paige said into the phone as soon as she was clear of the music and conversation. "Farrin?"

"Paige, hello."

Instantly, her stomach dropped. That businesslike tone was not a good sign.

"What? What's wrong? Is no one biting?"

"What? No. They're biting. Why would you say that?"

Paige leaned one hand against a cool, marble column. "You sounded like you were about to give me bad news."

"I sound like this because I'm worried you're going to say no when I tell you that you have to get on a plane this weekend and get your ass out here because you have ten meetings set for Monday and Tuesday."

"Ten meetings? Are you kidding me?"

"Not kidding. Do I sound like I'm kidding? This PTA murder mystery thing is liquid gold, Paige. Even Richard wanted to take a meeting, but I told him to go fuck himself. Not really."

Paige laughed, tears springing to her eyes. "I wish you had."

"I did tell him we'd only take the meeting if you wanted to. And if he brought apology croissants."

"Wow. I can't believe it. So this is really happening."

"It's really happening. When can you move back to L.A.?"

Paige took a deep breath. She had known this was coming, of course. And she was ready for it.

"I'm not. I can come for the meetings, obviously, and to get it all set up, but I'm not moving back." She stood up straight and fisted her free hand. "I think we should film on the East Coast."

There was a long pause. "But Paige, the *taxes* . . ."

"It doesn't have to be New York." Paige laughed. "Connecticut or even New Jersey would be better."

Farrin groaned. "Fine. It can be part of the conversations. But you need to be open to other locations."

"Other East Coast locations."

"I heard you the first time," Farrin said. "Send me your flight info when you have it. And Paige?"

"Yeah?"

"This is going to be fun. Welcome back."

"Thanks. It's good to be back."

She ended the call and then jumped up and down in her high heels and squealed. "Yes! Yes! Yes!"

"Good news?"

Paige was so startled she almost tripped herself. She turned around to find Dominic Ramos standing there wearing a dark blue suit and a deeply purple tie and smiling at her like he'd just caught her stealing.

He was even hotter in a suit than he was in his uniform. His hair had been recently cut, shorn on the sides and slightly longer on top. When he stepped closer to her, she could smell the spicy scent of his aftershave and she almost swooned.

"Really good news," she said.

"I've wanted to call you," Dominic said. "Everything's just been so crazy at work."

"For me too," she said.

His smile widened. "You look incredible."

"I feel incredible," she said, glancing down at her black, fit-and-flare dress. "And you clean up pretty good yourself."

"Thank you," he said, tugging on the front of his jacket. "Do you want to take that dress out for a spin on the dance floor and tell me all about your good news?"

Paige smiled a true, genuine, happy smile. It felt completely unfamiliar, and she never wanted it to end.

"I'd love that," she said.

nina

Under the table, Nina held on to Ravi's hand. She had never been very comfortable at parties or dances or conventions. For most of her life she had been younger than the other kids in her class, seen as a suspicious presence by colleagues. She had enjoyed going to hear Ravi's band play in college, not only because she got to watch her sexy boyfriend jam on his guitar (and know that all those other girls screaming for his attention were not going to get it), but because she could just disappear into the crowd. It was always too loud to talk, and everyone was too busy enjoying the music to care.

"We don't have to stay for dessert," Ravi told her. He knew her so well. "I could just grab our coats and we can sneak out."

The band transitioned from a slow song right into that old classic party tune, "Celebration." She was about to open her mouth to agree when she felt a hand on her shoulder. It was Paige, looking radiant. Clutching her other hand was Hot Cop.

"Hey, Nina. Do you two want to dance?"

Nina would have been embarrassed by how quickly her heart swelled if anyone could have seen it. "Yes! We'd love to."

She got up, dragging Ravi with her. He laughed as they headed for the dance floor, following Paige and Hot Cop as they wove through the crowd to find Lanie and her husband near the middle of the action.

"Hey!" Lanie cried when she saw them. She stopped dancing to fling her arms around Paige, then hugged Nina, too. Nina was so startled it took her a moment to reciprocate. "I'm so glad you're here!"

Her words seemed genuine, and Nina found herself beaming back. "Me too!"

"Let's dance, Ms. Treasurer!"

Nina laughed as Ravi took both her hands, lacing their fingers together, and got her moving to the rhythm—never her strong suit. It was the cheesiest song ever, and she couldn't dance to save her life, but looking around at Paige and Lanie and Ravi, she didn't care. She honestly didn't care.

It was time to just have fun.

acknowledgments

Thanks go out to you, lovely reader, for picking up this, my pandemic novel. I hope you enjoyed reading it as much as I enjoyed writing it. Hanging out with these characters definitely helped me escape the insanity of my remote-learning, two-parents-on-zoom-calls-in-the-same-office, what-the-hell-is-a-cohort? existence. But, perhaps I should thank you for reading my *first* pandemic novel, because I'm currently working on another and, yes, we're still in the middle of a pandemic.

Pause for a deep breath and long sigh.

I must also thank my incredible editor, Jackie Cantor, who never ceases to make me feel like a talented writer and always managed to point out exactly what needed tweaking, finessing, and outright cutting from this story. Jackie, I can't wait to see what you do next.

Thank you to my champion of an agent, Holly Root, who is somehow carrying everyone on her back through this most "unprecedented time." It's truly remarkable what you are able to do with a smile.

Thanks to everyone at Gallery, including Jennifer Bergstrom, Aimee Bell, and the lovely Aliya King Neil, who stepped in to help me bring this all home. Huge thanks go out to Andrew Nguyen, Lauren Truskowski, Bianca Salvant, and the entire sales team, whose support I felt even as *Wish You Were Gone* was postponed by—you guessed it—the pandemic. Oh, and then the supply chain.

Care to pause for another deep breath?

A huge, HUGE thanks to my supportive friends and family, especially Matt, Brady, Will, Wendy, Shira, and Jen—the only person who read this book before my editor did, and who kept sending me texts with totally wild theories as to who the bad guy was—which gave me the confidence to finally turn in the first draft. Also to all the librarians and booksellers who have been such cheerleaders this past year. You're the ones I think of when I don't feel like opening my laptop. So thank you for keeping this humble author working.